TURN AROUND, GEMINI

TURN AROUND, GEMINI

by

Shirley M. Byrne

Linda,

I hope you enjoy
the story.

Regards,

Shirley Byrne

ISBN 1-58721-232-3

1stBooks - rev. 04/04/00

About the Book

In 1954 twins were born to Emily and George Gallagher. Through the early years of their lifeTerry and Gerry were subjected to the most violent types of abuse from their father. The mother also suffers from the same abuse and retreats into a world of her own by writing in her diary. In the pages of the diary is the story of the family torn apart and violated by an abusive husband and father and others from outside the family.

Unusual deaths seem to follow the Gallagher twins, starting in their teens and on into adulthood.

When Gerry returns to close the family home after the death of her mother, from an illness, old wounds are opened when she finds the diary from the years past.

Living in San Francisco and working at a local library, Gerry Gallagher needs the help of her twin brother to help her with what she calls her "problems". When he returns to help her, the final debts are paid and a feeling of finality comes to Gerry for the first time in years.

Dedication

My utmost thanks to my husband, Bob, and daughters, Kathy Coarson and Patti Barsema. The confidence they showed in me gave me the courage to try a new direction in my life. They made me believe I could do any thing I put my mind to.

Prologue

A gloved hand pulled the door slowly shut from the dark, musty smelling hallway. All that could be heard was a tiny click as the door latch slid into its place in the door jamb. When the door was closed it sealed into that quiet room a sight that many people would not like to see, most could never imagine.

There was a slight giggle, then a quick, "Shh-h! Be quiet!."

Another sound came from the shadowy hall --a slight scuffing, then the sound of papers being rubbed together. When the shuffling noise stopped, a small roll of papers was gently placed between the doorknob and the door facing, held there for a few seconds by the same gloved hand, and allowed to expand to fit the space in the corner. Now the roll would hold it's own weight and stay behind the doorknob.

Then came the soft, padding sound of shoes going down the hall and decending the steps. There was not a squeak or groan from the old stairs as the feet slipped gently down and out the front door, two flights down. The noises from outside the building were the usual for two-thirty in the morning -- the sound of a trash can being dumped over by dogs or some of the local bums who frequented the alleys at this time, and the muffled voices of the drunks arguing on the corner.

As the last door latch clicked quietly into place, another giggle could again be heard, "Did I do it right? I was so nervous. I didn't get very far did I?"

"You did your part. That's the important thing. At least you tried."

"I'm so excited. I really helped, didn't I?. Well, Didn't I?"

"Shhh, don't be so loud. Yes, you helped. Now quiet down. We still have to get home. Enjoy the feeling now. Tomorrow will be just a regular day."

"Does that mean I won't remember? I hate it when I don't remember. I know I've done something, but it won't come to me. Will you tell me again tomorrow, like you do sometimes? Please? It was so good tonight. It's just not fair that I won't remember, but it feels right to repay a debt."

"Tomorrow you may think differently. Now, let's hurry. It's late."

"But . . . ."

"No buts. Believe me there's a lot that goes on that's not fair. You did your part. Be happy for now. When you wake up in the morning, maybe you'll have a good feeling that you at least tried to help."

Upstairs in the quiet apartment, a night light was plugged into a low socket next to the closet door, but the bulb was burned out. The stillness was as heavy as the heat that was beginning to build. The temperatures had been in the high eighties and these old buildings had no fancy cross ventilation or air conditioning.

The room held one main piece of furniture, a bed. The sight on the bed was one of dark red and a blur of liquid and bulging parts of what had, at one time, been the body of a fifty-three year old woman. Right now, this thing that lay across the top of the bed resembled a jumbled mass of unrelated pieces, even though every piece was still connected. It had the appearance of some large jumbled jig-saw puzzle.

Within the first hour the temperature had risen seven degrees. Now, in the total darkness of the small room, a soft scurrying could be heard with a tiny squeal coming now and then as the rats in the building built up their courage to explore this room that was usually lit, both day and night. The hot, sickly sweet smell began to build in the room as the furry movements on the floor finally moved up, onto the bed.

By six in the morning a soft <u>drip, drip, drip</u> could have been heard if someone was nosy enough to put their ear to the door and listen very carefully, but in this building no one bothered with anyone else's door. It was considered impolite, plus, it was dangerous.

The light was beginning to seep under the door, not bright enough to really see by, but it did give some idea of what the scene in the room looked like after just four hours of heat and rats. The smell was growing hot, sweet, and putrid. The vermin had lost all control at finding no resistance to their attendance in this room and were finally digging in and pulling at the innards for all they were worth. They each took some of this newly found treasure back to their nests and holes in the walls. The former resident of this room now covered approximately twelve square feet of the floor, since this was about all the floor space in the room. Downstairs, in the apartment just below, there was the beginning of a small damp circle at the light fixture in the center of the ceiling. It grew so slowly, it seemed to be a permanent stain, instead of a new, growing one. The sleeping man noticed nothing. He wasn't in the habit of checking his ceilings or anything else when he stayed in these places. As long as he could pay for the room, it was always the same. He asked no questions, and he answered no questions.

Outside, Thursday was beginning. Another hot, sweltering, humid day, in San Francisco. Today the temperature was supposed to reach the eighties again. The room upstairs should reach a steamy high in the nineties, at least. Today would be the first day the rats did not go back into the walls when the sun came up. This was the day they waited for all their lives.

By mid-afternoon, the scampering in the room sounded like an army of tiny feet, scratching, splashing, chewing and clawing. It was their day and they were not going to lose it.

November 27, 1953

Dear Diary,

This is my first time writing to a book. Mommy says it's silly, but I don't care. I bought this here diary at the dime store because I really needed someone to talk to. The other day I heard this lady at the grocery store talking about her diary, so I want to try it myself.

Well, here goes. I guess I will talk to you just like you were a real person. Maybe it will make me feel better. I never really had any good close friend that I could talk to about school things or just about how I feel about anything. I really need someone to talk to now, and Mommy won't listen.

Diary, I just got married four months ago. He's a really nice guy named George Gallagher. He went to school when I did, but he was in the class ahead of me. I surely did like him, when I was in school.

Well, he didn't seem to notice me much in school, but after he graduated and I was a senior, he started coming around the house. We got married July of this year.

Things have changed already. I don't have anybody to tell this. Sometimes when he gets mad, he hits me. I don't even know what makes him mad. He just gets almost crazy and starts in hitting me.

I try to be sure and not say anything that would make him mad at me. but then he gets mad just because I try to be nice. He says I'm too gushy sweet. That makes him sick to his stomach, so he hits me. Then, other times, he is so good and nice to me, I just don't know how lucky I can be.

Sometimes he brings me some flowers that he picked on the way home from work. I know he takes them from some yard, but like my momma always says, It's the thought that counts. I think it's real nice of him to bring me flowers.

I went to the doctor last week and I found out that I'm going to have a baby. I just can't hardly wait until next June. I am so excited, but I'm still afraid to tell George. I hope he don't get mad at me for having a baby. Mommy says he's not too right in the head, but I sure do love him anyways. He always had his choice of all the girls and he picked me. I never could figure that out. I know he fools around sometimes, but he always comes home. Sometimes he even tells me how nice it is here. Just so he don't get mean again. Even if he does, I'll always have my baby to keep me company.

I just can't wait until I have my baby in my arms. Then I can dress him up and show him off at the store and at the park. Of course, it might be a girl. I watch the ladies over at the park pushing their babies in their strollers. They're all dressed up with ruffles or little baseball shirts.

The other babies are dressed up so fine, I just am so excited, I can't wait until I can do that for my baby.

The doctor was so nice, he gave me lots of vitamins and even gave me some books and papers to read. I hope I can do this right. George says I mess up lots of things. I don't mean to be dumb, I just don't know a lot of things. Doc says I'll do just fine. I sure hope so.

Your friend,

Emily

Chapter One

It was a hot Friday afternoon. The hall on the third floor was busy with police, but they were moving around in a more quiet manner than usual. It was probably due to the mess inside the room that was scattered across the bed and floor.

As far as the police could tell, this pile of tubes and shiny masses had been, at one time, a female human being. Right now her age was undetermined, but she did have grey hair. She looked like she had been pretty flabby, too. One definite thing about her -- she was dead.

Outside the building, Lieutenant Frank Franklin's car pulled up to the curb. As he climbed from his car, he saw a uniformed man run from the door way down the outer steps and start toward the alley. It was Officer Gene Schwartz, but from the green look on his face, Gene was not looking for anything, but a little privacy.

As Schwartz came down the steps of the building, he took one look at Franklin, nodded his head toward the alley, and ran, holding up a finger that signified, Just one minute, please.

Franklin figured as soon as Schwartz's stomach recovered from whatever it was he had just seen upstairs, they could get on with the briefing.

"Must be a real dandy," he said to himself. "Shit, I guess that screws the weekend."

He felt this was not going to be the usual murder scene, but who ever said there was such a thing as a "usual murder".

Franklin was on his way back to the station, to finish up for the day, when the call came. The superintendent of the apartment building discovered one of his tenants dead in her room. He did not actually find her himself. The super called the station and waited for a uniformed officer before he opened the door. She must have been there for at least two days, since the smell was what had attracted him to the apartment. He lived in this area most of his adult life and he knew that death smell from years of bums and drunks lying around here. Most of the people in the vicinity were down on their luck and spent all their time in and out of hotels and apartment houses like this one -- real losers.

"Lieutenant Franklin, this is really bad," Patrolman Schwartz said as he came out of the alley, wiping his chin. "You've got to see it before I can give any kind of a report. It's really sick, I got the second call. The guy here that sees to the building -- you know, the superintendent . . ."

"Yes, Schwartz, I know what a building manager is. Get on with it."

Franklin had to push a little to get Schwartz into the events of the day. Officer Schwartz tended to ramble at times.

"Yes, sir. Well, I don't know who or what the problem was, but someone did a pretty messy job on this old lady. Her name was Mary Carlin. Her throat's been cut twice . . . well, really one-and-a-half times. One time from her left ear to the front of her throat. Looks like a botched job. The incision on her left side is ragged and torn. The right side is done from the right ear to the left in one clean sweep. A very clean and deep slice. Just in case that didn't do the job, she was cut from the right arm pit down through the navel up to the left arm pit. Looks like she suffered a trauma to the right side of the head, too. The blow to the head was probably done first. Just some poor old lady, and someone slits her like a fish. Her insides are laying all over the place."

Franklin looked up from his notebook and nodded to Schwartz, "That's okay, Gene, spare me the detailed description right now. I'll go up and look at her myself, and you can stay out here and get a handle on your stomach. Thanks for the warning."

Upstairs on the third floor, the officers in the room had to take turns coming out for a breath of fresh air - - or at

2

least a little fresher, the stale smell in the hall was taking on the aroma of the murder room.

After nineteen years with the San Francisco Police Department Lieutenant Frank Franklin still felt a twist in the pit of his stomach when he was called in on a mutilation.

As he started into the small dingy room, the first things he noticed were the slick puddles on the floor. Most of the Coroner's men had their hankerchieves or their hands over their mouths and noses. Some had the little white masks that people wore to protect their lungs from smog. Just looking around, he could understand why Schwartz had become sick at his stomach. Franklin couldn't smell much because of a chronic sinus problem, but his eyes told him how bad the smell must be. The old lady, as Schwartz called her,was just so much raw meat.

Franklin waved his hand over the area covered by the mess, "Does it look like the killer did this scattering?"

Entralls were spread over most of the floor, and that was not very large after the odds and ends of furniture had been put into the room, which was merely was a hole in the wall that held a small bed, one night stand with a small lamp, a hot plate sitting on a small dresser, and two chairs. One of the chairs had a pillow on the seat that looked like someone's grandmother had made it years ago. Not much else in the way of decoration. The bed was made, with the body and all it's mess on top of a well worn bedspread.

Having returned from downstairs, Schwartz stepped forward and answered, "No, sir, we figured the rats did the scattering. Plus you gotta remember that we've had three days of pretty hot weather. The room being closed up like it was, made it awfully stuffy in here. I think that helped rush the smell along, if you know what I mean, sir. It looks like the cutting was all that was done by the perpetrater, but the pests in the building were the ones that had made the mess."

Franklin grunted under his breath, "Perpetrator, I hate that word.

Perpetrator, sounds like he should be making coffee for Mrs. Olsen." He nodded at Gene, "Okay. See if the building manager is back downstairs. He was gone when I came in. I have a few questions for him. Find him and tell him I want his butt out front when I get there. I think he went back to his apartment. I also want you to stand at the door and make a detailed sketch of this room, as to furniture placement, measurements and contents. Details, I want all details. Even the smallest piece of paper."

"But, sir," the patrolmen sputtered, "the coroner's office and photographers will do all that."

Franklin smiled his nicest, and said, "I know they will, Gene, but I would like some feedback from another trained eye, and I feel that you will do just splendidly. You have a good eye for detail, and I don't want to waste a chance to use it to it's fullest."

The men knew that Franklin always tried the polite way first, and if this did not work, then there was yelling and swearing like you never heard before. It was usually easier to go with the first chance.

As the coroner's people worked, they took their normal procedures of measurements, samples and pictures.

The first patrolman began making a list of the personal effects of the woman, "What should I do with her stuff, Lieutenant?"

"Pack it up in something," Franklin answered.

"Yes, sir, I saw a box in the hall that looks like it should hold everything. She really doesn't have much. Just a couple of dresses, a coat and her purse is still here."

Franklin told him, "Check the purse for contents and count any money she had and put the amount on the list and put it all in the box. Get those books over there on the chair, the cups, and there are some papers and more things over in the corner on the floor. Bring the box to my

4

office when you bring the report to me. Don't forget to put the list of everything in with her things."

The main thing right now was to see if they could find any extra identification and locate any relatives she might have in the area.

"Before you start packing up this stuff, you might want to make the description and sketch I asked for," Franklin reminded them.

"Oh, yeah. I see what you mean. Horse before the cart and all that."

The super of the building had returned and was anxious to get this all over with and get these cops out,

"Lieutenant Franklin," he said, "I don't know much about her. Her name is . . .was Mary Carlin. She moved in about seven years ago, and she waited tables at some sleeze diner over on Eighth Street, paid her rent and minded her own business. She did have some company about two weeks ago. Looked like some kid. Didn't stay too long, but the old lady seemed to be happy to see the kid. I seen her talkin' to some bum out on the street once in a while, but I don't know if it was the same guy every time. You know the kind, they all look alike. He was a pretty hairy guy, but ain't they all?"

"Okay, thank you for your help. We'll see to Miss Carlin. The squad will do it's best to clean up the mess. If we have any other questions, I'll have one of my men get back to you."

The super was glad to be dismissed and get back to his soap operas.

Franklin wiped his nose, and thought how glad he was that he had sinus problems. The smell must be terrible, since some of the other guys kept their hankerchiefs out most of the time.

"Okay, get all the routine workups done and get this cleaned up. Patrolman Schwartz, I'd like you to get the report to me as soon as you can. Yes, I will be in on a

Saturday morning, if that is the question I read on your face - - and no, it may not wait until Monday."

Schwartz's son probably had Little League on Saturday morning. Somebody has to have kids. Thank God it was the young people having them.

As he eased out the door, Franklin thought there was no way he would go through the Little League and teachers' conferences. Just hearing about them from the younger men, made him thankful for, what he called, his "advanced years," all forty-two of them.

As Franklin started down the outside steps of the tenement, he wished he could find some grass, so he could wipe his shoes. Though he watched where he was walking in the room, he had this lousy feeling that his shoes were covered with the slime from those slick puddles. The trash cans by the curb had enough papers for him to use to scrape his shoes a little. At least he felt a little cleaner.

Checking his shoes again, Franklin slid into the front seat of his car. He muttered, "Tomorrow night I have a great dinner planned for Margot, and now if I can't get the reports finished on this damned thing, my schedule is going to be all screwed up."

The whole time his mind wondered what makes one human do such a thing to another. He wasn't surprised after all these years, he just couldn't understand why.

In the car Franklin thought, Someone decided they didn't like . . . what's her name ? Mary Carlin. What could be so bad to make someone do this to her? She sure didn't look like the kind of person that could cause another person that kind of anger, but in these times, who knows what anyone thinks. You certainly can't tell by looking at them. You can hardly tell if you do know them.

Feeling a little bit like Scarlett O'Hara he promised himself that he'd ponder that subject tomorrow.

As he drove away, he began to mentally file away some of the small details of information he had at this early stage of the case. The lady was certainly dead.

The main question in his mind, as he muttered to himself, was, <u>Why in the hell would anyone cut a person's throat one-and-a-half times?</u>

Chapter Two

Saturday mornings have two kinds of beginnings -- the bright, sunny kind when you could stay home and ponder the ways of the universe or the dull, dreary kind that only happened when a certain lieutenant has to go into the office to check on some paper work. This was the dreary kind, even though the sun was shinning on this great day in August.

This year started out rainy and was now making up for it with sunshine and heat. At least, the white haired old gentleman who owned the flower stand on the corner made it seem better with his multi-colored flowers, all sitting out in their crispy plastic bags.

Hopping down the stairs at the front of his apartment building as he stuffed his extra nasal spray into his jacket pocket at the same time, Franklin's only thoughts for the day were to get this little old lady put to rest, finish up with some paper work from a mugging on Thursday night, and finish paying some bills - - the bills were one of the things he always put off doing by pushing them back into the corner of his desk drawer.

<u>Maybe I should get married</u>, he thought. <u>Then I would have someone to pay the bills and keep all these finances straight.</u>

He shuddered at this thought, and realized he also would have three times the bills, so he figured he was ahead of the game by just paying the late charges on the few bills that accumulated each month. If it got too bad he could always get an accountant.

His worst bill was from the grocery store down the street. If he could ever bring himself to shop at the super market, he could certainly save some money. Gibson's Gourmet Grocery was not the cheapest store in the area, but they were the best-stocked for spices and meat, and they had some of the most unusual vegetables he ever enjoyed preparing.

Franklin had a few weaknesses, though he would never be the one to admit. Gibson's was his biggest - - well, at least his second weakness. Cooking was the religion in his life, and tonight's meal was being prepared for the greatest weakness in his life - - Margot Kent.

This police lieutenant, who could shake a bully into tears, could make a simple cheese sauce that would make a person eating Kraft Macaroni and Cheese feel he was committing a Cardinal Sin.

This morning he decided to take the bus to the station. He needed time to think about a few things.

Not too much to think about on the old lady, since he hadn't seen her belongings yet.

The mugging case was almost finished. The victim said he was just waiting for a bus, and someone jumped him from behind a wall next to the bus stop. If that was true, why did the mugger tear up all the pictures in the victim's wallet and leave his money? He also only hit him on the face. Usually if someone is just beating to hit, they slug you anywhere they could manage to get in a good one.

Franklin decided that the talk with the victim's wife was probably the key to the thing. The brother-in-law seemed a little unstable, and if his sister and her husband had been fighting, the brother-in-law just might think he's some kind of a knight in shining armor, saving the fair damsel.

The bus ride gave him the time to get himself in the right frame of mind for his reports and bill paying. This done, Saturday would be his for the finishing.

When he entered his office, he noticed the box from Carlin's room sitting on his desk. He immediately felt slimy again.

"Goddamn, Gene, why didn't you put that thing on the floor? It's probably got some of that slimy shit on the bottom."

Schwartz, dozing in a chair, jumped up , "Sorry, Lieutenant Franklin, I thought the bottom of the box was clean. We kept it right outside in the hall while we filled it, and I don't think it had any of the . . . you know--stuff, on it."

Franklin started taking the things out of the box, while Patrolman Schwartz checked them off the list he had made yesterday.

"Gene, is this everything that belonged to her?"

"Yes, sir, and there was some papers in her purse. You know this part. Her name was Mary Carlin, but you ain't going to believe this. She was only fifty-three years old. I found a red wig in the closet. I guess she wore that so's she wouldn't look so old. From all we could find out from any of the tenants, Mary Carlin kept to herself. Most of the time she worked the evening shift, walked home -- if you could call it home -- around twelve-thirty, and went up the stairs to her third floor room. She must have been eating at the diner, because there was no sign of food in the apartment. Just a small pot to boil water and she had a jar of Sanka on the corner table, a couple of tea bags, and a couple of cups. She had a few medicine bottles in the cabinet in the bathroom, but they're mostly over-the counter sleeping aids. One bottle from a druggist down in St. John's. I figured you'd want to check that out. The date was pretty old, looked like nineteen-sixty-five or nineteen-sixty-six."

Franklin wondered how many people kept pills that long. "Well, Gene, the pills can definitely wait until Monday."

Both Franklin and Schwartz checked the box for anything unusual. When the box was empty for the second time, they sat and stared at the contents that were spread all over the desk -- some yearbooks, all filled with class pictures and the usual hobby and sports pictures, several scrapbooks with pictures of school kids, a package of letters from some more kids and finally a small roll of note-book papers in a roll.

"Maybe she was a school teacher or something," Schwartz said. "Here are few pictures that look like class pictures. They're all of kids around ten years old. There's a young woman in some of these pictures that could be the Carlin woman, twenty or thirty years ago. Yeah, look at the lists of names under each picture on this page where the book mark was stuck. That's her right there."

Schwartz sat back down after handing the book to Franklin.

As Franklin reached forward, flipping some old sheets of paper that were full of tiny handwriting, he asked Schwartz, "What's this? Where were these? With her things, in her purse, or in that old dresser?"

Schwartz frowned and looked a little embarrased, "I'm not sure, sir. I think they may have been in the box when Pete grabbed it. It was just outside her door, in the corner. Should I pitch them? They look like something a kid may have written, and they look pretty old. The paper's turned yellow and it's kinda brittle."

"No, we don't throw anything away around here," Franklin said. "You know that, Gene. I'll get to them later, when I can check everything against the pictures we'll get from the lab boys. I've finally get to use one of those damned lists I'm always making you guys make."

"Yeah, I think they might like to hear that the lists really get used," Schwartz smiled as he sat back in the chair.

"I'll have to check this prescription with the drug store, but it's awfully damned old. How far is St. John's anyway? About fifty, sixty miles? Well, I'm sure it can all be handled over the phone."

Franklin started his usual workup on one of the large bulletin boards that hung on the right wall of his office. He put the boards up when he first moved into the office because he didn't know what else to put on the wall. He had an aversion to trophies and awards pasted all around, telling everyone that will look at them what a great cop you are.

Whenever a case was more involved than writing two or three pages of notes, it became fuel for Franklin's bulletin board. He loved cases that needed real solving -- not just pick up the guy and fill out reports. He did not get many of the complicated ones, but enough had come along to get him a reputation for making a jigsaw puzzle out of the more involved cases.

The guys in his division really enjoyed watching him when he started with the board. He actually made paper dolls, houses, streets or maps -- anything that pertained to the situation. Then he would spend hours shifting and rearranging the pieces until he came up with an answer. It was almost always the right one, too.

"I'll save my creating for later and just work on what facts we have here," he said.   All we know about Miss Carlin is that she waited tables at that greasy spoon down on Market and Eighth. She usually worked the evening shift, and she kept to herself. From all the pills she had in the room, we also know she had a sleeping problem, but who wouldn't living in a trap like she was in? We're pretty sure she used to be a teacher, so maybe she came from St. John's originally and someone there will be able to help us locate relatives and give us some of her history. She had to do something in the past twenty years since the date on one of the pill bottles. Try to pick out a picture from the murder scene that won't totally freak anyone out. I'll need something to help identify her in St. John's. Hopefully, someone will remember her."

"Here, Lieutenant, how about taking some of these yearbooks along?"

Schwartz said as he piled the books on the desk. "If they knew her, they sure would recognize the old picture before the one of her in her room."

"Yeah, that's a good idea. Better than seeing her sliced and diced."

13

After his phone call to Mary Carlin's boss at the diner, Franklin sat and stared at the items on his desk with a totally different opinion of Miss Mary Carlin. She had ceased to be the old lady and had gained some respect. She had held nine or ten jobs before she got this one and became friends with the owner, Manny Fry. It seemed she was a schoolteacher until about twenty years ago, but she never told Manny where.

Manny told Franklin, "She didn't really talk about the years before she came there, but over the the time we were friends. I just put a few things together. She talked a lot about teaching. She said that was the happiest time of her life. Once or twice, she started to talk about some guy. All I know was, he was married. She never said his name. I think he roughed her up once in a while. Sounded pretty mean, to me. She got pretty sad most of the time if she had a nip or two. Couldn't get her to say much about anything else in her past. I just had that feeling that she was a real sad person inside."

At this point Franklin wasn't too sure about Fry's judgement of character, but he took down his statement. He was sure, without seeing him, that Fry would have the same look that Franklin had seen over and over in these diners -- fat, greasy-looking with a dirty apron, and constantly wiping his hands on a stained dish towel tucked into the string tie of that same dirty apron.. He would check him out personally, tomorrow or Monday.

He finished the notes on Manny Fry then he reached into the drawer for his unpaid bills. After several attempts to put them into some kind of order, Franklin piled them neatly and shoved them back into the drawer. "I'll have more time on Monday or, maybe I'll really get myself an accountant."

The next phone call, at two thirty in the afternoon, was to Margot.

"If you're ready for something extra exciting that you thought you would never in your whole life be able to experience, be ready to be picked up at six-thirty this evening. Wear your best French perfume and have your appetite ready for French food and wine. This is going to out-do anything I've done before. I have some wine that has been waiting just for this meal."

A slightly impatient grunt was followed by, "Who the hell do you think you are, and what do you mean, calling me on Saturday afternoon for dinner on Saturday evening. Francis, if you don't stop taking me for granted, you will be eating your fancy meals and drinking your exotic wine all by your lonesome. Have you ever thought of calling me earlier in the week for something like this?"

He did not hear any of the sentence. He only heard the name Francis. When she used that name, he was in big trouble.

"Six-thirty", he quickly said and he hung up.

He thought to himself, <u>I'd better make damn sure dinner is good tonight.</u>

February 23, 1954

Dear Diary,

I'm so excited. Doc says I'm going to have twins. Can you believe that? Me, have two babies at one time.

George wasn't too happy about that. I think he must have had a bad day at work. He got a little mean to me and hit me in the stomach. When I told him it was going to be twins, he squeezed my neck so hard I passed out.

This morning when I went to the grocery store, Mrs. Jensen admired my scarf that I wrapped around my neck. I sure hope she couldn't see the bruise from George's hands. I don't know what to do about his temper. He hurt me pretty bad. Maybe he just cares so much, he gets carried away. I'm sure that's why he hits me.

Your friend,

Emily

Chapter Three

Saturday morning was laundry day, and today's wash was finished and put away with no conversation of any kind. The two voices were usually muffled from the other tenants in the building because of the sturdy structure of the building, but they still heard the noise now and then.

Since Terry had shown up last July, there were many arguments and the atmosphere seemed very strained at times. On other occaisions the sound of laughter and long sieges of giggles could be heard.   There was a very confusing aura in the apartment.

Most of the neighboring tenants did not hear any exact words. They just knew that the moods of the tenants on the second floor, front, had changed over the last year. The twins kept to themselves anyway, so it certainly wasn't any of the neighbors' business.This had been going on ever since Terry arrived. He wasn't there all the time, but when he was, the passions were from one extreme to another. The doorman, Ed Spatro, wondered many times why people, even brother and sister, lived together if they couldn't stand each other.

When Miss Gallagher was around, the smiles and friendly nods to the few neighbors she would meet in the hall, basement or elevator were always happily met. A large answering smile and greeting from Gerry made everyone feel good.

This good natured young lady was always enjoyed by the door man, Ed. He had a warm feeling for the timid "Little Miss," as he called her to himself. She was a fine tenant, never complained, there was a "thank you" or a "please" in every sentence.

She had lived in the building for about five years. Going to work every day and never bothering a soul, being such a quiet little thing. Even her friends from the library, where she worked, were about the same type. Gerry did not have a lot of friends, but the few that came to visit were nice young ladies trying to make a living, enjoy a few evenings together and leave the cold world alone, on the outside. That could not be too bad, especially in a city like San Francisco. Too many people here could only yell, complain and see the bad side of everything.

One thing Ed noticed, the friends weren't coming around since the brother moved in. That was surely a shame. Ed saw how much Miss Gallagher enjoyed having company in the years past. She did not really have much to do after work, and the company of her friends seemed to comfort her and fill her evenings.

The brother arrived last summer, and now he would go out at night with his bag and sometimes not return until the early hours of the morning. Ed wondered about this at first until he was told that the brother was a photographer and he was out taking picitures.

Gerry Gallagher had changed a great deal since then. She was still nice, but there was a different air about her. It was almost as if she'd become afraid of her shadow, or her brother. Except for last Thursday, she was always somewhat timid. That morning as she left for work, she was reciting something that sounded like Shakespeare and her mood was very cold and stiff.

Her response to Ed's, "Good Morning," was actually distant and uninterested.

When she reached the front door she shuttered slightly and said, "Oh, Good morning, Ed. Hope you have a wonderful day," and fairly skipped out the front lobby door.

Ed looked a little puzzled, but thought she must have been daydreaming when she first came out of the elevator.

Last night, on Friday evening when the brother came in, Ed tried to help him with his bag and received a very sharp, "Leave it alone, ol' man, I'm not that far gone that I need some old fart carrying my case for me.

Tend to the old and the sissys, if you need to feel important. Just stay out of my way."

Ed put on a painted smile and said, "Yes, sir, just didn't know if you wanted help this time."

The doorman never knew how this brash young man was going to act.

Sometimes he walked into the lobby and was at least halfway cordial. This meant he didn't yell. He just said, "Hello."

Ed Spatro had worked as door man at many places, but he liked his swing shifts and weekends in this apartment building and hoped he would be able to stay here for the rest of his career, so he was not about to make any waves.

Ed pushed the elevator button for Mister Gallagher, anxious to send him upstairs to the apartment and out of 'his' lobby. As the doors of the elevater closed, Ed gave the young man his usual sharp salute.

"What a perfect son-of-a-bitch," the door man whispered, as he returned to his desk on the window side of the lobby. "Just, positively, the most perfect son-of-a-bitch that ever lived!"

The elevator doors closed on the second floor and started downward to redeem a starchy, silvery-blue haired lady from the lobby, as the apartment door on the second floor, front, closed. The young man stood in the entry of the apartment for a few seconds and took a quick deep breath, seemed to gain some strength from the sharp intake, and entered the apartment.

I guess it's really going to hit the fan this time, he thought.

He picked up his small case and started down the hall, passing a large mirror on the left wall.

"Now, what have we done?" the small voice said. "Are you going to tell me about it, or are you going to let me worry about it?"

"My, my," the cold voice answered softly, "aren't we getting brave? When did you get enough courage that you would actually come out and start an arguement without crying first?"

"I don't want to start anything. I'd just like to know what has been going on. Have you been gone? I've had trouble sleeping and I'm forgetting things again." the shakiness in her voice was growing.

"Please, Gerry, don't start with questions now. I don't want to bother you with things that will only upset you. There is one more thing we have to do, and the sooner it's finished, the sooner you can get back to doing what you want. I'll leave, and you can go back to your hum-drum life."

The small delicate voice spoke again, "Please, don't be mad. I didn't mean to argue with you, I just can't remember some things and I know there must be something there to remember. It just won't come to me. You never tell me what you've done or what I've done. Why I can't remember? Maybe it's not very important, if I can't remember it."

Whenever he acted this way, Gerry's stomach would become upset.

She never could take the stress that seemed to come from the actions of Terry. He was always there to take care of her, but he always made her feel afraid. If he was not there, she was afraid, and if he was, she was even more afraid.

"You have to trust me. When I don't tell you about something, it's for the best. Will you believe that? Soon it will be finished and we can relax," Terry's voice calmed her.

"I hope so. I feel like I miss so much when I can't remember. It makes me feel like I've lost something. It's confusing. I've lost the memory of something, but I don't really care."

"Don't worry," Terry said as he proceeded to the bedroom. "Things will be just fine," When Gerry was little, her mother always said, over and over, "Twins are special.

You will only have each other when I'm gone, so be sure you take care of each other. You're all you each will ever have."

Even when they were in school, if someone picked on one of them, the other was there to stand up to the bully and give added support.

Almost always it was Gerry who needed the support. Gerry didn't know how many times she had felt nervous about something, and all she had to do was look around, and Terry was there. Then, she knew that everything would all right.

Today, she felt a little better. Terry's assurance last night made the nagging worries fade, at least for a little while, if she could only remember what it was that upset her.

She finished putting the clean linens on the bed and grabbed her purse. A walk in the park would make the day so much better.

On her way to the park, Gerry stopped at the little grocery store on the corner. Here she chatted with the clerk briefly. Then she went back to the produce section to get a bag of peanuts for the squirrels in the park. Glancing in her purse, she found she had forgotten to bring her book of poems, so she went to the magazine rack to get something to read while she sat by the pond.

After a few minutes, she found herself outside the store walking down the sidewalk towards the park. It always upset her when this happened. How on earth could she check out her purchases and not remember.

"Oh, well, Mama was a little strange. I guess I'm getting that way, too." she sighed.

She strolled into the park entrance on the northwest corner. She loved to walk down the winding path to the pond and around past the gazebo on up to the east side of the pond. Here, she would feed the squirrels for a while, and then get out her book of poetry or magazine. This was one of her most enjoyable times -- no worries and no confrontations, just quiet bliss.

As she reached into the small grocery bag for the peanuts, she noticed there were two magazines. The grocery clerk must have given her someone else's magazine. She was sure she only bought one. The new edition with needle-point patterns. To her amazement, as she unrolled the magazines, she saw that the extra book was one of those pornographic magazines that had pictures of men and women in disgusting positions. She was horrified.

Why would that clerk do such a thing to her? This wasn't the first time it had happened either. She was sure the bag boy had done this just to embarrass her.

She felt so dirty. She took only a short glimpse before she realized what the magazine held. Gerry quickly rose from the bench and went directly to the trash barrel that was sitting on the edge of the walkway.

This was enough to make her start walking back to her apartment, forgetting all about the peanuts and feeding the squirrels. The squirrels would be fed. Some small children found the nuts and began to feed them to the squirrels, but Gerry's blissfull day had come to an abrupt end.

As she walked up the outside steps to the lobby doors, she heard a very nasty cackle, almost a dirty laugh. She spun around, but no one on the street seemed to have heard it or was laughing in that manner. She was so upset, she went to the apartment and went to bed. Maybe a nap was just what she needed.

July 9, 1954

Dear Diary,

Would you believe it, I had myself a family all at one time. My babies are so beautiful. Geraldine Emily and Terrance George, born June 13, 1954. I just can't stop talking about them.

Even George messed over them, a little. I thought he would be mad because of all the diapers and bottles. I don't get to take very good care of him any more. You know what I mean, don't you? He got so rough while I was pregnant. It hurt so bad, I told him Doc said no more sex for awhile. I don't know what I'll tell him now. I sure don't like the funny things he tries to do to me. Sometimes I think he surely does have the devil in him.

When I brought my babies home, the ladies from the church circle came over and they couldn"t believe their eyes. I am so proud of my family, I just can't wait to start dressing them alike.

Some of the ladies say that dressing them alike will hurt them and that they should be allowed to be separate people, all on their own. I think that sounds a little silly. It certainly can't hurt to let them know how close they should be. They will always have each other, no matter what happens in their lives. That's what being a family is all about. Dressing them alike can't make a whole lot of difference. When they get a little older, I'll even let them take turns in picking out the clothes they'll wear. They'll like that, I know. I can't wait to see them playing and running around.

Good night,

Emily

Chapter Four

Dinner was in process, the salad ingredients were prepared, and the wine was open and breathing. The table was perfectly set with the proper glasses and dishes, which in itself, would have shocked most of the personnel at the station. This was a side of Frank that only a chosen few knew about.

He was a good sport at work, a friend to anyone that needed it, but when it came to sharing his private life, he drew the line. The fact that he had a very large investment account, inherited from a family business, was one thing that would really have surprised some of his cronies at the station. They knew he lived pretty well, but thought he just watched his pennies. If they could see his wine cellar they would have started asking questions. This was where his interest money went, on his wine and food -- certainly not to a good tailor. He grabbed his haggard-looking sport coat from the closet and took one last look through the small but neat apartment. He still could not figure out why he was always just a little nervous when he and Margot had these special dinners. She had been here a hundred times, but he checked to see that everything was perfect each time before he left to pick her up.

One of these days he was going to weaken and propose again.

In the half dozen times he had proposed in the last ten years, she always laughed and said the same thing. "Nope, not today. I love you too much. Why spoil things? And anyway, do you honestly think you could stand to have me fool around with peanut butter and jelly in your kitchen?"

He never answered her question, because he knew the urge would pass and he could rest easy for another few years before it would happen again.

One push of the door bell was all it ever took, and there she was -- five foot seven, a great face with green eyes, and the greatest brown hair he had ever seen. He never totally understood what made her so beautiful. All it took was about five minutes of conversation with her, and you were looking at the most beautiful woman in the world. Forty-one years old, she had never been married but could have been at least two dozen times. Six proposals from Frank alone.

"You're losing it, Franklin," she said as he took her arm to see her down the apartment stairs. "You are seven minutes late. I totally expect tonight's dinner, wine and....er, your gracious company to make me forget that you are getting old and forgetful. Not to mention, you always call at the last minute."

"It was a whole four hours ago," he smirked.

Franklin knew this would be a good evening together. She could sound gruff and be soft at the same time.

He held the door of the car for her, and as she arranged herself, the first thing she said after he got in was, "What happened with the police report I heard last night about a murder over near Eighth Street? Something about a woman being cut up?"

One of Margot's vices was the police radio she had in her bedroom. Frank gave her his shocked and hurt look and said, "This is going to be a night of fine dining and drinking and pleasurable company. I don't want to talk business. Maybe we'll talk about it over an omelet in the morning." With this Margot gave her typical whistling sound and said, "Tomorrow morning is not a fully decided issue, at this point."

Franklin always enjoyed it when she did this. It just meant that there would be more of a challange to keep her from talking about last night's murder victim. He liked to talk to her about his cases. Her mind was always ready for a puzzle, and more and more he found himself anxious to give her the details of his latest job. He didn't know how

26

many times she had seen some small detail that he and his men had missed.

Outside looking in, sometimes it makes a difference.

As he hung their coats in the hall closet, Margot went directly to the refrigerator to get the Chardonnay. Dinners here did not vary much. Perhaps this is why the deep friendship of Frank and Margot had lasted so long.

Margot took the chilled glasses from the freezer, poured the Stag's Leap as Frank started puttering in the kitchen. Margot seated herself on the kitchen stool with her wine and watched Franklin prepare the final touches of dinner.

Salad tonight was to be just a little different. Steamed asparagus tips were chilled, small bits of crab meat -- the real thing, not the pressed fish that was being used by so many people these days -- a light dressing sprinkled delicately over the top, made with just a touch of Poupon Mustard, white wine, a few capers and freshly made mayonaise. The sides of the plate were dressed with the leaves of marinated artichoke hearts and tiny ears of corn. Franklin enjoyed the fine art of dressing the plate as much as cooking the food. Then, of course, the eating was the final joy.

After the salad was eaten, a small bowl of cream of carrot soup was served. Franklin was not a soup fanatic but felt that it added a little to the time spent with a someone special over an interesting meal.

The rest of the dinner was simple. Tiny filet mignons with a red wine sauce, small mushroom caps with capers, and one small ground corn cake with a light rosemary seasoning were served, and raspberry ice for dessert -- simple, but elegant. The wine was not simple, it was just elegant. Chateau Mouton-Rothchild, 1975.

Now, sitting in front of the large window in the living room, it was their time to talk. Not more than a dozen words had passed between them as they enjoyed their dinner. This was always their way. They each knew the signals. A little more wine, add a little more meat to the other's plate, a smile or a nod when the first bite was taken of a new dish -- these things added more than any words could ever say.

"Frank, tell me how you keep your figure when you cook like this," she said, as they settled down on the large old couch.

He smiled at her and said, "Watch it, when you call me Frank, I know your planning on taking advantage of me. You called me Francis today and I thought I was really in hot water."

Resting easily on the couch he added, "If I ate this way all the time I would look like a house. I see you two or three times a month for dinner, and that's how I can splurge with my eating. I don't eat between times."

Margot grinned, "Sure, and the cabinets aren't full of goodies from the best gourmet grocery store on this side of San Francisco. I'll forget it for now if you'll tell me about your slashing victim yesterday."

He told her everything he knew, or at least all that he remembered. He described Mary Carlin and the scene Friday at her apartment.

"She worked at a diner on Market street for about seven years. Manny Fry is the owner. He sounds like a real greaser. I'll find out if my opinion from the phone call fits what he really looks like if I meet with him on Monday," he said.

He continued, "She probably came from down south of here, from St. John's. We found an old prescription bottle from there. No friends that anyone here knew of, except a visit from some kid about a week or so ago. She was also seen talking to a bum at the curb a couple of times. He may have been panhandling. No one knows if she knew him or not. This neighborhood is full of bums, who are regulars."

The more he told her the sadder Margot looked.

She said, "Can you imagine having such a little history left of yourself after your gone?"

Her interest gave way to her sadness for the forgotton people that made up a major part of San Francisco. She could walk down Market Street after a grand night at the opera or theater and only remember the ever-present figures, on their usual corners or benches, where they spent endless hours. They had their own possesions and these were not to be disturbed by the other residents of the street.

The first time Margot saw the "Wheelchair Bag Lady of Market Street," she couldn't believe her eyes. Here was a woman of undetermined age and cleanliness, definitely a bag lady who was the proud owner of a working, rolling wheel chair. Somewhere, somehow she had obtained this chair. Over the years, as she searched and dug through the various waste cans at the curbsides and in the alleys, she collected enough racks and frame parts to outfit her chair to hold her bags and all her worldly goods.

No one was sure how she came to have a working wheelchair or how she came to lose the foot that caused the need for it. Years ago she told some of the street people that she lost the foot in the Himalayan Mountains. She said it was bitten off by a Yeti. Most of the people around her had never heard of the Abomidable Snowman, so she quit telling them the story.

On the corner of Seventh and Market there was "The Sentinel" with his gleaming "Old Man of the Sea" beard and a clean scrubbed look to his face. The rest of him was distinctly darker in color. He sat everyday, never leaving his post on the corner, watching the masses of people go back and forth to their daily tasks.

When something made Margot sad, she always thought of these poor street people. She felt they were poor people, but she often wondered if they thought of themselves in this way.

Dinner was over, the conversation between Frank and Margot about the cutting victim and the sadness for all the itinerants of the area, slipped into the finished part of their evening. Now they silently rose from the couch, took their half filled wine glasses, and hand in hand, walked down the hall into the large, dimly lit bedroom.

"My side or yours," Frank said.

Margot's quiet voice answered, "We'll see."

The lights were dimmed to a shadowy haze. After all, they still had to see their wine glasses.

Chapter Five

It was around three-thirty, Sunday morning. The kettle was on the burner, and Gerry Gallagher sat waiting for the water to heat. This happened too often when she would wake during the night feeling as something strange had happened. It was as if the stress had built up and sleep would not stay with her to ease it.

She took the fingernail polish from the cabinet. This would be a good time to fix her nails.

What was affecting her this way? Things were so nice before her mother died, last summer. Gerry missed her a lot, but she really had no one to talk to about her mother. Most of this didn't make very much sense to her, but it was easier to just let the situation take care of itself. When that was done, things would get back to normal.

As she sat there, the kitchen took on the feeling of a small cage. The room hadn't seemed this small before. Each day seemed to decrease the size of the world around her. On some days she actually felt as though she was fading from sight.

As soon as the water was heated and the instant put into the cup, Gerry took a few cookies and her coffee into the cozy living room.

"Funny," she said to herself, "we used to call it the front room. I wonder when we changed it."

When she lived in that little house with her mother, things were simple. After Gerry graduated from high school, she worked at the St. John's library for a few years. Her mother worked there too, doing some cleaning. It made it nice to be together, even if they were working.

Now, Saturdays were spent dusting, washing the floors and windows and doing the week's laundry. Her fondest memories of Saturdays were of the three tubs of rinse water, all in their proper place in relation to the old reliable Maytag wringer-style washer. Every piece of wash

31

must be put in with things of the same color or close to it. First you did the whites, then the light colors, then the darks, and last were the towels. Was that right?

She was always puzzled after she left home. Did you do the dark things and let them fade on the towels, or did you do the towels first and let the lint get onto the dark socks and pants? Well, it didn't really matter much in these days of automatic washers. Each load had its own water. Things like this stuck with her. Some day she'd find some one to explain it to her, if it became a real problem.

She remembered the time when she was small and she had to stand on a box to help put the clothes through the wringer. One day she was careless and her arm got caught. Those were the days when her brother was always there to protect her. He was small, too, of course, but his yells brought their mother before any damage was done. She even remembered how Terry scrubbed his cheek when she kissed it for "saving her arm from being torn right from her body." He thought kisses were mushy stuff. At least that's what her mother told all the neighbors.

He was always there when she needed him. Now, she didn't understand exactly what was going on, but she knew that it would get better and that he would take care of things, just like he used to.

After finishing her coffee, she went back to her bed with those pleasant thoughts on her mind, and in no time she was asleep.

Franklin wasn't sure what woke him, the smell of the bacon and burned biscuits or the phone. He decided that Margot was trying to return the favor and cook his breakfast. This was almost always a disaster.

As he got out of bed to answer the phone, wherever it was, he grabbed his pajama bottoms that were tossed on the chair. Fortunately, he had planned ahead last evening before he left to pick up Margot.

"Yeah," he said into the wrong end of the phone receiver, then twisted it around. "Wait...yes, hello, Franklin here, who there?"

There was about a thirty-second pause while he listened.

"Yeah. Okay. All right," he said as he began to scowl even more than usual, because of being called on police business on this Sunday morning.

He hung up the phone without saying good-bye, flipped the sheets up on the bed, and turned to his closet. After grabbing trousers, socks, and a shirt, he headed for the kitchen.

Margot did not turn as he entered the kitchen, "Don't say it, I heard the phone ring. You have to go on a call. Does your phone ever ring when I'm not here?"

He looked as apologetic as he could manage and said, "Never. Now while I go take care of this small problem, why don't you eat everything you have cooked, and take a long, slow hot bath. I bought you some new bubble stuff for your bath. It shouldn't take long. Some bum got himself cut up. They're not sure when. Last night sometime or early this morning.

It can't be too involved. We'll go to the zoo when I get back."

With that he finished fixing his belt, straightened his collar and walked out of the kitchen, just in time to miss being hit with a very wet dishcloth.

"I hate the zoo!" Margot yelled at the closing door. To herself she whispered, "And I hate burned bisquits."

Grabbing the least black of the biscuits, and a cup of coffee, she headed for the bathroom, mumbling very unladylike words.

Franklin wasn't as sure of the time involved as he tried to sound.

Fred, from Division, was his caller. An old man had been found dead around seven this morning, down near the end of the line for the Van Ness buses. The old man was sitting on a bench, overlooking the water's edge in the lower harbor. It looked like his head had been jerked back and his neck broken. His throat had two wounds on it -- one short and shallow on the left side and the other, more terminating one was a very deep, clean cut from ear to ear.

As Franklin pulled up to the curb, he grabbed the <u>Police Business</u> sign for his car dashboard and flipped it up. He was parked on the end of the street, but the buses would have to make a sharper turn to make it around him.

<u>Such is life</u>, he thought.

As Frank walked down the slight incline to the park, he saw some of "San Francisco's Finest" happily going about their duties. yelling and making obsene gestures to each other. Fred was still trying to get some semblance of order when he spotted Franklin coming down the hill.

"Morning, Lieutenant. Sorry about the Sunday call." Fred extended his hand to motion to the bench with the old man's body on it.

"Here he is, sir. We haven't moved anything yet. The lab guys haven't done their thing, they're waiting for the photographer. He's got some money on him, just a few bucks, and a note with a phone number on it. It says to show up for work next Tuesday at a fish stand on the west side of the marketplace."

"Lieutenant, we already called the number on the note and they told us that this guy worked at the market Friday. He helped unload trucks for one of the grape growers. Nothing unusual in his actions. He walked around asking who needed help next week, and after he connected with someone, he started walking up Market Street. We haven't had a chance to talk to any of his friends from the market area to see what he did on Saturday."

"This guy wasn't a bum," he went on. "He had a job of sorts, working for one or two of the fruit-and-vegetable or fish stands over at Market and Seventh in the open marketplace there. A lot of these guys worked wherever they could get a little change. They made all their arrangements at the close of the day. He had a room some place over a furniture store in the warehouse district."

After all this explanation, Franklin said, "Good job, Fred. I was glad you called after I heard how his throat was cut. The only thing you haven't told me was his name and the color of his socks."

The detective looked at him and added, "Well, everyone called him 'Fuzzy' and he didn't have no socks on, ... sir."

The "sir" was added after a strange glance from Franklin.

Fred continued, "We figure it was done Saturday night or Sunday morning, early. We all heard about the other one with the old lady. We thought that this one might have some connection."

Franklin moaned a little at this last bit of information. "The old lady, as you call her, did have her throat cut like this guy, but she was also cut from one arm pit to the other. This guy has his throat slit, twice, almost. He's sitting on a park bench and one side of his head looks like meat loaf. I wonder if there really is a connection."

"Lieutenant, it looks like the head was hit over and over, after his throat was cut," Fred said with a puzzled look.

"Yeah, that occured to me, too, Fred. Strange, huh? Well, get all the information and his belongings to me at my office. Don't forget to see if you can find that hole he lives in. Give it a good going-over. I want all of his personal property from there, too. I'll look it over, and see if there's any connection."

With this, Franklin swung around just in time to see a bus make a slight scratch across the left rear panel of his car as the bus driver struggled to make the sharp turn with Frank's car in the way.

"Goddamn," Frank spat as he walked to the curb.

Grumbling to himself, he started his car. He decided to stop at the station and see if any new information had turned up on Miss Carlin. Someone might have found a relative in the area and he wouldn't have to bother with St. John's.

It was too nice a day to rush any place, so he started towards the wharf area. The office would be there and Margot was probably just adding hot water to the tub for the second time. She also liked a long nap after her bubble bath, so she wouldn't be expecting him for at least two more hours.

He started walking after he parked his car in the parking lot near Fisherman's Whart, right across from the window where you can buy the tickets to go over to Alcatraz.

Franklin stopped at a curbside stand down near the wharf and bought himself a container of Calamari. This was the way to start a sunny day. If he had time, he might get a slab of pizza, too.

As he strolled and ate his Calamari, his mind ran over the Carlin case. More and more it just seemed like some nut wanted to see how much of a mess he could make of a human body, and poor Mary Carlin was handy...but was she handy? She was killed in her room. That's not handy. She worked until midnight, and she walked home. It had to be between twelve and twelve-thirty in the morning when she got to her place. That surely is not handy if you're just out prowling.

There was no apparent struggle. There was not much in the room, the chairs were all upright, the bed was not messed, except for her being on it, and there were coffee cups out on the side table .. two coffee cups with saucers.

That was the thing that had bugged him. He realized that he had almost botched things in not noticing this before. If it was just going to be her in that room, there was no reason for her to have two coffee cups out, and both were clean. There was no time to make the coffee.

She must have known her visiter. Did the murderer act that fast, or did he just not want any coffee?

"Damn," he muttered.

How could he have missed this. Now he knew he had to get to the office, just to get his thoughts and ideas down on paper, and to look through the victim's belongings again. All of the Carlin information coupled with the killing of the bum in the same general way, made him anxious to get back to the office.

An ice cream would travel well in the car, so Franklin ran in and bought a double cone of banana and rum-raisen. As he got into his car, he moaned a little as he glanced at the scratch. He also decided that it was his own damned fault. He was just finishing the cone as he parked outside the station.

On the way into his office, several officers glanced up at him and then to each other.

"This must be something special to get Franklin here on Sunday," one officer remarked to the other uniformed man across the table.

Franklin wasn't much worried about what their thoughts were. He was more aggravated with himself for missing the coffee cup thing at Carlin's on Friday. Reaching into the closet, he pulled the Carlin box from the shelf and carried it over to his desk.

All the items were the same as they had been twice before, but somehow he felt that there had to be something there. Most of the books were yearbooks from St. John's Elementary School. The pictures must have been from there, too.

Then there were those scruffy pieces of paper that Schultz thought had been in the box when he got it out of the hall. The writing was dim, and it looked pretty old. There was a date at the top of one of them, looked like <u>May 1958</u>, but he couldn't be sure. This piece was cheap, lined stuff, probaby from a pad like they used in school, the size of notebook paper, but it did not have the holes.

He could make out the words, "You're not going to believe this, but George didn't get mad about me being pregnant. He did tell me to do something about it. I feel real bad about this, but I just can't have another baby."

Farther down the page, Frank read, "He went out for awhile and came back with that teacher. Can you believe, he really brought her right here into this house." The writer sounded a little upset.

The paper looked like a letter to some one, there was the beginning of a salutation at the top but all Franklin could make out was, "Dear Dia... "

He couldn't make out the name. Some of the other pieces were smaller and looked like they came out of a small notebook. On the top of one he could make out quite distinctly, "Dear Diary." That frosted it. These were pages from a diary, and they were signed by someone named Emily.

Here was another page that was quite readable, "Dear Diary, I feel bad today. Next Monday that teacher is going to take me over to Longtown.

She says there is a doctor over there who will get rid of the baby. The fancy word is abortion. I don't like the sound of that word, but that's what I have to do."

The diary entry went on to say that the doctor was a veterinarian.

It looked like Franklin was going to miss out on his eggs and cold burned biscuits. He knew he had to make the phone call, and he dreaded it. He reached for the phone and dialed his own number.

The phone rang about five times, and a firm, feminine voice answered, "Francis, you are dead meat."

There was a very small, quiet click, and then a dial tone. He was so interested in the pages, he just hung up and started studing the old papers before him.

March 16, 1958

Dear Diary,

I'm worried about the babies. Sometime they fight so bad I just don't know what to do with them. I can sit and play with them for hours and never get tired of looking at them. I'll bet I'm just as smart as those teachers. Especially that uppity teacher. I sure hope the kids don't have her in school when they get older. I just don't think I could stand to have her with them all day long when I know how she spends most of her nights.

I'm almost sure she's the one George sees after work. Last week some of the ladies in the grocery line were talking about her, but when they saw me behind them, they stopped talking about her.

I guess everyone knows what George does outside our house. I wonder if they know what he does inside it.

Good night my friend,

Emily

April 4, 1958

My dear, dear Diary,

I think I'm pregnant again. Why can't Doc see my problem when I tell him I can't have another baby? George will get crazy again, I know for sure. He wasn't so mean when he found out I was pregnant with the twins, but he's gotten pretty mean since then. I dont think I can stand to go through that if I can help it.

I'll get the test results on Wednesday. Doc told me he can't do anything about it, if I am pregnant.

Maybe, since we've had the babies, George will feel better about it. He loves the babies, I know he does. Sometimes he's just a little mean to them, but I'm sure he really loves them, down deep. Why just last week he played catch with them.

I hope he's changing. He hasn't been mean for a while. You remember what he does those times? How can he do such a bad thing to me? I've never said no to my wifely duties, but to force me, and in front of the babies--I almost don't mind that he sees that teacher for most of his sex. She must have been the one to teach him all those nasty things he does to me.

Dear Diary, I'm so glad I have you to talk to, I'd just go crazy if I didn't have a friend like you. Sometimes I just feel like you're a real person.

I tried to make friends with some of the women at church, but most of the time they are busy and can't spend any time with me. I think it might be that they're afraid of George and they are trying to stay away from me. I talk to Mrs. Jensen at the grocery store, but I can't make much of a friend when I just have a few minutes while I go through the line. She would probably avoid me, too, if she knew more about George. I guess most people just don't like him much.

We never had any friends to visit with, or maybe play cards, like some people do. I heard some of the ladies at church talking about starting a card club, but when I asked if it was hard to learn how to play, they acted like the club was full and there wasn't any room for another couple.

George wouldn't go anyway. He says he hates those nosy biddies from church. That's what he calls them. I don't know how he knows if they're nosy or not, but he sure don't like them.

With my love,

Emily

April 20, 1958

Dear Diary,

George brought that woman over today for Sunday Dinner. He says she is an old family friend. I sure never heard that about her before today.

Well, it wasn't too bad. She seemed a little nervous and sure paid a lot of attention to the babies. They didn't care for her much. They don't like the fussing some people do. She helped clean up after we ate, and then George took her home.

He's been gone for two hours, but I don't really care. I'm going to try to be asleep before he gets home. It sure makes things easier sometimes.

He wakes me when he comes home if he's in a bad mood, but I don't think he will tonight. He had a silly look on his face when they left, and if he thinks he's fooling me, he surely is crazy. I don't care, as long as he leaves me alone.

I must get to bed now, so I can get to sleep real fast.
Good night, Dear Diary.

Love,

Emily

May 25, 1958

Dear Dia...

You're not going to believe this, but George didn't get mad about me for being pregnant. He did tell me to do something about it. I feel real bad about this, but I just can't have another baby. I keep thinking that I shouldn't have to be away from my babies that I already have. It's hard enough with just two, and I guess I'll have to do something with this one.

George says so too. I told him I thought Doc wouldn't do anything. I was afraid to tell him I asked Doc to take care of it without talking to him first. George says not to worry, he can find a way. He sure is being nice about this. He hasn't been mean or anything. I think his crazy times are over.

He went out for awhile and came back with that teacher. Can you believe, he really brought her to this house again. We sat and had tea and talked like we were just friends having a visit.

I guess she's not so bad. I couldn't believe he brought her here, the first time, but he said she was the daughter of an old friend. I'll bet.

I guess that's all for tonight. It was kind of nice having company, even if it had to be that teacher. Maybe she's not so bad. The babies didn't pay too much attention to her. They don't like to be bothered. They don't see many other people around here.

Good night friend,

Emily

May 26, 1958

My dear friend,

I feel so bad today. Next Monday, that teacher is going to take me over to Longtown. She says there's a doctor over there who will get rid of the baby. The fancy word is abortion. I don't like the sound of that word, but that's what I have to do.

She says the man is a vet. That is a short name for a doctor who takes care of dogs and cats. I sure don't like the idea of some dog doctor working on me, but she says he does this kind of thing all the time. She keeps calling him "Doctor Charlie". I don't know if that's his first name or his last. Here I am going to have my own baby killed, and I don't even know the doctor's name who's going to do it.

The teacher says we can go Monday night, so no one will see us go into his office. I guess he'll do it right there where he takes care of the dogs. I sure hope I don't get no fleas. I know that will make me even sicker, if I see one of those little bugs. I can't hardly stand to see a bug near me.

I feel like I should be going to church or something, but I don't want to talk to anyone there, because they will tell me what a wicked woman I am, for having this abortion.

What do all these other women do. I'll bet their husbands don't make them have sex all the time. None of them are always getting pregnant. There's got to be a way to keep from getting that way besides those fancy pills they all talk about. George wouldn't let me take those things, even if we had the money. That must be what those fancy ladies take to keep from having a whole house full of kids.

I sure wouldn't give up my babies that I have, but I can't take a chance on having any more. I'm so scared. I hope this doesn't hurt. I never did like to hurt, and now it seems like that's all I ever do, is just sit and hurt from

44

something. It's always because of George. I just can't think of any time he didn't make me think of something but hurting. I'm not saying that thinking about my babies makes me hurt, but there sure is a lot of pain with them, too.

They act so funny sometimes. Yesterday, Gerry started strutting around here like she was some kind of a queen or something. She talked so strong and bossy, not like her usual self. Mostly, she's been such a good girl. She scared Terry, I could tell. He kept telling her to quit being that mean sister. I've never heard him call her that before, and I don't know what he means when he says mean sister. It was like he thought she was a different sister. Poor Terry, he must just be tired. They have been fighting a little more these days.

Terry has been acting strange around his daddy, lately. Like he don't want to be left in the room alone. I don't know why. I guess I don't really want to know. If it was for a reason I didn't like, and I said something, George might beat on me again. I don't want to think about that right now. I've got enough trouble. Terry can handle his father, besides, what could George possibly do to his own son that a mother wouldn't like?

I guess that's all for now, my dearest diary. I'll write tommorrow or the next day, when I feel like telling you about my operation. This will be something nice. I've never had an operation to talk about. Now I have one of my very own.

Goodnight sweet diary,

Emily

June 2, 1958

My dear friend,

Well, it's over. That vet doctor did that abortion thing to me. I'm still pretty weak, but he said to rest plenty and I'd be fine in a week.

I'm sure glad the babies don't know about this. They might wonder why I didn't do that to get rid of them.

I guess since I waited to tell George so long when I got pregnant with them, he didn't even think about doing that to them.

Sometimes when George beat on me while I was carrying them, I thought he was doing it to hurt them. Even before they was born, he was acting different. Like he enjoyed making me hurt.

He hasn't hit them hardly at all, lately, leastwise, since they learned to not cry every time he yelled. The crying seemed to make him just that much madder. He would really slam into them, for that. Now they just stand or sit, whatever he tells them to do, When he hits them they don't cry, or look around, or anything.

Gerry's a little different. She acts like she's standing there sleeping with her eyes open. Nothing comes out of her mouth and she don't cry or say a word. Terry gets into a little more trouble because he talks back. One time he even tried to hit George.

Last night Terry made her mad and Gerry sounded like one of those army generals on television -- you know, giving orders and being real firm.

Terry always calls her the mean sister when she acts like that. He said one day that the mean sister takes care of fights at school, when they need her. Sounds to me like he's making up odd stories. Don't you think that's just from a good imagination? I'm sure proud of my babies, they can make up games and stories real good.

46

I guess I'll go to bed now. I'm tired and the babies are in their room playing. They wanted me to come in and read to them, but I couldn't pass up a chance to write to you, my sweet Diary.

Goodnight,

Emily

June 11, 1958

Dear Friend,

I've been feeling pretty good, and George has been kind of nice to me and the twins.

He's still seeing that teacher, but I don't care much. She's not so bad. When she comes over on Sundays, I pretend I have a lady friend to talk to, and I never had that before.

I just wish she wasn't so bossy. This time she told the babies to go back up to their room and put on some nicer clothes for dinner. They looked at me a little funny, but I nodded my head for them to do what they was told. I heard them fussing at each other when they got up there. When they're down here, they act like they like her. I don't think they really do.

George also leaves me alone more now than he used to. I guess having her around isn't so bad.

He did get mad at the twins last week and he beat Terry pretty bad. I really think that Gerry was the one that started the fire in the trash can. I was almost sure that Terry was upstairs. Gerry said she was taking a nap and she didn't play with matches around there.

Sometimes I can't keep up with either of them. I really like talking to you, my dear friend. You never argue back, and you are always here to listen to me.

Your best friend, Dear Diary,

Emily

April 3, 1960

Dear Diary,

It's Sunday night, and I feel pretty good. Today we had company for dinner again. Mary Carlin was here. She's still coming over for Sunday dinner once in a while, and it's not too bad. She helps the babies set the table and helps me. Sometimes she acts like she's the boss around here, and I don't like that very much.

Today she set the table with them, and they sounded like they had fun with her. They even played "turn around" on her. She thought that was the best joke she ever saw. Gerry was mashing the potatoes and then Terry slipped in and took her place.

Mary went over and said, "Gerry let me help you with that" and the kids laughed and laughed.

Then they started their sing-song, "Turn around, Turn around! We got you".

Then she told them not to play in the kitchen. They looked like their feelings were hurt.

The school called again. I tried to talk to Terry and make him understand that he has to follow the rules of the school. He gets so mad and I can't make him understand that they have to make all the children at the school do things together. He wants to go off by himself and do his own things alone. He doesn't even want Gerry with him on some of his free time.

When they have recess, he usually tries to sneak out of the play-ground. I don't know where he goes from there. He's probably playing some more of his tricks. Last week one of the teachers had all four tires on her car go flat and they tried to say Terry did that. Now how can a small boy like that make those big tires go flat, when they didn't even have holes in them. They just like to pick on him, I think.

Gerry got into trouble again. The principal said she beat up on one of the boys. Can you believe that? How could my sweet little Gerry do that. The principal said she was dressed like Terry when she came back after school and she hit that boy with a baseball bat. The reason he knew it was Gerry was he saw Terry still sitting on the wall by the school gate talking to some of his friends.

I think Gerry might have done it, but if she did I'm sure the boy deserved it. Gerry has more nerve to do things if people think she's Terry.

I've seen her be a little more brave a couple of times, even with her daddy. Of course, some of the time, she says she didn't do anything. She will stand and tell me that, when I've stood and watched her. Some times she gets so mad her face turns red. How can a little girl be so mixed up? She really believes she didn't do these things.

If the twins are dressed alike, George can't tell them apart, half of the time. That's why he usually spanks both of them. That way he's sure the guilty one will be punished. I wonder if one of them has ever been punished twice and the other one got nothing.

I think it's pretty funny. A father who can't tell his own babies apart. I never told anyone this, but I've had a few times when I can't tell which one I'm talking to. It doesn't bother me, because I love them both so much. They know I love them and they don't care if I call them by the wrong name.

One day last week they did get mad at me. Terry wanted me to work with them on one of their school projects, but I told them I was going to be busy writing to you. For some reason, when I write to you, it makes them mad. Terry said I loved you more than I did them, but we know how silly that is. Why I'll always have them, and the only way I can keep you is to be sure and write to you all the time. You're the only true friend I have and I just can't lose you.

50

Goodnight, my dearest friend.

Emily

November 9, 1960

Dear Diary,

I think I know a real secret, but I'm not sure. George has been really crazy for a few days. He hasn't hit me or anything, but he doesn't talk, and he's been home almost every night for most of the last weeK. He stopped at the tavern, but he's been home after that.

Yesterday one of the twins came home from school and said Miss Mary was sick and would be gone from school for a week. I'll just bet she had to go see Dr. Charlie. I think that's really funny, if it's true. That old vet sure is making money off of Mister George Gallagher. That should teach him to stay at home and behave himself more. A man doesn't have to do that kind of thing all the time. Once he has a family, he should quit doing that stuff.

That's what Mommy always said, and I surely do believe her. Why Daddy was the nicest, dearest man, and I'm sure he didn't make Mommy do those nasty sex things all the time.

I remember how nice he was when he was around Mommy. He would always help her up the stairs, open doors for her, and do all those important things that a man should do for a lady. Momma surely was a lady. She would dress up on Sunday in her best dress and a nice hat. She even wore nice little white gloves. When I was little, she let me wear gloves when I went to church with them. Daddy was so kind. I wish my babies could have a Daddy like I had.

If Miss Fancy Pants, Mary Carlin, had to go see Dr. Charlie, she is just getting what she deserved. That is the only reason I can think of for George to be the way he has been this past week. I really think this is funny, don't you?

Ha, Ha, dear Diary.

Ha, Ha, dear Emily.

See, Diary, I can have you laugh with me. Goodnight, my dear friend. We won't share our secret with anyone else.

Emily

Chapter Six

As the two sets of blue eyes starred at each other, there was a heavy stillness in the apartment.

"Have we done something?" she asked, quietly. "Something bad? I can always tell by the way you act. We've done something again, and I've forgotten, haven't I? Please don't make me ask all these questions."

Whenever he acted this way, Gerry's stomach would become upset. She could never take the stress that came from the actions of Terry or her own forgetfulness.

As she walked out of the hall, a mocking voice followed her, "You don't know anything unless I want you to know it. Don't start in on me or I'll leave right now. Then what will you do? You don't know how badly you handled the last two opportunities I gave you. You almost made a grand mess of everything. Well, at least you tried. I'm not trying to be mean, honest. I'm trying to help."

The low muffled voice muttered again, cleared his throat and said, "You don't even know what I'm talking about, do you? I leave you alone for a few years and I'm surprised that you lasted this long without help."

Tears formed in Gerry's eyes, as she slumped to the couch.

"Please, Gerry, don't start sniveling, you know I can't stand to hear that noise. You sound just like Mother when she cried. I hated that sound."

Gerry took a few deep breaths and blew her nose. The tears gently slowed and she became quiet.

Terry rose from the couch. As he walked through the hall, he said to himself, "The darkroom. That's where I'll go. I need to go down to the darkroom."

He went back into the kitchen, picked a key chain from the rack in the corner and left the silent apartment.

As Terry closed the door, Gerry wondered when Terry became interested in photography. She remembered that it was her hobby when she was still living at home. Sometimes, the fact that she forgot a lot made her nervous. She reasoned that if she forgot something it must not be very important.

The darkroom was made from the storage space each renter was allowed in the basement. The owners of the building didn't care what you did with your storage space, just as long as you kept within your own area.

When Terry came last summer, he wanted to build the darkroom, so he could have some place of his own. Gerry arranged for a plumber to pipe water into the storage area. Terry made a few trips to the local hardware store, where he purchased a few cabinets, some supplies, and picked up a few other things.

The enlarger and all the developing equipment came from an ad in the "Second Hand News" and this small room became Terry's haven.

His pictures were good -- in fact, exceptionally good -- but most of them showed a troubled and downtrodden world. Some were even violent and shocking.

Terry was only at ease in the darkroom, his private piece of the world. After each session of developing and making his prints, he would mix more chemicals for the next session of his work. The chemicals must be at a temperature between sixty-five and seventy degrees when he used them and since they had to be mixed with water that was from eighty to one-hundred and twenty five degrees, he usually mixed his developer, fixer, and stop-bath at least one day in advance. The basement temperature was perfect and kept the chemicals at a constant sixty-eight degrees, perfect for use later.

Terry made sure today's batch of prints were wiped properly with the Squeegee and clipped on the line to dry. He made sure they hung without touching each other, then began to make his list of needed chemicals.

With this done, he tidied his work station, checked the room and walked out, locking the door behind him.

It was about four in the afternoon when he walked over to enter the elevator and go upstairs. As the doors slid open the doorman, Ed, came out of the elevator. Standing in front of the door, Ed stopped to greet the young man.

"Good afternoon, Mister Gallagher, having a fine day in your dark room, are you?"

Terry was upset at missing the elevator, and with a slap at the button, the young man grunted and went back to reading the shopping list in his gloved hands. Ed figured that the chemicals were pretty harsh to make a person wear those rubber gloves down here. Terry wore the gloves most of the time.

He often thought to himself, <u>Please, God, let that crabby young man put one of his rubber gloves over his head and take a deep breath.</u>

After the door slipped shut, Ed glanced around, making sure no one else was in the basement, and gave the snappiest salute ever. He saluted the closed doors of the elevator. If anyone had been there, he might have noticed that all the fingers were not aimed in the same direction. Only one finger was raised in the salute -- the middle one.

Ed clicked his heels, gave a sharp military turn and walked away smiling, exceptionally pleased with himself.

Chapter Seven

There were nine diary entries in all. The dates ran from 1958 to 1960. Franklin did not understand this. Why was someone else's diary at Mary Carlin's place? What did it mean? Could Mary have been keeping the diary for this Emily and then threw it out, just before the murder.

The box was from some grocery store. At one time it had held carpet cleaner He wondered who in the hell ever cleaned or even had a carpet in that building. <u>Probably brought groceries or something home in it and was just too lazy to carry it all the way down to the trash container.</u> Most of the people, around here, just pitched their trash out the window, and into the alley.

The first thing to do was place the entries in chronological order.

Then he took some of the items from the box and started arranging them on the bulletin board.

The writer, Emily, talked about her abortion. Frank could read most of the dates. They started in 1958; the last number was smudged a little. The person who took Emily to have the abortion was named Mary. He finally found one that used the whole nam -- Mary Carlin. It sounded like Mary was fooling around with Emily's husband.   A few entries were quite a few pages long, about George coming home late, smelling like a brewery. Here the other woman is mentioned as Mary again. Frank read more entries where the full name of Mary Carlin was used.

In some pages Emily talks about twins. She must have had them before Mary took her for her abortion. Seems the little rotters were quite a handful, always getting in trouble and switching places to confuse the teachers and neighbors. There wasn't very much mentioned about them that showed happiness. In fact, not much of any kind of happiness showed in these pages.

These pages seemed to center on Mary and George. Sounds like George was quite a ladies man, she complained about the way he pawed her, and then she complained about the time he spent with the other woman, Mary. Evidently Emily just doesn't like George very much by this time.

The little she wrote about the kids sounded like he was pretty rough on them. Emily didn't go into much detail on that part. Sounded like the father may have abused the son. Most of this is about her thoughts on Mary Carlin. Some of it sounded like she knew Mary, and some did not. This helped Franklin with the dates on the diary pages.

Franklin's notes contained lists made up of different items culled from the loose pages in front of him. The main point revolved around Mary.

She had been the honored subject in at least this part of Emily's diary.

There were probably more pages centering around the other people involved around Emily's life, but here Mary Carlin was the star.

"Well," said Franklin to himself, "these papers are important to something, but is it the murder of Mary Carlin?"

They were probably tossed out there by Mary Carlin herself. Franklin wondered why Carlin would have Emily's diary in the first place. These pages were from various dates and from various types of notebooks. There must have been writings between these dates -- so why just have pages on Mary Carlin left there.

"Good question," he answered his own thoughts.

Franklin stared at the diary entries. He couldn't tie them into the murder. They were too old.

<u>People don't go around cutting up retired school teachers just because she kept old year books,</u> he said to himself.

He knew there had to be a reason and it would come out some time.

Franklin drained the cup of cold coffee and turned to glare at the pot on the hot plate, in the corner of his office. It was empty too. This was one of the finer appointments of his elevated position as a lieutenant He shared his office with a detective, who was on leave of absence, and they had their own hot plate with which to boil away the instant coffee made in the large pot in the cop's lounge.

During the week, one of the secretaries brought Franklin's coffee in about ten minutes before he was due in the mornings. The largest problem was that he didn't really come in at any precise time, so he either had three-hour-old coffee that had become syrup, or he did not have any. The cup he had just finished was from the deli down the street, cold, but still liquid.

He stacked the albums and photos, and placed them in the box. As he went through the items that had come from the purse, he noted the contents of the wallet -- about fourteen dollars with some change, a cheap lipstick that was almost white.

Shades of the sixties, he thought.

The wallet was the type that had a place for bills inside a fold and papery plastic holders for credit cards, of which there were none, and a few dog-eared photos. There was one of a man, two women and a couple of kids. It looked like they were sitting on the front steps of a small white frame house. The kids held what looked like a hula hoop between them.

God, he thought, most of the guys working here are so young, they've never heard of a hula hoop.

No matter how he looked at this picture, it told him very little. There was nothing written on the back, so there were no clues as to who these people were. The man stood on one side, beside the kids, then the two women. The woman in the middle and the man had their arms around the kids and the other woman seemed to only be there for the picture. This might be old George with Emily, the diary writer, the twins in between and Mary Carlin, standing dutifully off to the side.

The phone rang to startle him out of a semi-haze, as he stared at all the diary pages on the board.

"Yeah," Franklin said as he held the phone to his ear with his shoulder, "Franklin here."

On the other end was the patrolman that had answered the call from the superintendant of the building where Mary Carlin lived. "Lieutenant Franklin, Schwartz said you were asking some questions about a box that was outside the door where we found that cutting victim Friday. Well, sir, when I got there, the super was downstairs. He said he had the key to the room, but the smell was so bad in the hall that he was afraid to use it. He gave the key to me. When we got up to the third floor where the victim lived, I went to open the door and there was a roll of papers stuck behind the door knob. Kinda like some kind of advertising. I just took the wad and tossed it into a box that was in the corner next to the door. Then I used the key and opened the door. You know what we found after that."

As the patrolman paused to catch a breath, Franklin whispered, "Well, well, a calling card perhaps."

"What did you say, sir? Was that all you needed to know? Schwartz said you were mostly interested if the papers came from inside the room or out in the hall. If they're the ones that looked like a roll of pages from some kind of a notebook, they were there in the hall, behind the door knob, like I said. I figured some kids left them there."

Franklin smiled and answered, "Thanks a lot, you have answered some of the puzzle. Not totally, but at least now I know that these papers might have something to do with the murder."

Franklin looked at the pages and started to read them again before he had even hung up the phone.

As he returned the pages to the board, he said, "Here are the final belongings of a human being that has been sliced out of this world."

What could he learn from this small pile of nothing?

After he placed all the albums in date order, he stood reading the pages of the diary again. He was sure that something here showed him a part of Mary Carlin's life that hadn't been talked about lately. What more had she been to these people in the picture and in the diary?

If she was the other woman, why did the wife tolerate having her around as if she were her best friend? Maybe she was. That surely had happened before. If she was a school teacher, she could have been a teacher to these kids in the picture, who must certainly be the twins mentioned in the diary.

As Franklin looked at the picture, he thought the children looked about five or six years old.

It was silly to think a person would fool around with someone while she was so close to the kids and the wife though. That was really looking for trouble. It seemed like there would definetly be something to be learned from a phone call to St. Johns.

With any luck there would still be someone around that could remember something about Mary Carlin. After all, teachers leave their stamp on the community where they teach. Some students are always left to say, "I remember her, she made me stay after school." or some such silly memory.

This should be simple, he was sure, as soon as he tied a few facts together.

Without bothering to look at the clock, Franklin pulled the small stack of bills from the corner of his desk and started sorting them. The check book was still in the pile so he decided this would be a good time to finish with his domestic chores of paying his bills.

When these were finished, he noticed that the stubs of some expense statements had been crammed down into one corner of the drawer and started pulling them out. Before he knew what had happened, he had cleaned out the drawer and put everything back in such a neat order, he was not sure if it really was his desk.

"Oh well," he sighed, "it has to be done some time."

Not quite sure what had possessed him to become a neat freak on a Sunday, he was satisfied with the look of his office as he stood up from the desk and looked around at the newly tidied surroundings. He felt that he had put in one very productive day, even though it was a Sunday.

Sometimes this was the best time to do things like this. Most of his regular activity was done during the work week, and things were just a little quieter here on weekends. That made it easier to really study and ponder on some of these queer cases. It also made it easier to get his personal bills paid when he didn't have the constant interruptions of the usual work day.

He finished around half past five and decided to call it a day. He had not had anything to eat since the ice cream cone, and he could really use a shave. His beard was beginning to drive him crazy. He put the remaining items on his desk back into their box and placed the box in the closet. He felt like he knew all he was going to get from these small pieces of Mary Carlin for today. Maybe tomorrow would bring some more light onto the happenings of the weekend.

As he walked out the door to the street, the smell of evening hit him. This was one of the great things about San Francisco, that cool smell that he loved so much. Sometimes it smelled like fish, but that too was San Francisco. He looked forward to going back to his apartment. There was nothing like a hot bath and a few glasses of wine before going to bed.

Tomorrow would bring the answers he needed, and he could start the week with a clean slate.

He'd call Margot in a few days. Everything would be all right, then. It always was.

Chapter Eight

The first thing Franklin did Monday morning was call the St. John's Police Chief. His questions around the office had turned up a wealth of nothing. He decided that this town did not really exist, because only one other person in the station even knew there was a St. John's. This was getting off to a great start.

St. John's was a small town, downstate from San Francisco, about sixty miles. Not much ever happened there, but the residents thought they were just about as citified as anyone from New York or Chicago. The town was situated on one main road, on the west side of a small river named El Verde. The name fit, too. Its usual color was that of pea soup.

The river was about as spectacular as the town of St. John's, and it did nothing very special but run by the town. A few small marinas lined it's shores near town, where you could rent a boat to fish or one to just putt-putt around in on a Sunday afternoon.

Most of the people of St. John's worked in neighboring towns that had larger, more industrialized business centers. There was a bottling plant in the next town and several small manufacturing companies that boasted about one hundred employees each. This was the hub of the working community of this area. Most of the residents had lived here all their lives and could not think of doing anything different from what their parents had done before them.

As he hugged the receiver to his ear with his shoulder, Frank punched in the number and started going over his list of questions he would ask of this Chief Michaels from St. John's.

"Hello, St. John's Station, may I help you?" the voice on the other end answered.

"Yes, sir. My name is Lieutenant Frank Franklin from San Francisco Police Department, and I have some questions about a former resident of St. John's. Would I be able to speak to Police Chief Michaels, if it's at all convenient?"

Franklin asked this in his most official voice. He always saved this way of talking for the first time he had to speak to someone of authority, especially if the authority had something he needed and he wanted to make them think he had more pull than he really did.

"Can you hold, please, Lieutenant Franklin, I'll see if the chief is free."

Franklin smiled. That meant he'd see if the chief wanted to talk to some stranger who called and said he was a cop and wanted to ask some dumb questions about someone whom no one remembered. He would probably get shuffled around through a half dozen guys before some desk cop gets stuck with the questions.

"Hello, Chief Michaels, here, I understand you are an officer from San Francisco and you have some questions about one of our former residents. How may I help you, sir?"

With that Franklin shook his head. He couldn't believe his ears until he remembered the size of St. John's and realized that the chief and the person who answered the phone might be the whole force in that town.

"Chief Michaels, I thank you for sparing me some of your valuable time. Last Friday we received a call from the superintendant of a somewhat run-down hotel. After an inspection of the room in question, we found one of his tenants was the victim of a brutal murder."

"From her belongings we were able to ascertain that at one time she had resided in St. John's. It seems she was a schoolteacher there for a period of years. School yearbooks with her name and pictures were among her things. Do you have any knowledge of a Miss Mary

Carlin? Her papers show her age at fifty three." Franklin panted after such a long speech.

"Mary Carlin? I'm not too familiar with the old residents of the area, but I'll look into some of our old records and see what I can find. I'll get back to you tomorrow with anythin' I can find out about her. I'll need any dates and any addresses you may have. The best source of information around here is to just go over to the park and ask some of the old timers if they know anythin'. If they don't know it, it don't exist." the chief laughed.

Franklin could not quite figure out why that was funny. Life in a small town gave you different things to laugh about, he guessed.

"Yes, Chief, the dates in the year book are from nineteen-sixty to nineteen-seventy-four. There are some other dates involved that might have something to do with this. You can also consider the years from nineteen-fifty-eight to around nineteen-sixty. These may have something to do with the lady we found. What we need here most is someone who was still in contact with her and maybe knew what she was doing and who her other friends were up here in San Francisco."

Franklin checked off his notes as he finished. He had mentioned all he had on the victim. Now it was up to Chief Michaels to find out who, what, and where about the lady's past life in St. John's.

"And Chief," he added, "I surely do appreciate your taking time personally to talk to me today. This has really been a messy thing to find her like we did, and it would be good to find the person who did this before it happens again. I'm sure your nice little town doesn't have to worry about such happenings, and I appreciate your giving me your time and help."

Franklin almost purred, he sounded so smooth. When he had to worm around this way to a stranger -- or to anyone else, for that matter -- he always made sure the door to his office was closed. He positively did not want anyone from the outer office to hear him gushing like this.

"Lieutenant Franklin," Chief Micheals said, not above purring himself, "even in our small town of St. John's, we've been known to have a grizzly murder or two. Why, sir, just last summer we had the most disgustin' and heart tearin' spectacles you have ever seen. Even I, in all my years as an officer of the law, have never seen anythin' so beastly and inhumane. If you have a few moments, I would surely like to get your opinions on some of the happenin's of last summer in St. Johns."

"I'm awfully sorry, Chief, but right now I have three people sitting here waiting for instructions on what to do about Mary Carlin's murder," he lied as he made a sweeping motion to three empty chairs, "I'd love to hear about the crimes at a later date, perhaps next week, when I have a little more time to listen and appreciate the story behind the events. Would that be all right? I look forward to any information you can find on Mary Carlin. I'd really like to find someone who knew her in the past and has had any contact with her recently. Please call my office as soon as you can with any information. Thanks a lot, Chief."

Franklin looked at the phone as he hung up. He sure didn't need to hear about some wife cutting up on her husband because he looked at the barmaid, or there was always the mailman delivering more than letters in these small towns. Life needed to be sparked up with a little "special delivery" once in a while. Such is life in the fast lane of a small town.

As he nodded his thanks to his three imaginary people waiting in his office, he again started to put the remainder of Mary's things back into the box. These would make sense some day, but right now they were just so much junk.

Hitting the button on his intercom, Frank yelled, "Anybody got some more Baggies out there?"

He pulled a fresh map from the pad of street maps of San Francisco and a map showing the city and neighboring towns. These always came in handy, if for nothing else than to look like he was really working out some type of strategy.

He pinned the maps on the bulletin board, along with the other things. He then placed a pin in the appropriate spot for Mary Carlin. Then he slipped one down in the town of St. John's, just to give the board more movement and depth.

Last weeks map had two markers in it. The red one was for the guy that was mugged on the corner, and the blue marker was supposed to be the location of his brother-in-law when the mugging took place. The victim's wife swore that her brother was with her in her car down by the waterfront, watching the fishing boats come in.

How many fishing boats stayed out after dark, Frank did not know. It wasn't impossible, but if she had just said "watching the boats" it would have sounded more likely. The husband hadn't been down to file formal charges yet, so nothing had been done as far as questioning the brother-in-law, or even talking to him.

Most of the background information had come from neighbors who said that there was bad blood between the two men. They had been fighting for years over some of the silliest things, and it seemed that things had just gotten out of hand. Hopefully the "muggee" and the "mugger" would settle things privately and not bring the police into it.

Frank hated the typical "domestic situation". He had avoided them like a plague when he was a cop on the beat. None of the cops ever wanted to get into the middle of a husband-and-wife argument. No one ever won, and the cops always lost. If they hauled the husband away, the wife would get mad at the cops. When they hauled the wife away, then the husband would get mad at the cops. Do nothing to anyone, and both sides would get mad at the cops. The typical domestic situation was definitely a no-win situation.

It was almost lunch time, so he leaned out his office door and called, "Anyone going to the deli?"

Chapter Nine

As he hung up the phone on his end of the line, Chief Ralph Michaels gave a snort to himself. "Next week, my ass. Some smart-ass lieutenant from San Francisco thinks just 'cause we're in a small town, we don't know 'bout murder, and we don't have the same problems the big city departments have."

The officer sitting at the desk in the corner looked up from his paper work and asked, "What's he want, Chief. Did someone from St. John's get into some trouble up there?"

Chief Michaels tossed the pad he had been writing on over onto the desk of Bill Hays, his assistant and one of the two other men on the force in St. John's.

"Here, Bill, see if you can find out anythin' on a woman by the name of Mary Carlin. Fifty-three years old, used to teach school here 'round nineteen-sixty. Seems like she's got herself cut up pretty bad and pretty permanent," he said. "Go over and ask at the school, and you can stop by the park and see if any of those old coots over there can remember anythin' more than their own names today. Sometimes they can come in handy, and some days they ain't worth a damn to anyone but the pigeons. Some day those pigeons are going to start shittin' on those old men like they do 'Old John' over there," This last was said with arms extended as if they were holding the reins of a horse. "Old John" was the nickname given to the white-shouldered statue of John Alfred Cornley -- a large, stately man seated on his faithful horse, Rob.

St. John's was not named for a saint, but for this do-gooder who lived out here during the gold-rush days. There was not much gold in this area, but at one time there was a siege of the fever, and John Alfred Cornley spent most of his time and money seeing to the sick and taking care of their families -- thus Saint John's. It started out as Saint John's Settlement and over the years just became St. John's.

Chief Michaels' fear of growing old began to show up every now and then. Some of his fear was apparent as a gruff manner when he talked to the old people or even talked about them. It was as if he felt they grew old on purpose. He was very much afraid of getting old himself, even more afraid of the alternative.

Michaels hadn't lived in this town long by the local residents' standards. He moved here from some midwest or southern area, which he never named in general conversation. After serving on the police force of this unnamed town for about twenty-five years, he resigned and moved to California. The residents didn't know why Michaels had moved out here, but they had been satisfied with him in the past nine years that he had been their police chief.

He was fifty-seven years old, and touched up his hair with Gretian Formulae -- not black, but the shiniest reddish-brown ever made. When they were standing in front of him, no one in the town even dared to look at the part in his hair to see what the natural color of his hair was, but when they happened to be walking around behind him, there was always a quick glance at his roots.

As the Chief flopped down into his chair, he grumbled, "No one ever thinks that somethin' important can happen in a town like St. John's, just 'cause we're small. Hays, I'll tell you this, some day we'll get that mess from last summer figured out. I don't care if we are small. No one can just walk into a town like that, and take two lives away, just like they don't matter. No, sir. Somethin' will come up some day, and we'll have the S.O.B.s that did that. I guarantee it."

Hays squirmed a little, made a few bubbling sounds in his throat as if to clear it, and asked, "Chief, do you think old Mr Hendrix' pecker was that small 'fore they cut it off? Now, don't go getting mad, but since you brought up the

72

subject, I thought maybe we could talk about it now. You never did say much last summer. It was such a mess, with him being nailed to the kitchen table and all, but to see that old man laying there staring at his own pecker that was just sitting up there on his chest like that, and him all bloaty like he was -- that was really spooky, Chief."

The chief sputtered a little, not knowing if he should be stuffy and businesslike or relax and get the talk over with. He knew it would have to come out sometime, and he was surprised that Bill had waited this long. He figured that if he did not talk about it, Bill would not have the guts to raise the question. Well, now the subject had come up, and they might as well get it out into the open. Most of the residents didn't know exactly how the old man died. The newspaper release only stated that some hippies came through town looking for money and cut up the old man.

As for Doc, they thought it was the same hippies killed him earlier in the month, looking for drugs and money.

"Bill, do you realize that speculatin' as to the size of a victim's private parts before they was--- er, removed, is not really an official part of police work?" the chief asked. "When we found Hendrix, he'd been dead for over a week. The temperature had been hoverin' around eighty-five degrees for 'bout ten days. He was nailed to the kitchen table through his hands, with a rope holdin' each of his legs to a separate table leg. He was spread out 'bout as far as you can get one old man of seventy.

"It looked like someone carefully unzipped the old man's pants, pulled out his joint...I mean, his penis, and whacked it off just as clean as you please, probably with his own butcher knife."

"Now, you tell me, Bill Hays, would you have a big pecker if someone did this to you, while you watched them? Even an elephant would have somethin' resemblin' a small dill pickle, if he had to watch this being done, knowin' full well that while you are a lyin' there, watchin' your own pecker stare back at you, you are most definetly goin' to bleed to death."

As Michaels started his story, Hays was pulling a sandwich out of the lunch pail in the drawer, and Michaels, knowing Bill's love of dill pickles, couldn't pass up a chance to get to his assistant. He timed his statements and answers to Hays' questions just right, waiting for him to reach into the ever-present lunch pail for the, also-ever-present Baggie, full of dill pickles.

"Chief, sometimes you do some really shitty things to me," Hays complained.. "You knew I had pickles in there."

He enjoyed it when the chief picked on him. It made him feel just a little closer to the gruff but somewhat proper old man. He did not really feel that fifty seven was old. It was just when you put that age on the chief, it seemed older. He couldn't explain the feeling. It was somewhat like having a special uncle.

Bill Hays sat there finishing his lunch and began to chuckle to himself. "Hey, Chief, did I ever tell you the story about the mute guy that picks up this hooker, and she asks him to come up to her room?"

"No, Bill, you didn't. Do I really want to hear this?" Michaels answered, knowing full well he was going to hear it no matter what happened.

"Well, this guy, he ain't been around too much, but he knows all about diseases and the like, so he knows he should protect himself. So he motions for the hooker to wait outside by the curb, and he goes into this here drugstore on the corner. Since he can't talk, he motions to the druggist that he wants to buy some rubbers. Now, this here druggist can't understand what any of these motions are, and the mute guy is making all kinds of motions and signs and things are getting pretty anxious. Did you hear this, Chief?"

"No, and I don't think I want to."

"Well, anyways, the mute guy is worried that the hooker will leave and the druggist is afraid that this guy will

74

get wild, because he can't make himself understood. Finally the mute guy whips out his pecker, lays it on the counter, and puts a five dollar bill down besides it. You sure you ain't heard this?"

"Hays, stop or go, but get it the hell over with."

"Okay , Chief. Well, damn, this here druggist finally thinks he understands, his face lights up, he unzips his pants with one hand and flips his own pecker out onto the counter, while he reaches for a yardstick with the other hand. While both peckers are stretched out there on the counter, he measures them with the yardstick, the druggist's is longest, so he grabs the other guy's five dollar bill, and sticks it in his pocket. He figures he won the contest. The mute guy takes one look at him, flips himself back into his pants, zips up, walks out the door to the hooker, gives her a backhand, smack across the mouth and walks down the street, into the night."

Hays leaned back in his swivel chair and grinned, while the Chief just stared at him.

"Bill, I've heard some sick stories in my day, but I think that must be the sickest. I'm goin' over to the diner for lunch, and I then to walk to the bank. Shouldn't be gone too long. While I'm gone, I want you to run over to the school, look up Mary Carlin, and if you have time, stop at the park and ask the "Know-It-All Group" what they remember about her. She was probably a sweet young thing when they were just startin' to be dirty old men -- and, please, don't tell them that dumb joke. If she was here, I'm sure some one there will know her. If the school has any pictures, get them too. Maybe we can show this Mister City Cop that we don't just sit and whittle down here."

"While I'm thinkin' about it," he went on as he walked to the front door, "when you get back, take out all the old case files from the two murders last summer. We'll spend some time on them this week. I don't think we have anythin' else pressin' on our schedule, do we?"

Hays scratched his arm, leaned back toward the desk and answered, "No, sir, nothing pressing and all of the other stuff will all be done by the time you get back."

As Michaels reached the door, Bill noticed that the chief's shoulders were shaking as he tried to get outside before he lost control of his laughter.

The chief closed the door to the police station, and turned left towards the river. The St. John's Bank was just one street from the bridge and this was something he did almost every day. He liked for the townspeople to see him walking around, seeing to their town. He would save a small amount of banking for each day, if he could, even if it meant just cashing a check for a few dollars for his lunch or dinner.

He would then take his casual walk over the bridge to the bowling alley on the east side of the river and have a coke with the owner, while they watched the ladies' leagues. These blue haired old ladies surely knew how to throw a bowling ball.

This was the biggest sport in this community. There were leagues for every age -- Senior Citizens, Teen Club, Young Mothers, Young Fathers. When the town was small and the income matched it, there was always the challenge to find something inexpensive to do, to keep the citizens happy and busy and...out of trouble.

This was his home now, and the reminder that someone came into it last summer and killed two of its residents disturbed Chief Michaels. Last summer he felt the whole town had been violated. In a way it had, because as quickly as it happened, just as quickly, the town forgot, and everything went back to the usual daily events. No one talked about it, no one pressed him to find these horrible killers. It was as if someone had just pulled a couple of weeds, and no one really cared.

Michaels thought that this might be the time to renew his search into the events of last summer.

Chapter Ten

Franklin finished the sandwich that he had brought in from the deli down the street.

"Corned beef on rye with swiss cheese." He wiped a spot of Poupon mustard from his chin. "Not too shabby."

As Frank tossed the foil from the sandwich and the paper cup that had held his coffee into the trash can, Fred Murphy walked into the office, making himself comfortable as usual.

Murphy flopped down into one of the three chairs facing Franklin's desk, tossed a large manilla envelope over to Franklin, and said, "Here's the belongings of Fuzzy, the throat-cutting victim at the harbor yesterday morning."

"Why the hell do you keep calling him Fuzzy?" Franklin asked.

Fred smiled. "That's what the people over at the market called him, don't you remember?"

"Here's his stuff. He had a wallet, not much money, about three dollars, some paper clippings, and some old letters or something. I had a team go over to the place Fuzzy called home. They came up with a few old shirts, an extra pair of boots, probably stolen -- they were in pretty good shape for him -- and some more clippings. There were a few more pictures, some old identification cards, no credit cards, an old voters registration card, and a few old photographs. Not much to show for a lifetime."

That statement struck Franklin as odd, since Margot had said almost the same thing about Mary Carlin. He supposed all the people of the streets, and the ones who were only close to the streets, were just about the same. If they had more they would not be in these places, working a day at a time, or waiting tables for a bunch of old has-beens and winos. Maybe Carlin and this bum had more in common than he had thought at first. At least they ended up about the same.

Frank opened the envelope and dumped its contents onto his desk. Here he was, going through someone else's belongings again. This job certainly did have a way of sticking his nose into everyone else's business. Sometimes he felt that was all he did, just snoop in other people's closets.

The wallet was old, torn and faded. There was a blood doner's card in it with the name of George Gallagher. Fuzzy probably gave blood at one time so he could buy his next bottle. Most of the bums and semi-bums did this at one time or another.

Murphy sat and waited. He had worked with Frank before and knew that when Frank was ready, the loaded questions would follow. Franklin did not disappoint him. It was a full five minutes before anything came from the lieutenant's mouth, and then they were not made for a gentle person's ears.

"I'll be goddamned. This guy came from St. John's, too." Franklin said, almost to himself. He glanced up at Fred and repeated, "This guy, he came from St. John's, too."

He grabbed the phone, punched in a number, and moved over toward the bulletin board where his most recent addition had been placed.

"Get Peterson up here, will you," Frank yelled to an officer sitting at the desk just outside his office door.

"Here Fred, look. This old man came from the same town as the first cutting victim, Mary Carlin. The guy in the diary pages, his name was George, too, wasn't it? This can't be a coincidence. This has to mean something. Start writing down everything you saw, heard and felt from the first time you got the call and walked up to the body. Let me see it as soon as you're finished. Better yet, do it right there. Don't move from that chair."

Fred's eyes were about as wide open as he could get them, since Franklin had started talking as fast as he could and barking orders to everyone he could see, or he thought could hear him.

"Frank, what happened? " he asked. "What did you find?

"Here, look, Fred, the voter's registration. It's from nineteen-sixty-four, and it's for the town of St. John's. Somewhere in San Francisco there's got to be a connection. These two people here in San Francisco with no connection that we can see, but I'll bet they were connected at the hip twenty years ago. Now, they're both down on their luck. They both end up very dead by the services of a very sharp knife. I think the broken neck was just an added insult. Probably happened when the murderer pulled his head back to slice it. Each killing is a little different. Maybe, the hate was different, too. He also took some severe blows to the head after he was already dead."

As Frank stared, the expression on his face went from hard study to one of total enlightment.

"Well, Shit. This damned Fuzzy has to be our George from the diary pages. It's just got to be. Look at these pictures. I can't beleive this. The fronts of these houses are the same."

Frank was beginning to accelerate and Fred was having a hard time following his line of thought.

"Fred, grab all the stuff that came out of that envelope and bring it over here by the board. I want to get it up where we can see it at the same time we view all the belongings of Carlin."

"Okay, Frank, but slow down, you'll give yourself a coronary, and me too."

Fred was beginning to sound out of breath, just being in the same room with Frank. When he started on a run like this it usually affected everyone around him.

Carlin's board now held the four photo albums hung in clear plastic bags, the pictures, and the nine entries of the diary.

Murphy said, as he moved closer to Mary's board, "Look, Frank. Besides pictures matching, Fuzzy had some of these loose pages from some note book, too."

Gallagher's board started with the voter's registration card. Next to it was the blood donor's card. Four small photographs that were badly bent and cracked. There were two small clippings torn from some newpaper, with no dates on these. He had read these as soon as everything was posted. Two dirty envelopes with letters that were just about as unreadable. They had Gallagher's name and a post-office box number.

Now came the real excitement for Franklin. Here in one small flat package were several neatly folded pages of what looked like the same kind of diary pages as had been found outside Carlin's door. These were certainly familiar. It was more of Emily's diary.

He had spent four hours Sunday staring at almost identical pages that came from the box that held the only things left of Mary Carlin.

"Damn," Murphy said, as he moved closer to the boards. "look what we've got. These are the same things, like those on Carlin's board."

Franklin felt light headed he was so excited. While Murphy pinned these up to the board, one at a time, the room became very quiet. Murphy was the only one who didn't know about the other pages, and started to look around very suspiciously when he noticed the whispering.

"Frank, maybe we got ourselves a real live mystery. Not just a couple of bums getting cut up."

The doorway was beginning to fill like a traffic jam, since all the commotion alerted everyone in the outer room that something was really happening.

As the commotion continued, someone noticed a small voice coming from somewhere, "Frank, what in the hell is going on there? Are you on the line? Will someone pick up the damned phone? What's going on? Hello...? Hello!"

Frank had dropped the phone as soon as he had finished dialing Margot's number and forgot about it as soon as he saw the diary pages.

He ran back to the desk, grabbed the phone, "Margot, it's very important. Can you get right over to the station? I need your kind of thinking. We have another murder, and there are more diary pages. The second victim is also from the same town, downstate. It's really important."

She only said, "Twenty minutes." and he heard the click on the other end.

He understood completely. This was why they continued the way they were. Deep down, the understanding didn't need to be talked out when an emergency was there. She would respond the same way he would, if the need came to either of them.

She was trained to understand and know people from what they did, not necessarily what they said. She could figure out more from just looking at the way a car was parked than from listening to a long speech about why it was parked. If she could study these letters and diary pages, something could be learned about the writer of the pages, at least. This might lead to some notion as to who could be cutting up these people and why they would want to do such a thing.

"Fred" Franklin called, "let's get all we can down on paper. Where was most of this stuff?"

Fred took up a pencil and tore off a sheet of paper and wrote as he talked. "The wallet, with three dollars, was in his right hip pocket. The small photos were folded up and slipped inside one of the compartments of the wallet. There was an old rubber band around the wallet to keep everything in and together."

Franklin walked back up to the bulletin board saying, "Where did you find these diary pages? They don't look too messed up. He couldn't have been carrying them for too long."

"Well, the diary pages, as you call them, were folded in half and in half again. The crease was fairly new, but the paper wasn't dirty, just old. You could say they weren't on him, they were with him. The papers were just lying in his lap, under one hand. It really looked like they had been put there after the old man was killed."

"There must of been some flapping of his arms when the murderer cut his throat. You could see where the first cut didn't work. It started under in the center and went to his right ear and didn't do much. It didn't go all the way across the neck and it certainly wasn't deep. More like it was sawed. The one that really did it was the deep swoop across the whole neck starting from the right ear and going across to the left side. Very deep, too. I'm pretty sure the murderer stood behind the victim."

"The papers would have blown away if he had just moved his hand a little, but I really think he was dead before the cutting. There wasn't as much blood as there should have been, and the broken neck could have killed him. The beating looked like an afterthought."

They both stood there, moving their heads back and forth, comparing and staring at the two sections of the board.

"Fred, you're right. He surely would have tried to get away if someone was sawing away at his neck like that. If the neck broke high enough, it would cause instant death. The first slice was a fizzle, so it had to be done again. The first cut almost looks like it was done by someone weaker, both in muscles and stomach. But, hopefully, we only have one cutter here and not two. I think he just misjudged the first time and had to try again. Any comment from the coroner on that?"

"Not yet, sir."

Franklin reached up to the board and took down Carlin's picture of the man, the kids with the hula hoop,

82

and the two women. He walked to the other board and held it up next to the small pictures from Gallagher's wallet.

The pictures were worn, so it was difficult to really see any detail, but the porch in the background definitely looked like the same one in Carlin's picture.

Gallagher's picture was of two small children and one woman. Now things were beginning to hum. He put the photo back on Carlin's side and took down the newspaper clippings. It could be a few more minutes before Margot got here and he just couldn't let all this momentum sag.

The clippings didn't have a byline or city name. They had been torn through that line. Someplace some elderly man had been killed. The article was pretty vague as to how and failed to give any discription of the murder.

The authorities believed that a troop of "Manson like" hippies had come through town, looking for money and kicks. The second clipping was just about the same. One clipping mentioned the murder of a local doctor. The other mentioned the killing of an old man and also mentioned the murder of a doctor the previous week. They had to be the same town -- St. John's, maybe? The paper reported in each article that the authorities believed the hippies were looking for drugs. Nothing of any consequence was turned up in either case.

Franklin turned each clipping over, looking for some other way of tracking this down. There was an ad for a local grocery store, and the sale that it advertised was for the last week of July, 1986.

"Well," he said to Fred Murphy, who now sat staring at the empty desk top, "we have a date for one of these clippings -- and this other one, the doctor's, happened just one week before."

"Frank, do you think these clippings about some other murders have anything to do with the murders? I mean, if these were last year, why would someone wait for a whole year to wipe out these two?. We still don't know where these other murders took place either."

Frank leaned back into his chair and tried to relax. "No, but there has to be a connection between our two victims. These clippings, maybe. Who knows?"

"As soon as Margot gets here, I want everyone to clear out. She'll need all the quiet she can get in this place, and I want her to be able to concentrate fully on all the evidence we have."

Chapter Eleven

Margot Kent was a psychologist with the San Francisco Police Department. Working as consultant to the Juvenile Department and the Psychiatric Division, she was available to most divisions when something, such as this strange pair of murders came up.

The fact that she and Frank Franklin had been seeing each other for the past ten years just added a little spice to the speculation about their relationship around the offices -- his office and hers.

"Okay, let's get this show on the road, Frank. What kind of case is this new one, and where do we start?"

As she removed her purse from her shoulder and dropped it into the corner, Frank motioned to the boards.

"It's all over here, he answered. "At least all we have, so far." Her brief case open and papers and pencils taken out, she was ready for work.

"Start," she said.

"First victim. Mary Carlin, female, age fifty three. Lived in one room, third floor, alone. Found there in her room Friday around three in the afternoon. Dead from two knife wounds across the throat. More cuts that extended from the right arm pit down to the stomach area and back up to the left arm pit. There was a bruise on her right temple, probably a blow to the head to quiet her before the slicing.

"She worked as a waitress at 'Manny Fry's Diner' over on Eighth Street. Pictures of her room with and without the body. One bed, two chairs, one night stand, and a hot plate. Small chest of drawers. There was no refrigerator in the room. Super says the tenants weren't allowed to cook in their rooms. The hot plate was all right, just so they only used it for instant coffee or tea. She must have taken her meals at the diner. Stomach like concrete, huh!

"Here, look at the lab pictures. Two coffee cups out on the night stand. I missed that on Friday when I was up there. She may have been entertaining."

"The pictures, over there, came from her wallet. The yearbooks were under the night stand."

"These pages from someone's diary seem to be the major key to the situation. They weren't found inside the room. They were rolled up and tucked into the space behind the doorknob on the outside of the door.

"The first officer to the scene found them when he came up to the door. He said they were tucked behind the doorknob. He tossed them into a box that was in the corner next to the door. Do you think someone was leaving their calling card?

Margot added a few notes and said, "If it was left like that, there had to be a reason. Maybe a message to someone. Go on, Frank, tell me more."

"These pages look like they came from a diary. They're all signed by an Emily, and Mary Carlin is mentioned in all the entries that were at the Carlin apartment -- sometimes as "that woman" and on later dates by name. The dates are scattered over many years, starting in nineteen-fifty-eight. Seems the pages that referred to Mary Carlin were torn out and left there at her door as the murderer left the body inside the apartment."

"What on earth did she do in the diary, kill someone? No, no, never mind. Sorry I interrupted." Margot went back to taking notes.

"Yeah, now, we think this murder took place Wednesday night, or rather it would be Thursday morning around one o'clock, or so," Frank said.

"Victim number two. Gallagher, George, age sixty-one. Nickname, "Fuzzy". Found sitting on a park bench overlooking the end of the harbor. His throat was cut, almost exactly as Mary's was, one and a half times but from behind. His neck was broken. We think that was from being snapped back hard and fast when the cutter started to slit his throat. Then the back of his head was made to resemble meat loaf. It was totally apparent that he was dead, so this last assault must have been made as a last attempt to just defile George. He worked the market over near Seventh Street, whenever he could get a day in. The venders use these guys as part timers. They're the ones who gave us his nickname."

Margot made a motion to wait, as she reached for another pad of paper, then waved Frank to continue with in his report.

"Well, George, "Fuzzy" lived in a hole in the wall over an old deserted furniture store. Found some more identification in the room, extra clothing, and some old newspapers. The papers on him included an old voter's registration card from St. John's -- Mary Carlin's home town, I might add. There were a couple of ancient photos inside his wallet, and these showed the same house as in a few of Mary's pictures.

"Now for the kicker. Folded neatly, just under one hand, were some more pages of dear Emily's diary. These contain mostly references to good old George, here."

Margot walked across the room and stood close to the board. "Do you mean these two were killed by the same person? They each had the same 'calling card', as you called it."

"Looks like it, don't you think?" Frank responded as he pointed to the two boards.

As Frank began again, Margot whispered to herself, "Crazy, crazy!"

"I haven't had time to read the pages of the diary George had on him, but I thought I could do that while you started on Mary's pages. I'd like your impressions of the pages we found at her place before you look at his. What Emily must have been like, and so forth. They give us a pretty good picture of Mary Carlin twenty-five years ago, too. This hopefully will give us a lead as to which way to go from here."

87

"Frank," Margot said as she began to remove Mary's diary pages from the board, "have you read all of the pages left with Mary Carlin?"

"Yes, and she's mentioned in every one of the entries. I'll lay odds that Fuzzy's mentioned on all of his pages, too. After we get through all this, I guess the next thing to do is to get down to St. John's. I hope you have enough time to spend on this case. I'd like for you to stay with it to the finish."

Margot was listening to him and looking a Mary Carlin's board at the same time. "Sure, I've already checked it out with the Department superintendant. I'm assigned to you for the duration of this case."

"My, my, aren't we sure of ourself?" he snickered.

"You sure have a hell of a lot of room to use that term. Now shut up and let me read. I'll use you as a sounding board when I get finished. Oh, by the way, while I'm reading, why don't you find your nasal spray? You sound like your talking in a bucket."

Franklin reached into his pocket and took out his inhaler. His nose taken care of, he walked back to George's board. He removed the diary pages and returned to his desk to do his own studying.

The two sat for about thirty minutes reading, over and over, the pages of someone else's life, things that were so private that they must be put down on paper and closed away each night from the eyes of the world, and now strangers were seeing into the deepest thoughts of Emily's life. It made them both feel as though they were prying into the very soul of something holy --or unholy, as it turned out.

During this time, Margot muttered, "How could she?... You don't really believe that, do you?.. Don't do it?.. Good girl. Go tell her. How can you let her keep on doing that?"

She was also taking notes furiously as she read the pages at least three, sometimes four times. Frank hadn't said a word, but he read George's pages over and over, and when Margot looked up at him, he was visibly shaken.

"What on earth is in your pages? You look terrible. My pages were more sad that anything."

Frank wiped his face with both hands, then opened a drawer, pulled out a small towel, wiped his face again, and wiped his hands as though they were covered with mud.

"We'll get to mine after you tell me about Carlin's pages. I'm glad I read these others before you, I can tell you now, to be prepared for some weird reading. It is not a pretty picture. It should be interesting to hear about the Carlin pages first. Shoot."

Margot picked up her notes, sat back and said, "You realize that this is just a quick analysis of these pages. To do a good job, I should devote more than thirty minutes, but I can do that later.

"Now, for my first thoughts. The writer of the Carlin pages sounds like she married right out of high school. Even though the spelling is correct and her punctuation is so-so, her word usage is lacking. I can hear her talking as if she were not a very educated person. I think she must be a very shy and sad person. There were situations that called for a confrontations and she seemed to step away from anything that could cause friction.

"In the beginning Emily referred to George's staying out late. She progressed from talking about 'that woman' to 'that Miss Carlin' and finally to calling her Mary.

"Sometimes Emily tells the diary about some of the new and disgusting things George tries to do to her and that he probably learned them from 'that woman'. Several times she mentions his coming home drunk and late, but he didn't bother to hit her or make her have sex with him. This sounds like the pages in between must have been extraordinary, if they describe any of this."

"They do," Frank interjected.

"Anyway, Emily mentions twins. Seems this Carlin woman was a teacher in the local school, and Emily was forced to take her twins to school, even though she wanted to teach them herself. As I said, she had a high school education, but I think she was of average intelligence. She just was a quiet and undemanding person. Just from reading the diary, I'm sure she even pronounced words such as reading and writing as readin' and writin'. She sounds very meek and afraid of being involved with the world. So sad too.

"In some of the later pages, it seems that George forced the friendship of Emily and Mary Carlin. In one entry, Emily talks about George not getting mad when she told him that she was pregnant again. In another he told her that Mary would be taking her to some doctor in the town to get an abortion. Emily didn't sound like she was too sad about having the abortion. She had already asked her own doctor about it, and he refused.

Here she also states that she thinks that George's crazy times are over.

"In a few more pages she talks about the doctor who did the abortion. He was some vet, named Doctor Charlie. Mary took her to Doctor Charlie and seemed to know him. In one page dated several months later, Emily wonders if Mary had to use Dr. Charlie herself. She said George had been pretty grumpy and that Mary had taken a week's leave of absence from the school because of illness. No one knew what kind of illness. Emily sounded like she thought if was pretty funny.

"Evidently Emily has accepted the situation with Mary and George.

She even said in one entry of the diary that it didn't seem as bad as it had at first, now that George was spending most of his evenings with Mary. It sounds like he gets most of his sexual favors from Mary, and this sits pretty well with Emily now."

"One thing that strikes me strange is the way she still refers to the twins. She always calls them her babies. When Emily first mentions Mary, it's nineteen-fifty-eight, and she calls them babies. Here she's still calling them babies in nineteen-sixty. I also noticed that she still refers to her own mother as 'Mommy'. That in itself is no big thing, I'm sure many people do that. It's just that most people change to a more mature reference for a parent as they age."

"Okay, that's just a brief run-through of the pages that I have from the Carlin body. Do you want to tell me about the diary from George's body, or should I read them myself without any coaching or opinions from you?"

Franklin wasn't quite sure if he should prepare her for the pages he had just read or let her have them cold and see what she could make out of them. He was sure she could handle the information, even if it wasn't from a pretty world.

"Some of this stuff is pretty nasty. It could ruin your rosy outlook on the world," Frank said as he pushed George's pages across to Margot.

She smiled and reached for the pages he had just stacked and shoved across the desk toward her. Again she settled down with pencil in hand and began to read. After Frank's comments about the nastiness, she was just a little more on guard with these entries.

Strangely, there was not one sound from Margot as she read these diary pages. Most were just as the others had been, pages describing the boring life of a probably boring person. Her life centered around her twins, but in these pages that had been found on her dead husband's body were the words of a desparate, fearful woman. In her life, as in these pages, the husband whom she had loved so much in those early days, just out of school, had turned into a cesspool most of the time.

Again, these were only the pages that referred to her days and nights with George, and this was not the best of times. Most of her writing about her husband described an animal, who enjoyed beating and humiliating his wife, and doing things in front of the children that most children never learn about, even when they become adults. Then, as the years progressed, he began doing these horrible things to the children, themselves. How this man lived as long as he did, was a surprise to Margot.

She read the pages for the fifth time, laid them down and reached for the same towel that Franklin had used when he finished reading them. The paper seemed to transfer to the holder, the dirt that this man had inside him.

December 3, 1956

Dear Diary,

George did the most horrible thing. He's been drinking again, almost every night. Last night when he came home, he was real mad. I think that woman he's been seeing and him had a fight. He must have left before they did it. You know -- had sex.

I forgot and locked the front screen door. When he came home, he was so mad, he broke the screen. He was just like a madman, yelling and throwing things. I just stayed in bed and acted like I was asleep. When he came into the bedroom,he put on the lights and started hitting me before I could even get out of bed. I thought for sure he was going to kill me. He punched me so hard in the stomach, it made me throw up. That just made him madder.

Diary, I wish he had killed me. He went in and got my babies out of bed. When he came in with them, they was scared, but like usual, they didn't cry. They sure are good babies. Then George made them sit in the chair next to the bed and came back to hitting me some more.

This time after he punched me in the stomach, he yelled that if I threw up again, he'd hit the babies. I was so scared. I just kept on swallowing. Then he tore my night gown off and threw me on my stomach and did that nasty thing he does to me sometimes.

Dear Diary, God didn't mean for having sex to be in that place. I'm so ashamed. My poor babies had to sit there and watch. They was scared, but they didn't cry. Not one tear.

I'm so sick today. I don't know what George will be like tonight. Most of the time he acts like nothing different happened. I guess that's best. Then we don't have to talk about it.

I'm so glad the babies have each other. Like I always tell them, twins are special. You'll always have each other. I don't think I'll be writing much, I'm just so sick. I sure am glad I have you.

Good night my dearest friend,

Emily

May 16, 1959

Dear Diary,

Today I really feel happy. I don't know what caused the change in Gerry, but I surely do enjoy it. Even Terry has noticed. She's quiet and polite, again. She sits and waits for me to finish what ever I'm doing, and then she asks for help in what she's doing or maybe when she asks for a piece of candy. She doesn't fight with Terry any more. She has turned into the nicest quietest little girl you ever saw.

Of course, Terry is still a stinker, but it wasn't the same as Gerry when she was bad. Something was really wrong with her head, I think.

She was almost like an animal some of the time. You know, just like her daddy.

Well, it's all over, and Gerry is nice again. It feels so good to go to the park. Now the other mothers have even noticed how polite Gerry is, and they don't make their kids stay away from her like they did before.

Just last week, in the park, Gerry was trying to hit some little girl that was sitting down and watching the ducks. Gerry said they were her ducks and the other little girl couldn't look at them. We were lucky. The girl's mother didn't see Gerry when she took that stick and poked her in the back. I told Gerry she was being mean and don't you dare to try to use that stick on that little girl, again. She tried to hit me with the stick, but I threw it into the river.

This week is all different. She is so good, I'd swear I have a new little girl. I'm so happy with her. Of course, I always did love her, but there were sure times where I didn't like her at all.

I remember when she was real little, I used to wish she hadn't been born. Sometimes, I wished she had been a boy, like Terry. I can expect that kind of acting up from a boy, but you sure don't like it from a girl. I sure wouldn't punish my babies for just being kids. I'm sure they don't mean any harm. They're just being playful.

Sometimes, they acted just like their daddy, but I know I don't have to worry about that any more. Since he makes them watch him being mean to me. You know, doing that bad sex stuff. I'm sure they will grow up to be nicer than he is. They would have to be nicer than he is. When he makes them come into our bedroom, they still seem to disappear into their own heads. I think that's their way of not seeing what's going on.

I don't like to talk about that nasty stuff that George does to me. I like it better when he doesn't come straight home from work.

Tonight the babies wanted me to read a story to them, but I told them they would have to look at their pictures. I couldn't miss my time with you, dear Diary. I don't get to write to you every night, and I just couldn't miss a chance, with George being out. Sometimes he yells about you, but I just keep you hid under the towels, where he won't find you.

Good night my dear friend,

Emily

March 7, 1963

Dear Diary,

Today was just another dull day. The twins got into a little trouble again at school, but it wasn't for anything real bad. They been playing "turn around" again. Their teachers have been complaining to that old crab Mr. Welsey, the school principal. He just don't understand the twins. Twins are special. They need to be treated just a little different.

They traded clothes again at recess. I guess this made their teacher mad. It's not really such a big deal, they was just having a little fun.

I don't know why they have to bother me about it all the time. The last time they played "turn around" in school, I got a real nasty letter. The principal wanted me to come to school for a conference. That's what he called it. That's just another fancy word that means he wants to crab to me about my babies. I just threw out that snotty letter as fast as I could -- specially when George hates that school so much. He would have a fit it he saw that the twins were geting in trouble at school.

They sure don't need any more trouble from their daddy. Last night he got mad at both of them and took them out back, to the old shed. He actually tied them to the center post and whipped them. I was sure proud of my babies though. They didn't cry one tear.

I felt a little bad when he made them stay out there all night. I got up early and went out and got them. George said I could when he left for work at five this morning. He said to go get them and make them clean themselves up real good. He wanted them to be a shining example of clean and neat children at school.

That sounds like he's getting more of those fancy words from Mary Carlin. I guess it isn't so bad having him take up with her. He leaves me alone most of the time. He don't bother the kids too much, leastways not as much as he would if he didn't have her to do -- you know, those sex things. I feel pretty lucky now that I have had time to get used to the idea. Maybe most wives would like the idea of their husbands having a girl friend to take the pressure away from them.

Well, my Dear Diary, like I said, things have been pretty quiet and boring around here. Oh, I forgot to tell you, the drapes in the front room look fine. They look almost store bought.

Good night, my dearest friend,

Emily

July 22, 1964

Dear Diary,

This is another sad time for me. I wonder why God decided to give me so much pain. I'm sure nobody else has the kinds of problems I get. It's just not fair.

The first thing is, I think Gerry is killing chickens again. I'm not sure, but it looked like blood on the baseball bat.

Then last night when I was finishing up on some mending, I heard an arguement in the kids room. When I got up there I found Terry on top of Gerry trying to have sex with her. She was crying and really giving him a battle. I screamed at him to get off of her. She was almost crazy. He says he hasn't been doing it to her nearly as much as his daddy does it to me -- and to him. When I heard that, I almost fainted. How can a daddy do such a thing to his own son?

When George came home I asked him about it. He started beating me. Diary, I didn't think he would ever quit. When he did, he went upstairs and beat both of the babies. He said that Terry had to be taught to keep his business private. I heard him yell that Terry was not to tell any other person what went on in this house.

I'll bet George would get in a lot of trouble if people found out what kind of person he really is. He has to be different than most men. I just know other men don't do what he does. It's not natural. It says so in the bible. One place in the bible says that man should not lie down with animals or something like that. I heard George tell some man he tried that too one time. He scares me. Sometimes I can get sick to my stomach when I think about what he does.

I'm not going to think about him any more, my sweet diary. I'm going to sleep now.

I sure hope he changes soon.

Good night my friend,

Emily

May 22, 1965

Dear Diary,

It's happened again. George is having one of his crazy times. Early yesterday morning he woke everyone up and made us get out of bed. He said the government spies were coming to take away all his secrets. He says he's been stealing papers from the plant and he's going to sell them to a foreign government. Now he says our spies found out and they are coming for him. What kind of papers can you steal from a fertilizer plant?

We spent all morning looking for hidden microphones and hidden cameras. The babies thought it was fun until their daddy heard them laughing and went into their room and started to hit them. He split Terry's lip and poor Gerry fell against the bed and got a bump and black spot on her forehead.

They was only playing. They thought their daddy was just being silly and playing a game for a Saturday morning. They sure found out different after that.

He tore the whole house apart looking for things he called "bugs". I told him I don't have no bugs in my house, cause I cleaned good everyday. That made him so mad he hit me in the mouth and called me stupid.

I sure was glad when he left for the day. I guess he went down to the tavern. He headed in that direction, and he didn't come home last night. This afternoon he come in around three o'clock and wanted to know what was for dinner.

I made his favorite, pork roast and mashed potatoes and sauerkraut. He acted like nothing had happened, and we kept it that way. He still had that mad look in his eyes that he gets when he's like this. I sure don't like it when he gets his crazy spells. My mommy said he was funny, but I didn't think she meant this way.

101

Thanks for listening to me, Diary, I sure do need to talk to someone, and it feels so good to have you.

Love,

Emily

September 21, 1965

Dearest Diary,

Why can't things go smooth, like they should? Yesterday George brought home a used television, and the babies were so happy. It don't get a real good picture, but we can see enough to enjoy the programs.

Here we all sit just watching television, and things could be going so nice, but George is on one of his bad times. He can only rant and rave about what he thinks is going on. It gets so tiresome, but I can't say anything or he might hit me.

I wish I could live without being afraid that George is going to hit me or do worse. I know he does things to the babies that I don't want to talk about, but it makes me so sad. How can a man do such things to his own kids. Such a dirty thing to his own son is disgusting.

The worse thing is that Terry is still doing it to Gerry, and I can't make him stop. He's just a baby hisself, and he's doing those nasty things to his own sister. George taught him those things, I know, but how can Terry do it without feeling bad? Course, George don't seem to feel very bad when he does something bad. I guess Terry is more and more like his daddy than I thought.

He is going to be just like his daddy -- just plain mean. I used to think Gerry was the mean one, but she changed again. She's nice and quiet, most of the time. Sometimes Terry complains that she's that mean sister again. But she don't do that much anymore.

Today I sure taught him a lesson. He had his little pee-pee out, and I caught him playing with it. I showed him how bad it can be to play with it.

I rubbed it for him until it got kinda hard, then I smacked it with the ruler. That will teach him not to do nasty things with his body. He got so swollen, he couldn't go to the bathroom, but he's got to learn to have pure thoughts.

I hate to admit this, my dearest Diary, but I sure never enjoyed touching George that way, like I did touching Terry. Course, George was always so mean with his. He just liked to hurt me with it. He never let me touch him, gentle like.

I guess I'll have to watch Terry more and make him behave.

Sleep well, my friend,

Emily

March 16, 1966

Dear Diary,

I'm starting to hate my life. I'm really lost. Here we sit just watching TV and things could be so nice, but George is having one of his bad times. Seems like all he ever does is rant and rave and smack us around. He just gets crazy so easy these days.

It gets so quiet around here, but I can't say anything or he might hit me again. The kids have been going to school with bruises, but nobody has said anything about it, yet. I sure hope they don't notice the marks.

I wish I could just live without being afraid that George is going to hit me or do worse. I'll bet none of the fancy ladies over at the church have bruises like I do.

I don't feel so good tonight, Diary. I think I'll go to bed early.

Good night my only friend,

Emily

November 27, 1967

Dear Diary,

Things are bad around here again. Today George came home early, and the first thing he did was make Gerry go to her room. She didn't do anything bad, he just made her go up there by herself. I kinda figured he was going to do that dirty stuff to me, but instead of making me do things, he just went upstairs. He said he was going to work on the shelf in Gerry's closet.

I don't know what got into him about doing some work around the house. He hasn't done that for years. He said he had a new idea and he wanted to try it out. He looked pretty pleased with himself, when he said that.

Later, I found out that it was just a new excuse to get at Gerry. George is doing that stuff to her all the time now. I told her last week that she shouldn't feel so bad. That was just her daddy's way of showing her his love.

When I went upstairs, George was just coming out of the closet. When I looked in the closet, there was Gerry all crouched down in the back corner. From the looks of the closet, he's been taking her to the back corner and doing sex things to her for a while. I haven't looked back there for a long time.

It isn't really a closet, it's an old store room, but we use it for a closet. There's a blanket and pad back there in the farthest corner.

That's probably why Gerry has such a fit when I tell her to hang something in the back of the closet. I guess now I'll never get her to hang things up for me. I always end up having to do everything myself. I'll have to hang up all the fresh laundry on wash days.

No one ever gives me enough help around here. George won't even carry his own boots upstairs after he gets home from work. He just drops them by the front door. He leaves all the mud or dust on them for me to clean. No one in this family knows how much they put on me.

Responsibility. That's what it is. That's my new big word for this week. I'm trying to improve my words, and I have to learn a new big word each week. Responsibility -- that means to take all the work and blame for things, while no one else does anything.

I must go to sleep now, my sweet diary.

Good Night,

Emily

"Well, I can't say you didn't warn me," Margot said to Frank. "I think I need to catch my breath before I start on this one. I didn't finish my notes completely. He appears to have been one of the meanest, vilest men that ever walked this earth. I can't say that too many people are apt to miss him."

She took a sip of soda from the cup she had brought in with her and began again.

"From what I read in the diary pages that were with him, Mister George 'Fuzzy' Gallagher was a deeply disturbed wife and child-abuser --maybe a bully in other areas, but we have no way of knowing that right now. In one entry Emily mentions how George laughs at something that should be sad. One time he actually cried when something extra funny came on the TV. The mood swings and the animal-like cruelty and tensions he showed are frightening.

"He also talked of some of the people of the town being against him and their plot to get rid of him. He said he would show them one day, but nothing was mentioned here about anything he did to get back at them. I think that was just one of his more empty threats.

As far as these pages show, only Emily and the children are the ones that he vents his anger on, but as we know, these are only Emily's diary pages. It would be interesting to know if he ever hurt Mary Carlin or any one around San Francisco.

"Well, to continue, what he did to Emily was the first sign of his disturbed mind. He needed someone to cower in front of him, to make him feel dominate and more important. What he did to the children was just a more sadistic part of his sick mind. How he could do these things one day and then go on as if they didn't exist or had never happened is the best description of his sickness.

"First the sexual abuse of his wife, then to his own children. Emily actually explains to Gerry that this was her daddy's way of showing love. The disassociation by the mother must have been devastating for the children. Emily only wanted her diary. Those poor children.

"George has the feeling of the people of the town spying on him and. again, his ability to act as if nothing had happened after one of his terrors that he put his family through. For those young children to have to watch him as he beat and raped his own wife, then their own abuse, must have had some very long lasting effects on them. Just the fact that he would not allow them to cry could have been a traumatic experience for them. The body needs its releases and tears are the best doorway that exist for anger and sadness .

"Then to start abusing the son and finally the son abusing his sister. This is almost too much to grasp. The horror of growing up in this home makes me....enough. I'm beginning to preach instead of analyze.

"To summarize, Mary Carlin, the teacher and other woman, has also became a questionable friend. She took our writer, Emily, to have an abortion, took care of the husband's sexual needs, and appears to have had at least one abortion herself by the help of dear Dr. Charlie

"George 'Fuzzy' Gallagher -- husband, father, lover, and one very mean, sicko-type dude. Fits of rage, distant from children most of the time, rarely showing any playfulness toward them. He found most of his spare time to be happier away from his wife and spent this with Mary Carlin or at one of the local bars. Had a great need to beat his wife occaisonally and sexually assault and humiliate her, both privately and in front of the children. Later he abused the children themselves.

"Again, we don't know if he did this to anyone else, since we don't have their diaries. Is this about what you wanted to know?"

With this Margot went over to the coffee pot and poured herself a very thick cup of black liquid of mysterious origin.

Franklin nodded in agreement at what she had said. When she poured the coffee, he made a face and said, "Now, there, you are dealing with a deadly substance. Pour that stuff out and make another pot. We've got some more work to do. I'd like for you to look at the other things on the boards now and add any ideas to your notes. I may have to make another phone call to the police chief down in St. John's and see if he can ask around about the Gallagher family, too. If all this was going on, someone has to remember something."

After the afternoon of talking and studying all the pages from Emily's diary, Frank decided he would drive down to St. John's in the morning. Talking face to face usually produced more then the telephone, and he now needed more results.

Chapter Twelve

The trip to St. John's was a pleasant addition to Franklin's job. His driving was usually through city streets with traffic on all sides or down some deserted side street that would make even the best of drivers nervous.

The trip took about two hours and Franklin spent most of it getting all of his facts mentally in order.

Mary Carlin's books from the school and George 'Fuzzy' Gallagher's clippings and voter's registration all connected them to St. John's. The diary pages referring to George and Mary connected them to each other. The pictures were too old to make a positive identification, but they looked good to him. Now if he could get some information from a local resident here that could connect them in San Francisco, he'd be on his way to finding a murderer.

Franklin turned off the interstate about fifty minutes ago and now was working his way along the winding country roads. At first they were four lanes, now down to two. The farms out here were medium-sized to small, but they all had a cleanness to them. Somehow that made the air smell better.

One more turn up Church Hill Road. This was the last road marked on his map. A small pet shop at the intersection, and then a drive-in theater off on the right. This had to be the most popular spot in St. John's. After passing the Big Joe Miniature Golf, the road sloped easily downward and there was El Verde, the river in all it's pea-soup glory. Then came a small marina on the southeast side of the river and a bowling alley and restaurant on the northeast side.

As he crossed the bridge, he noticed the small bank the fellow from the pet store had mentioned. He said to go past the bank about two thousand feet. There was the fire station on his left, and the police station was right

111

across from that, next to the barber shop. That was certainly easy enough. Towns this size were easy to find, and it was easy to find places in them.

As Franklin opened the office door, a small bell, hanging from the top of the door frame, tinkled to announce his entrance.

A young man in a tan uniform sitting at the desk behind the counter looked up, "Yes, sir. Can I help you?"

"I'm Lieutenant Frank Franklin, San Francisco Police. I called yesterday morning about Mary Carlin. Your chief of police said he'd get all the information on her he could find in the records here and possibly some additional information from some of the older residents."

"Yes, sir. I'm Deputy Hays. I worked on that myself, but we expected you to call back. There isn't all that much information for you to drive all the way down here."

Franklin forced himself to droop his shoulders to look a little more humble and maybe a little less formidable.

"I thank you for wanting to save me the trip, Deputy Hays, but another murder has been committed, and we're pretty sure the second victim comes from St. John's also. We need some information about him, too. With Mary Carlin and this George Gallagher coming from here, I felt it better to come down myself and talk to you about both of cases. Personally, I hate telephones. They don't establish the personal contact that I like to have when I'm working with the police force of a different city."

Hays ate this up. Here stood the big-city cop, all stooped over and humble, asking for the expert help of Officer Bill Hays. He could not understand how the chief could think this guy was uppity. He probably only had courage to talk big when he was behind a telephone.

"That's Okay, Lieutenant. No problem. I have the file on Mary Carlin right here. We can go through this, and maybe I can fill you in on your other murder victim. I'm sure Chief Michaels will talk to you about both these people if he has any additional information. He probably will want to tell you about our murders from last summer, too. They were really something."

"Well, I'm in somewhat of a hurry, right now. My boss, you know. He told me to get my ass down here, get the dope on these people and get my ass back, as soon as I could. I'm also supposed to look around, see their homes -- you know, stuff like that." Franklin was so self-effacing, he was afraid he might gag.

"Sure, Lieutenant, I've had bosses like that before. Chief Michaels is really a saint compared to some of them."

Totally aware of Officer Hays' apparent youth, Franklin could not resist asking, "Oh, how many chiefs have you worked for?"

"Well, not a lot, but he's a good guy."

Suddenly Hays knew this Franklin was not to be taken as lightly as he first thought.

Franklin felt better. In the easiest manner he kept the same stature and told this youngster not to mess with him This was a special trick he used often.

"Okay, Officer Hays, let's see what you came up with on Mary Carlin, then we'll discuss the other victim." Franklin opened the file, "Very neatly filled-out reports, Officer Hays. Your work?."

"Yes, sir. Thanks," Hays said somewhat shyly.

Franklin began to read aloud, "Mary Carlin, born here in St. John's in nineteen-thirty-four, went to local elementary and high school, attended County College, returned here to teach school. Taught various grades in elementary school from nineteen-fifty-six to nineteen-seventy. Mostly the third and fourth grades. Never married, though some of the old-timers say she had a boy friend. Some said he was married."

Hays interrupted with, "The usual story. Married boy friend with a family, probably used to come around her place for a change of pace-- or--," here Hays snickered, "a change of piece. One old fella, Tom Jerold, says she was

113

a great looker. I guess that's old-time talk for a great piece of......"

"Hays ! That's enough." Chief Michaels was standing just inside the door as he roared Hays' name. When he heard the unprofessional statement start from his deputy's lips, he knew it was time to let his presence be known."I think the lieutenant can read the report and then <u>we</u> can assist him with answers to any questions he might have."

Michaels smiled, touched the tip of his hat brim in a greeting type of salute, and said, "Good mornin'. Lieutenant Franklin, San Francisco Police, I expect. So glad to meet you, sir. I had no idea you was comin' down, I could have had some rolls and coffee ready. Hays, go across the bridge and get some coffee and...."

"Nothing for me, Chief," Franklin said as he stood to shake hands with the chief. "I'm very happy to meet you. Officer Hays has been kind enough to get me started on the Mary Carlin file."

Hays noticed Franklin's stance was totally different when he stood to meet the chief. He had the feeling this was done with great purpose too. This surely was an old cop trick, and he had fallen for it. It made him like the guy a little more. Hays enjoyed a joke, and he could laugh at himself as well as laughing at the next guy.

"Chief", Franklin asked, "Can you add any personel feelings about Mary Carlin?"

"No, sir I can't. Seems she left around nineteen-seventy-one. Just moved away. Didn't know her myself. I've lived here only nine years. She was a teacher over at Keller Elementary. As Hays started to say in his own colorful way, we've heard she was a very attractive young woman. The part about the married man -- yes, Bill, I heard almost all of that, too, --that's rumor from the Park Bench Bunch. You might want to go over and ask them some questions. I'll walk over with you later and introduce you, if you'd like. They're a bunch of old-timers who play checkers all day. Anythin' worth knowin' 'bout anythin' around here, and one of them will know it."

"Thanks, Chief, that might be a great help. I'll do that in a few minutes, but now I have another victim on my hands. We think he's from St. Johns also. The only thing we have for sure is the name George Gallagher. No dates that are definite. I have some information that give me approximate years from nineteen-fifty to nineteen-sixty-six. This is only conjecture. I'm not sure these dates even pertain to this George, but it sure seems likely."

The chief looked across the desk at Officer Hays and asked, "Doesn't Gallagher ring a bell? We've had somethin' about a Gallagher. Nothin' violent, but I'm sure it's come up recently."

Bill Hays rose from his desk and opened the bottom drawer in the last row of black file cabinets. The tag on the front of the drawer said, Births and Obits.

The inside of the drawer had two sets of alphabetical files in it. The last half was tagged Obits and some imaginative person had marked the edge of each tab with a wide stripe from a black marker. Hays pulled out the G file, thumbed through, and pulled out a newpaper clipping on an Emily Gallagher.

He returned to the chief's desk. "Here you go, Chief."

" 'Emily Gallagher died peacefully at home after a long illness. Mrs. Gallagher was alone at the time of her death on June 10, 1986. A life long resident of St. John's, she lived alone since her daughter, Geraldine, moved away in 1976. Mrs. Gallagher was a widow, preceeded in death by her husband, George, in 1967. Her only survivor is her daughter Geraldine' That's the only thing we have on a Gallagher."

"Yep, that's all we have on a Gallagher," Bill repeated.

"Thanks, Bill," Franklin was warming to this boyish but sharp young officer. "But, what about a son? I have good reason to believe there was a son in the family. Here it says the daughter was the only survivor."Hays   started, "Lieutenant...."

"Frank will be fine, if you don't mind, Chief," he said nodding to Michaels, as if to ask his permission.

Hays turned also, as if to get the chief's permission to call Frank by his first name.

Chief Michaels nodded and smiled at Hays. His smile seemed to say, "Yes, of course, you dumb shit, you can call him by his first name."

"Frank," Hays began again, "that looks like our only Gallagher, and there's no mention of a son, living or dead. I think the George you have must be this one, but he sure dies a lot, for one person. If that's him, he was married to Mrs. Emily Gallagher, who died last summer.   Guess George is something else to ask the old timers about."

Franklin was disappointed and puzzled. "Well, I think I've found my Emily Gallagher, diary writer, and this must be George Gallagher. murder victim -- but certainly more than a little confusing. This says he died in nineteen-sixty-seven, and I have a body that looks like his up in San Francisco. I'm afraid I'm back to square one.   I wonder if my latest victim was using the identification of the real George Gallagher. If so, he's been using those papers for a long time."

Chief Michaels rubbed his chin, looked over at Hays and said, "We're goin' over to see the Park Bench Bunch. Maybe they can give some more information on Mr. Gallagher."

As they left the station, the church bells were tolling noon. Franklin's stomach had been telling him it was lunch time for thirty minutes.

Walking west, they came onto the town square. It wasn't a real square, but a triangle. Three small streets formed the park inside the triangle. There were several benches, a gazebo with four tables, one water fountain, and the   statue of John Alfred Cornley, seated on his faithful old Rob.   Mister Cornley was seeing to the needs

116

of some of the residents of the park -- the pigeons. The statue's shoulders served as a roost to about a dozen pigeons each, and the shoulders and back seemed to be draped in white, evidently a gift from the pigeons in return for a place to sit.

As they walked into the gazebo, all the old timers but one turned and called greetings to the chief.

"Fellas, I'd like to introduce Lieutenant Frank Franklin of the San Francisco Police. He needs some help from the city of St. John's, and I figured you gentlemen would be the perfect ones to give it to him. y'all knowin' all there is to know about St. John's, and all that."

The chins all went a little higher, and the backs all straightened -- again, all but one.

Frank nudged the chief and asked, "What's wrong with the old man on the end? He hasn't acted like he even knows we're here."

"Him?" Michaels returned, as he pointed to the old man on the end.

"That's Sam Cleary. He probably don't know we're here. He's been like that for about twenty or thirty years."

"What happened to him?" Frank asked.

"What I heard, he was working on his car radiator one evenin' with the car runnin' and the garage door shut. The hood fell on him, and the jar must of set off the horn. Miz Cleary finally got tired of listenin' to the horn blast, come out, and found him. The fumes got to his brain, and the horn got to his ears. She's been bringin' him over here with the other guys for as long as I been here. That's nine years. I've heard that story from a lot of people, for years, but I can't figure out what made the horn go . Well, Lieutenant, start askin' your questions."

"Gentlemen," Franklin began, "as you know, San Francisco has its share of violence and crime, and I have two murders that have background information leading to St. John's. I know Officer Hays has talked to you about Mary Carlin, and I'd appreciate anything additional you've thought of since he talked to you yesterday. My questions today are about a man named George Gallagher. The chief's extraordinary filing system has given me an obituary article on a Mrs. Emily Gallagher. It said her husband, George Gallagher, preceeded her in death in nineteen-sixty-seven. Do any of you have any recollection of the Gallaghers?"

Franklin thought he noticed a jerking in the silent old man, on the end of the bench but turned back to the others and waited as they mumbled amoung themselves.

A crusty old sailor-type wearing a fishing captain's hat cleared his throat and cackled, "Old Georgie didn't die then. That was just a polite lie we use here in St. John's to say the bastard skipped."

Chief Michaels grinned and goaded, "Now, Jed, I'll bet you're just makin' all that up."

"Naw, sir. George Gallagher was a bastard, if there ever was one on this good earth. Used to beat those kids and his poor little wife. She was a sickly little thing. I always thought it was from the beatings. My wife, Elsa, God rest her soul, used to work at the grocery store. Gave those sweet kids a lollypop whenever the boss wasn't lookin'. You shoulda seen those kids. Two peas in a pod, they was. Elsa told me Miss Emily came in there too often with lumps and bruises. Tried to hide them under a scarf most of the time. My missus said so."

"And 'bout him dyin'?" he went on. "The only way he'd go was screwin' hisself to death. Long time he just went to the next town and then -- I don't know when it started -- he got hisself a local girl. That went on fer a long time. I always had my idea on who that was,too. Funny you askin' about both Mary Carlin and Gallagher. I always figured it was old Georgie she was seein' on the sly. Sure don't know what she saw in him."

"All we heard was Gallagher skipped town, and that was the last we ever heard of him. Just up and left, he did. Elsa said she thought they would be better off now. Yes, sir, Georgie Gallagher, Bastardo Numero Uno."

At this last mention of George Gallagher, the old man on the end stiffened and muttered, "That rotten kid, I sure showed that little bastard."

They all sat and stared. Nothing had come out of Sam Cleary for years, and now he came out with a whole sentence.

Frank took notes as the old timers offered a few more comments on Miss Carlin and George Gallagher. One mentioned Miss Emily, and how long she was sick before she died last year.

"Gentlemen, do any of you know anything about the son?" Frank asked.

"No, sir. I remember them when they was kids, but that's all. Just two peas in a pod, they was. Two peas in a pod."

"So you said. Thanks." Frank moved around to the side of the covered area, "What about last year. Did you see the daughter very much, when she came back to clean?"

"No sir. like I said. No one saw the daughter away from the funeral, but the chief."

With his notes finished, he thanked the men in the park, and Frank and the Chief started back to the station.

"So," said Franklin as he and the chief walked, "I sure want to thank you for all your help. As soon as I get back, I'll check on the daughter.

With all the connections in this case, she may be in danger, herself. You're absolutely sure the mother's death was just from her long illness?"

"Sure am. She'd been sick off and on for as long as I knew her. I made the call to the daughter myself. She was really broken up. Came right down from San Francisco. We had the funeral here in town at St. John's Free Church. Most everyone attended. Even if they didn't know her. St. John's is like that. Miss Gallagher came back the next month and cleaned out the house and put it on the market. It's still for sale. Would you like to see it?"

"Yes, Chief, I think I should. I'd like to compare it to some pictures I have. They're pretty old, but I should be able to see if it's the same place. Would you mind going with me?"

"No problem, just let me tell Hays where I'm goin'."

Franklin drove, taking the abbreviated directons from Michaels. "Left....now   down   one   block....left again....right....and there it is. Second house from the corner."

Of course in a town this size, there were not that many turns and complicated streets to use.

The house was the one in the picture. Franklin could tell this before he got out of the car. They came in from the road drove down a slight hill to a small circle drive in front of the porch and front door. At one time it could have been a great-looking house, but thirty years of neglect had taken it's toll. The porch was fairly roomy, with an old wooden settee on each side of the door. The screen was almost gone, looked like it had been torn off the hinges. In the diary Emily mentioned the night George tore it open when she forgot to unlock it. Two old planters hung on each side of the steps, long empty of anything, even closely resembling flowers.

Franklin pulled out the pictures that came from Mary's room.

"They stood right here," Franklin said, to no one in particular. "Okay if we go inside, Chief? I'd just like to get a better feel for the family. It might tell me something."

Franklin made notes as they walked into the front entry. This went into a hall that ran straight to the back door. The living room was on the left and the dining room on the right with the kitchen directly behind. Stairs went up to bedrooms, he supposed. He'd soon see.

The furniture was large, stable overstuffed type, and at least thirty five to forty years old. The Gallaghers probably

120

bought everything used, when they set up housekeeping. The place was neat, it just had a heavy coating of dust and cob webs. A few tracks through, probably real estate people showing it and the daughter last summer.

The bedrooms, both of them, were the same way -- in order but full of cob webs, dust, and spiders. No personal items but some books, again, all old. Franklin was sure this place had looked just like this when all the Gallaghers lived here, minus the dust, maybe.

Franklin went down to the kitchen and started looking through the cabinets. There were a few cans of vegatables, salt and pepper shakers and a small bowl of solid grey colored mass. It must have been sugar at one time. Surprisingly, even the ants didn't like coming in here.

The mother must have lived in some of this dirt. It was too much for just one year.

Under the sink were the usual cleaners, a dried bar of Ivory Soap still in it's yellowed wrapper. A waste paper basket had a grocery bag in it. One cheese wrapper, a small cracker box. English muffin wrapper, and a few scraps of paper -- probably from Geraldine's lunch.

<u>Why didn't she clean out the kitchen?</u>   Frank wondered.

The personality of the house fit with the ideas Franklin received from the diary pages and from the Park Bench Bunch. What a sad, dreary family.

Franklin took one last trip upstairs and glanced into what must have been the twins' room. Here he did see a few children's books but no toys, no remberances of childhood past. This bedroom was on the front left side as you faced the road, overlooking the roof of the front porch. It even had a trellis to climb down. Franklin wondered if the kids ever slipped out after bedtime in true Mark Twain fashion. It really was a great room. It was large and airy with windows on two sides. A large closet stood in one corner. It looked more like a small store room. There were two sets of marks on one closet door.

Must be how tall the kids were at special times.

It was the only room in the house to show even the slightest sign of happiness.

Franklin went back downstairs and joined Chief Michaels on the porch.

"Well, Frank, did you see enough?" The chief asked. "Was there anythin' to help?"

"Nothing to write down," Frank replied as he gave the settee a shove and sent it swinging.

"I just wanted to get some new impressions of the family. It leaves me a pretty sad."

They were almost back to the station when Frank told Chief Michaels, "Chief, my thanks to you and please extend my thanks to Officer Hays and your Park Bench Bunch. You've all been very helpful. I'm sure of Mary Carlin's connection. I'm also certain my George Gallagher is, or was, your George Gallagher. I have a feeling talking to the Gallagher girl will help. While I have you right here, could you give me your impressions of the girl? Another thing, we still don't know what happened to the brother."

"Frank, I don't know anything about the brother. I can ask around and I'll have Hays do some more record searching. As for Miss Gallagher, she was the saddest little thing. 'bout thirty, small little girl, beautiful long red hair. Very timid and soft spoken. She came as soon as she could. We all helped her with funeral arrangements. Then she came back a few weeks later, cleaned out the house and went back to San Francisco."

"All the clothes were her mother's.," he continued. "They went to the Salvation Army. She burned a lot of stuff out back of the house. That's about all that happened. Didn't talk to her much. She stayed out here by herself. I put her phone number and address in with the papers I gave you, there in that bundle.

"Where did you get the information on the brother? I didn't know there was one."

"Oh, just something mentioned in some papers Mary Carlin had at her apartment." Franklin replied, sliding over the question.

"Oh, here. Hays made a few copies of things for your file. It's all in the big envelope.   Put in a few copies of what happened here last summer too . Thought if you had time, we could talk about it sometime. Now there's more to those stories than is in the paper. We had to leave out some of the information so the general public wouldn't know all the facts. Besides, some of the details were just a little too disgustin' to print in the paper. I'll tell you more if we get together -- if you're interested, that is."

Franklin drove Chief Michaels back to the station. Leaving town, Franklin felt disappointed in the trip. He did not really learn much on either victim. As he drove, he considered all the information he had collected from Chief Michaels and Officer Hays.

When he first planned to go to St. John's, his prime suspect was the elusive Emily.   He thought he would just go down to St. John's, arrest this wronged woman and toss her in jail for the rest of her sad life. These were pretty rotten thoughts he was having. She probably got onto Memory Lane and thought about all the mean things George and Mary did to her in the past, then came to town and sliced them out of this world.

"Boy! Was I wrong! No way in hell a nice, quiet old lady who's been dead for a year can come back and make a mess like this," Frank said as he fussed with the car radio.

As he drove along, Franklin wondered about the daughter. Reaching over with his right hand, he shuffled through the notes and copies Chief Michaels made of the newspaper clipping of the obituary on Emily Gallagher and other things.

"Here it is," he said to the stearing wheel, "Geraldine. She lives on the southeast side. Age thirty-two, lived in San Francisco for the last ten years, works at the South

City Library. She worked at the library in St. John's too before she moved to the big city."

Frank hummed and beat out the time to some music on one of the local Mexican stations, all the time going over his conversation with Michaels and Hays.

<u>That Hays was quite a card. Had a funny story for everything.</u>

From the exchanged looks between the two St. John's' officers, Franklin believed they were having a few silent laughs at his expense too.

"I'll bet Chief 'Ralphie' Michaels was sure some good ol' boy when he was younger," Frank whispered. "You can smell the corn pone, catfish, and home brew just listening to that slow, steady way of talking. Not much accent left, but he's still got a lot of shit-kicker left in him. Probably never said a <u>G</u> in his life."

Things sure weren't falling into place as easily as Franklin had hoped. An interview with the daughter was the next thing on his list. If she was the last of the family, she could also be in danger.

October 21, 1965

Dear Diary,

Oh, how I hate to tell you what has been happening around here. George is wild, Terry is in such a bad mood, and Gerry just sits and waits for her brother to tell her what to do.

She has gotten to the point where she won't do anything on her own. I guess that's my fault. I keep telling them both that they have to take care of each other, but Gerry doesn't seem to do any of the taking care of when it comes to her and her brother seeing to each other.

Terry is such a joke player. He thinks it's fun to sneak out and play pranks on the neighbors. George keeps spanking him and sometimes he spanks both Terry and Gerry. Just because Terry plays a few jokes on the neighbors doesn't mean he's not a caring boy. He just likes to do tricks.

There have been a few accidents, but that's not really Terry's fault. Like the time he threw Mr. Cleary's cat off the roof. That was just a natural thing for a baby like Terry to wonder about -- I mean, the statement that cats have nine lives. He heard that someplace and wondered if it was true. Mr. Cleary is a little crabby with kids, and I guess they all like to play tricks on him.

Gerry is so sweet. This week at school she made a real pretty picture for me. I was going to keep it with these books of my diaries, but Terry tore it up into little pieces. He's sure can be a handful when he gets into one of his moods. Sometimes I think he may end up like his Daddy.

George got real mad at him last night, and he really gave him a bad spanking. It wasn't really his fault, but he sneaked out again to play a trick on Mr. Cleary, and that mean man had made a trap. I mean a really bad trap. Can you imagine a grown man leaving a great big bucket of yellow paint stuck over the door of his garage, just waiting for someone to open the door? Why, my poor baby came in just as yellow as the sun. George beat him for going out. He beat him for trying to do something in Mr. Cleary's garage. He beat him more for getting caught in such a silly trap.

I thought he looked pretty funny standing there all yellow with just two eyes peering out. He sure made a mess of the trellis and his bedroom, too.

My poor Gerry got a spanking too last night. George says it was her fault that Terry went out. If she was better company for him, he wouldn't want to be going out all the time. He just hit and hit, but she didn't shed a tear. I sure don't know how she does it sometimes. You can just almost, see her shaking inside, but she keeps herself in control, like a good little girl.

Terry never cries neither, but he's not such a good little boy. Me and George keep telling him he's got to be a better kid, but he don't pay no mind to that kind of talk. He's got his way of doing things. I guess we can never change him. I do wish he'd stay in the house at night.

I guess that's all for tonight. Things sure do get tiresome around here. I wish I had me a friend that could talk back. Not that I don't love you, Diary, but I sure do wish you could talk. Sometimes I would just like for someone to ask me if I like something, or not. I sure do feel a little left out of the world sometimes. Even when I give you some words to say to me, it just don't feel quite the same. I'm sorry. I guess I shouldn't complain. I have my babies. No matter what they do, I still love them. They're not bad, just a little playful.

Good night dear diary,

Emily

Good night, my friend, Emily. Your friend, Diary.

That helps a little.

October 27, 1965

Dear Diary,

Sorry I haven't written since last week. Nothing special happened until now, and I have been a little lazy. I got those new curtains made for the babies' room. They sure do like them. Maybe I can make the bed spreads to match.

If Terry comes in with any more paint on him like he did last week, I'll be the one to tan his back side. Of course, I wouldn't hurt him like his daddy did. He's really a little too rough on the twins.

Since they've gotten bigger, I keep thinking that he will be a little more loving with them. Last night George was kidding with Terry about something. The next minute he lost his temper and smacked him right across the face. Gerry stood there and shook, I think she was afraid she was going to get the next one. Terry didn't shed a tear, and Gerry didn't move. She stood there and waited for her daddy to leave the room.

Then when he did, she and Terry went back to their books like he had never been in the room. They did say something to each other, but I didn't understand what the words were or what they meant.

Last night we had some bad news in the neighborhood. Mr. Cleary -- you know, the crab that trapped poor Terry with the yellow paint. Well, he had an accident with his car. Seems Mrs. Cleary kept hearing a horn blow and blow. When she went out to see what the trouble was, she found her husband stuck under the hood of the car.

They think the hood slipped and trapped him under it. The vibration made the horn to go off. Poor Mr. Cleary. He couldn't hear nothing, or say nothing, when they took him away.

He was in, what they call, a comma. You know, when a person acts like he is sleeping, but nobody can wake him up. I read a story once about some poor little girl that was in a comma for months. When she woke up, she was just fine. Maybe it's spelled coma. Oh well, anyway, her mama said she always believed that she would wake up and be fine. That sure was a lovely story.

I found that story in one of the books at Doctor Hedley's office the time I had the funny rash on my private parts. Remember how George yelled and hollered when I told him that Doc said I couldn't have -- you know, sleep with him. That's what polite people call it. Sleep with. I don't know why they call it sleeping with someone. When they say it that way, they sure don't sleep. I guess there is supposed to be a polite way to say everything.

Anyways, they took Mr. Cleary to the hospital in a real ambulance with the siren going and flashing, and everything. I never seen one of those going full-blast so close, before. I never knew anyone who was even in one . The siren sure was loud when it took off.

The babies sure got a kick out of seeing the flashing lights and hearing the siren. Gerry was reading in her room,and Terry was out doing something, Lord knows what. That boy, he sure can come up with some new things to do. He said he was going over to watch somebody get what he deserved. Probably one of his friends was in a fight with another boy. Terry's such a stinker, sometimes.

Gerry just sits and listens to his every word when he comes in from playing with his friends. She sure does idolize her brother. I'm sure he feels the same way about her. Sometimes I feel a little left out. They act like they are the only two people on the earth.

They still use some of their special words. I sure am glad I found out that a lot of twins talk their own special words sometimes. The first time I figured out that this was their special talk, it had me real worried, but the nurse at the school says that a lot of twins make up their own words and special signs. I guess that's what keeps them special to each other. I keep telling them that they're special to each other, and never forget it. They'll always have each other, no matter what happens to anyone else.

Funny part about that accident, Mrs. Cleary said she thought she saw a youngster run out of the back door of the garage just as she came from the kitchen door. If there was any one in the garage, you'd think that they would have helped the old man instead of leaving him stuck in the front of his car.

The lady at the store -- you remember Mrs. Jenson -- said that the gas fumes from the engine had addled his brain and the horn had ruined his ears. He might stay in a coma, or comma, whatever it is. Even if he does wake up, he will probably be funny in the head.

I'm glad I don't have to take care of anyone like that.

I guess that's all for tonight.

Good night, my sweet diary,

Emily

Chapter Thirteen

Frank decided to make his visit to the daughter a cold call. Most times an unannounced visit from the police gave more information than one with a call first. This was one of those times.

He walked toward the front door of the apartment building, and before he could reach out for the door, it was opened from inside.

"Good evening, sir. I'm Ed, the doorman. May I help you?"

Franklin looked up and saw the pleasant smile of Ed Spatro, the doorman, as he politely tipped his hat.

"Yes, you can, Ed. I'm here to see one of your tenants, Miss Geraldine Gallagher. She is not expecting me. My name is Lieutenant Frank Franklin of the San Francisco Police Department," he said, as he pulled out his identification. "If you would call and see if she will allow me to come to her apartment, I'd appreciate it. Please assure her this is just a routine visit, I have some questions about an old family friend."

Franklin choked a little on the old family friend statement, but that phrase sounded better than "Her old man is dead".

Ed nodded as he reached for the house phone.

Franklin could here the voice on the other end and it didn't sound like a shy, timid voice to him.

Ed put the phone back on it's cradle and turned to Franklin. "Lieutenant, her brother says you can come up." He paused and added in an embarrased voice, "If you have to."

"Her brother?" Franklin returned.

"Yes, sir, her brother.   Terry Gallagher. He lives with her."

"Oh, yes, of course. I, ah.... just wasn't expecting to see him tonight," Franklin said as they walked to the elevator.

He had the distinct impression that Ed did not like the brother, Mister Terry Gallagher.

Ed pushed the elevator button marked 2 for him and Frank smiled his thanks. As the door closed he nodded another "thank you" to the snappy salute he was given by Ed.

Frank stood in the center of the elevator, hands down at his sides, and starred at the doors. His body hadn't moved a muscle, but his mind was racing.

The brother, here. Well, that sure takes care of one big question. Why hadn't the brother been mentioned in the obituary? Did he leave with the old man when he skipped? The kid would have been too young. If George was leaving to get away from responsibility, he sure as hell would not take a kid with him. Why didn't he show up last year for Emily's funeral?

As the elevator doors opened, a movement in a doorway to his left caught Franklin's eye.

"Over here, if you're Lieutenant Franklin." The voice had a bored sound to it.

Frank saw a lean young man in jeans and oxford shirt with a cable-knit sweater vest over it.

Frank thought, Good looking young man. Fair complexion and slightly long red hair.

The hair would have been considered short by anyone other than Franklin.

As they stepped into the apartment, the young man stepped back to the couch.

He motioned Franklin toward the large, comfortable looking easy chair across the room and said, "I'm Terrance Gallagher. Ed said you wanted to talk to Gerry. She's out for the evening. Can I help you?"

Franklin noticed that Terry Gallagher made it very awkward for him to reach out and offer his hand in a

132

normal greeting of handshakes between men. Frank knew you waited like a gentleman when greeting a woman. Mister Gallagher just did not want to shake hands.

"Thanks, Mister Gallagher. Now, I don't want to alarm you or your sister, but I have reason to believe that you both.... um, may be in some danger. From what person or direction, I don't know, yet. I'm in the process of establishing a connection between two murders that have taken place here in San Francisco."

The young man raised a hand as if to interrupt. "But, we don't have any connection to any...."

"If you please, sir, let me fully explain. We have found connections to the small town of St. John's and I'm sorry to say we have very good reason to believe one of the victims may have been your father, George Gallagher."

"My Father is dead, sir," Terry said, changing the subject with such a cold voice that Franklin was almost startled. "He died in nineteen-sixty-seven. Who's your other victim?"

"Her name was Mary Carlin. She'd been living in San Francisco for the past fifteen years or so. She waited tables at a greasy spoon diner over near Market Street. We understand she was a school teacher in St. John's about the time you would have been going to elementary school. Do you remember the name at all?"

"Mary Carlin, sure. Miss Carlin was one of my teachers. She was a friend of my mother's when I was a kid. She used to come over for Sunday dinner sometimes. My mother didn't have any other friends. That's why I remember her so well."

When Terry spoke of his mother, the whole caliber of his voice changed to a soft, loving tone -- another suprise for Franklin.

The words 'Mary Carlin' were spoken with no emphasis or emotion at all.

"Mister Gallagher," Frank said, "are you sure your father died in nineteen-sixty-seven? I've spoken to some of the town's people in St. John's, and they say he just left town in nineteen-sixty-seven. Perhaps this is what your mother told you. You were pretty young then, weren't you?"

"I've always believed my father died in nineteen-sixty-seven. I can't believe my mother would lie. She never lied. She was a wonderful woman. A saint."

Terrance Gallagher was standing in front of the couch, by this time. The flush to his face told Franklin that this was one very excitable person.

"Please, Mister Gallagher, I'm not trying to hurt your mother's memory. Perhaps she was the type of mother, loving and thoughtful, who would tell a small white lie to save the feelings of her small delicate children. This sounds like the kind of thing she would do, doesn't it? We know -- I mean we've heard from the people who remembered her -- she was a kind and loving mother., always ready to make any sacrifice for her two children. There are just two of you, aren't there?"

Franklin was using a voice for a four year old and it was working.

"Yes, that was my mother."

Terry sat back down on the sofa and was beginning to relax again.

Quickly his shoulders came up, and his chin assumed it's previous beligerant angle.

"Is this all you came about? If these people from St. John's think that your victim is my father, I guess they could be right. Why come here to bother us about it. We thought he was dead long ago, so it certainly doesn't make any difference, now."

The chill was back in his voice.

Frank replied, "We at the department feel you and your sister may be in some danger. When will I be able to talk with her? Will she be home tomorrow night after work?"

Franklin noticed that Terry did not respond to the statement about him and Gerry being in possible danger, even after he mentioned it for the second time.

"Yeah, I guess so. That should be okay. I'll leave her a note so she is sure to come straight home after work. Make it around six-thirty."

Most people do not assume the authority to set times when the police can have an appointment. This young man showed no such qualms. He told Franklin when he could see Gerry; he did not ask. Franklin let it slide. Why make waves at this early stage? Give this haughty young man a little rope and see what he did with it.

"Mister Gallagher, if I may, I'd like to ask a few more questions of you. What year did you leave St. John's?"

"I left when Gerry did. I'm a photograhper. I came back to be with my sister last year. She needed me after the death of my mother."

Franklin thought it a little strange here, he noticed Terry said "my mother" not <u>our</u> mother.

"Gerry is somewhat weak-natured, he explained. "When anyone uses the term 'Weak Sister', that's who they're talking about. I came to be with her and see to any of the problems she couldn't handle. Mother's death upset Gerry greatly, and when she's is upset, it affects me too. I find it much easier to handle things for her. I know if I'd let her learn to solve her own problems when we were children, she could face things better now, but this is the way it is and I can't change it."

"Did you attend your mother's funeral?" Franklin asked.

"No, sir, I didn't. I wasn't aware of it in time. I, ah....met Gerry at the house in St. John's and helped her clean out the house after the funeral.

Then I came back here with her. She's still having some problems that I have to help her with, then I'll be going."

"No one from St. John's mentioned your being there -- after the funeral, I mean," Frank said. "Did you talk to anyone while you were there helping clean out things? I know it's a small town, but maybe there was just one person who saw you."

"I didn't see any of them either. I really don't know why this is so important. We cleaned out the clothes and any personal things that were left. Gerry called the Salvation Army about the clothes that were usable. Those were put on the front porch with a note to take them. Gerry burned some old junk, while I sorted some other things from the bedrooms. I really didn't talk to anyone myself. Gerry talked to the sheriff. I refuse to call that fat old asshole 'Chief'. I think he made up that title himself."

Franklin noticed the stiff cold manner was back. Terry Gallagher was one very cold, brassy S.O.B. Every tone was cold steel cutting on ice, when talking about anything and anyone except his mother. The pale blue eyes were almost frightening. Franklin wondered if this could be his murderer. He certainly seemed to have the temperament for it.

"I think that will be all this evening," Frank said. "I look forward to seeing you tomorrow night at six-thirty along with your sister. Thanks again."

"I may be out. I'll see. I'll leave the note for Gerry," Terry answered with a note of finality.

Franklin raised his hand to offer it in a handshake, but Terry reached for the door and opened it for him instead of shaking hands.

"Nice talking to you, Lieutenant," he said, and closed the door behind Franklin before he could answer.

Frank did notice a smile on Terry's lips as the door closed -- the only one he had seen the whole time of talking to him.

Franklin walked across the hall and punched the _Down button at the elevator. The orange glow of the button just stared at him.

"What are you looking at?" he asked the button.

As if to answer, the light went off, and the elevator doors opened.

Franklin stepped into the elevator and turned to face forward. He wondered what one thing in life had trained every person, whoever used an elevator, to stand quietly facing the front and stare at the doors or the numbers of the floors. An elevator was usually treated with an almost religious quiet. Even when people got on in groups, they quieted down, stood back, and stared forward.

"Pavlov's dog", he whispered to the walls.

Coming out, Frankin walked across the lobby to the desk by the front door. "Ed, do you mind if I ask you a few questons? Nothing that will jeopardize your position here, I assure you. Just a few questions to clarify a few points that were brought up by Mister Gallagher."

"Of course not, Lieutenant. I sure do like Miss Gallagher, and I'd be happy to do anything I can to help her."

Franklin noticed Ed didn't mention liking, or disliking, the brother.

"Ed, how long has Miss Gallagher lived here?"

"About ten years, Lieutenant.

Franklin noticed Ed never lost his "at-attention" posture. He probably felt a man in uniform should always look bright and alert.

"Has her brother been here long?"

"No, sir. Showed up last summer. Around July, I think. I can look it up if you'd like. We're supposed to keep a record of things like that. Can't have someone renting out an apartment for one person, then later moving in a whole tribe of people. Do you want me to look it up now?"

"No, no, not yet. If it becomes necessary later, I'll let you know. What's Mister Gallagher do for a living?"

"He's some kind of photograhper. He put in a small dark room down in the service area. That's allowed, you know. They took their storage room and fixed it up for him and his pictures. Just as long as it doesn't break any fire

137

or safety rules of the building. Lieutenant, if I'm not being too forward, Mister Terry Gallagher is not a nice person. He's crabby and yells and I think he even picks on his sister. Sir, she's changed so much since he showed up. She was always a nice, quiet young lady, but now she seems to be afraid all the time. Like she don't know what's going to happen next. I think she doesn't know what he's going to do to her, and she's afraid of him. I hope I'm not out of line, sir."

Franklin reached over and patted Ed's shoulder, "Ed, you can be assured, I'll keep this in the strictest confidence. Do you mean she changed after her brother moved in? Maybe it was just her mother's death that effected her."

"No, sir, when her mother died she was so sad and seemed kind of lost, but she didn't have that confused look to her most of the time. Well, except for last Saturday, when she seemed almost happy again. Like she used to be. I was thinking, maybe her brother was going to leave. He mentioned it last week one night when he came in. Said to me, 'Thank God, I won't have to look at your constantly smiling face for long. It really gets tiresome.' He's not usually very polite to me, Lieutenant, but I'm getting used to that. Guess that goes with my kind of job. Most people here are pretty nice. When they receive a smile, they usually give one in return. I don't know what his problem is."

"Is he always like that to you, Ed? Crabby, I mean."

"He sure is. Never a good word. But Miss Galagher, she's just the sweetest thing. How did you like her?"

"What do you mean? She wasn't in. I didn't get to talk to her," Frank answered.

Ed looked a little puzzled. "I was sure she was there. The brother didn't tell me she was out when I called upstairs for you. I saw her come in about forty-five minutes before you got here. I guess she went out, again. We do have more than one entrance."

"Thanks again, Ed, you've been a big help. I'll be seeing you tomorrow night around six-thirty. I have an appointment with Miss Gallagher."

Frank offered his hand and the doorman smiled in appreciation. It was nice to be treated as an equal, not just something that opened doors and punched elevator buttons. He took Franklin's hand and shook it vigorously.

Frank had gotten more information from Ed than he had from Terry. It would be very interesting to meet Miss Geraldine Gallagher. Chief Michaels had described Gerry as a timid, shy person, agreeing with Ed's picture of her, without the mention of confusion. That was also before the brother arrived.

When he got into his car, he made a few notes and headed home. Tomorrow should be interesting. Margot was coming into the office for more studying of the diary pages. This new information might bring together some new points.

Chapter Fourteen

Gerry was not happy about the prospect of talking to Lieutenant Franklin tomorrow night. After quite a long explanaton about why Franklin was coming on Wednesday night and what he would be asking, Terry still wasn't sure she understood.

He tried to make it simple, but she appeared worried.

"Gerry, if you're relaxed, you shouldn't have anything to worry about. I wouldn't have talked to him if he hadn't surprised me."

"I know. We just weren't prepared. I can't remember too much about what is going on, so there really isn't much to think about. If I know, I'll talk about it. If I don't, there's no problem. Isn't that right?"

"Sure," he said without much conviction. "Just remember we both have everything to lose. We can't be separated on this thing. Just do as I say."

Gerry went to bed a little earlier than usual that night. After staring into the darkness for quite a while, she decided sleep was not going to come. Maybe a cup of tea would help relax her. As she left the bedroom, she tied her robe snugly around her waist and glanced into the hall mirror that hung on the wall just outside the bedroom door.

Out of the hushed quiet of the apartment a voice sneered at her, "Boy, are you getting vain. Now you get up in the middle of the night to look at yourself. Why are you up again?"

Catching her breath she quickly turned her head away from the mirror. Why did he treat her this way? They had no one else on this earth to call family, and he jeered and harrassed her with cutting remarks. He was so patient just an hour ago. Now he was like this.

Her feelings were so mixed. Terry used to be so protective of her; now it was a constant battle of wits. She only had his well-being at heart. Why didn't he understand this?

When he came to help her with her problems in the past, she tried to say and do the right thing. She always tried to help him. It seemed like he spent his whole life cleaning up after her when she had a problem. She felt as if she never did anything right. It frightened her to always be wrong. It also comforted her to know that Terry would always show up and help her with anything that bothered her.

Right now she couldn't quite remember what her problems were. That was why Terry was here. He would take care of everything, and she could get back to her nice quiet life and her work at the library.

Terry said the police were coming tomorrow night at six-thirty, to see her. What could they want? He tried to explain, but right now she still did not understand. She couldn't remember doing anything too unusual. She would have to wait until tomorrow to find out what the questions were.

She left the hall and entered the kitchen to boil water for tea. She was unusually nervous since Terry promised to leave soon. She did not know if she was happy about this or sad. She needed him so much at times, but when he came to take care of her problems this time, she became very frightened. Sometimes she felt as though she would never be alone.

As usual, he didn't tell her how he was handling anything. It was strange that she should continue to use the word "problems". She did not remember what her problems were. Terry told her last Saturday she was helping take care of them, but again, she didn't remember doing anything different -- and, how could she take care of a problem if she didn't know what it was?

He never explained things in detail.

"I'm going to leave soon," he said, "and then where will you be? You should learn to handle your own life."

Gerry often felt that she was the one who would be going and Terry was staying. Her confidence had lessened each time Terry arrived. She could not remember why. All her friends at the library were asking questions now.

"Why are you so nervous, lately? Are you getting sick? Are you sure your brother isn't mistreating you. Sometimes you look so confused when we mention his name."

<u>They'll never understand how it is between us</u>, she said to herself.

The girls had never met Terry, and naturally, they were very curious about him. Most of their questions were really to just learn more about him, but they only served to make Gerry more nervous. The main reason the girls were so curious about Terry was not knowing he even existed before Gerry's mother died last June. When she came home after cleaning out her mother's house, she started referring to Terry, how he always came when she needed him.

They also didn't know what kind of problems she could be talking about. She became more quiet and more into herself that usual, although a few times Gerry was abrupt with them and on a few occasions had spoken quite sharply to them.

As she sat in the kitchen, she remembered the box of papers sitting in the pantry. She started to open the pantry door to pull the box out. Terry's voice rumbled, "Leave that alone. I told you to stay out of there. I'm not going to have you rummaging through those things. You'll just get yourself more confused."

"I just wanted to look through the papers and books. Maybe something will be in there about....you know. The accident."

"Shut up," he bellowed, "I don't ever want you to say that again. It wasn't an accident, and you know it. Don't talk about it ever again. Do you hear me?"

Gerry stood in the center of the kitchen, shaking and holding her arms tightly to herself, totally frightened. "Why can't I look at the things that were mother's? They were her last tie with reality. There were so many things mother didn't tell us."

The pantry door was slammed shut, and Terry snapped, "That is the end of this conversation. Stay away from that box. It's going to be burned, and that will be the end of that portion of our lives. Do you understand?"

Gerry picked up her cup of tea and walked out of the kitchen toward the living room, nodding her head yes like a small child that had just been scolded by her parents. "I'm so sorry. I'm so sorry...."

Then her head turned to the hall, and she brightened and said in a happy, childlike voice, "Why don't we ever play 'turn around'" any more?"

"We are, you fool," was the only answer that came back to her.

Smiling to herself, Gerry said, "Oh, I'm so glad" and with that she turned to the bedroom.

After finishing her tea at her bedside, she placed the cup on the night stand and crawled into her bed. The tea finally made her sleepy, <u>Now, maybe I can get some rest.</u>

The dream started slowly.

First, Terry was sneaking out of the window.

"Mother told us we shouldn't do this anymore. Boy, Terry, you're really going to get it, this time."

"Not if you don't tell, snitch," The boy of eleven could climb down the side trellis as easily as a monkey. He should. He'd been climbing down this wooden ladderlike structure for at least five or six years now.

"Please, Terry, don't go out tonight. If Daddy finds out he'll whip you again, and me too, probably. This time he might even use that stick on your backside. Remember how it cut you last time. You still have the scars on your back and shoulders."

144

"Forget it, snitch. If you tell, I won't tell you all the neat things I do when I go out at night. Remember when I told you about throwing the rocks at Mister Cleary's windows. Well, tonight I'm going to get that cat of his.

I hate that old cat. It's smelly and it poops in our yard. There's some gas in the old can Daddy uses to fill the mower, and that old cat and me are going to have a hot old time tonight."

"Oh, Terry, no! Please don't hurt the cat again. It already walks funny from when you threw it off the roof."

"Yeah, whoever said a cat always lands on it's feet sure was wrong about that one. It propably is just as dumb as Old Man Cleary. I'll sure fix him tonight."

The conversation came back to her so clearly. She could hear his voice and the hatred in it. Gerry couldn't understand why Terry hated so much. Every time he got caught, their father beat him until he bled, but a few nights later, Terry would sneak out and find some other person to harrass or torment in the quiet of the night. Most people had a pretty good idea who the culprit was, but out of what they considered, a kindness to Emily Gallagher, they went to the father to complain.

Then Emily could not understand why George was constantly beating his children. Most of the time they were both punished, because Terry would wear clothes that fit either of them and the neighbors did not know which of the twins was   tearing down clotheslines, filling the mail box with cow manure, or breaking windows with rocks, not to mention crippling some of the neighborhood pets. Of course, Gerry had her mean times, too.

The dreams were hazy and sometimes even fun. If they were of a picnic or a good day at school, they would leave Gerry fresh and happy in the morning. This didn't happen too often. Most of the dreams were ones of the conflicts between them and their father or the neighbors.

Gerry's mind flew through a sea of clouds. "Oh, Terry, come home. Mama will be here soon. Please come back into the room. Fly home. Don't do anything bad."

Terry's face slid into the bedroom over the window sill. She could just make out the clothes he had worn when he left, but the color was different.

"Why do you look all yellow all over?" she asked. "Are you hurt? Let me call Mama."

"No, I'm full of paint. That damned old man fixed a bucket of yellow paint so it would spill all over me. Now Daddy will know, and I'll get in real bad trouble. That Old Man Cleary will pay for this. I'll kill him. I'll kill him. I'll kill him."

She could still hear the horrible loathing and hatred in Terry's voice. She became so frightened she hid under the covers.

Somehow in the dream it was already the next day and Daddy had the switch out, but he was hitting Terry on the hands over and over. Gerry was told to stand on the back porch and watch, along with Emily.

"And don't you cry, either of you," Daddy yelled.

The next thing Gerry could see through the clouds was Terry laughing as an ambulance that took Mister Cleary to the hospital. The old man had been working on his car in his garage when the car hood fell and trapped him like a huge mouth biting at his waistline. Then the horn went off. He was almost killed from the gas fumes coming from a leaky part of the motor, and the horn hurt his ears. Gerry could not understand why this would make Terry so happy. She could still remember the look on his face. He was smiling so hard, as though he had a big ice cream cone that would never be empty.

As Gerry floated across fields of flowers, she heard Terry call to her, "Gerry, Gerry! Turn Around! Turn Around! Turn Around, little sister."

She awoke with a start. As she sat up in bed, Gerry felt clammy and chilled. She must have kicked the covers off of the bed as she slept and dreamed about her childhood. Why couldn't she dream more of her mother. She missed her so much.

She slowly relaxed and drifted back to sleep. This time she entered a totally dreamless state, and the night was gone to her.

Chapter Fifteen

Franklin walked in the front door of the station and strolled over to the stairs, giving a wave to Officers Johnson and Doyle near the front desk.

"Have you heard about Frank's bulletin board?" Doyle asked, as he leaned back to get another file from the cabinet. "The guys upstairs say he has a beauty this time. Just like in a dime novel."

Johnson paused in the middle of the report he was filling out and glanced back at his partner, "When was the last time you bought a novel for a dime? Come to think of it, when was the last time you bought a novel, period?"

Frank was anxious to get into the office this morning. Last night he struggled with sleep. First he went over his trip to St. John's. Then he rehashed the meeting with Terry Gallagher. He did not think this young man was lying, but Frank was sure he was leaving some great holes in anything he offered to tell.

Tossing the morning paper on a chair, he went to the coffee pot and poured himself a cup of the mystery liquid of the day. At least by coming in this early, he found the coffee was fairly good. It even poured easily.

Frank took his cup with him, pulled a chair out in front of the bulletin boards, sat down. Now he stared at the papers hanging before him.

The diary pages were hung in chronological order, but were hard to read. "I'll have to make a chart of the pages, by date and happening."

He proceeded to make some small cards with the information gained from his trip to St. John's. He put each bit on Mary Carlin and George "Fuzzy" Gallagher on separate cards and pinned them to their respective bulletin boards.

As he sat and stared, he asked the boards, "Mary Carlin, messed around with a married man, right?. We know who that was, don't we, Fuzzy? She left town around nineteen-seventy-one. But, Fuzzy left four years before that. Hmm! why did she wait so long? Evidently they didn't plan on meeting and being together. She was a school teacher. On that subject we didn't really add anything new down in St. John's."

"Now, for George. He's the man who died twice. Once in nineteen-sixty -seven, thanks to the kindness of the town editor. That was sheer goodness toward Mrs. Emily Gallagher. The second and more final time, last weekend, was thanks to our mysterious cutter."

"What can happened to cause old wounds to open and old hatred to seek this kind of vengence after all these years? Something had to trigger these murders. Why wait for twenty-five to thirty years before getting satisfaction? The only connecting circumstance was the death of Emily, and that happened last June."

Frank decided the murderer did not know where to find them -- but, if that was the case, how did he find them now? Did he wait until he found them both so he could do them in together? There were many unanswered questions.

Were Mary and George in contact with each other here in San Francisco?

"That's something to check out," he muttered as he made a note to remind himself of this.

Frank went to his desk and started another list, "Where do you look if you want to locate someone in a city as large as San Francisco?"

The first on his list, and most logical, was the phone book. He doubted if either would be listed. He was right -- nothing for either Mary or George.

Then he thought, "Could they have been listed in some back issues of the phone book, before they were so down on their luck?"

He would check this out with the phone company and check some old books. Mary Carlin may have a phone at one time. George probably never did. His type needed every cent just to stay alive from one day to the next.

Frank went back to Mary's board. Some of these letters from George were dated in the late seventies. They gave a box number at the Union Square Post Office.

If the murderer saw these letters, he would have had an idea that George was from near that area. Maybe he didn't know he was around, until contact was made with Mary.

He checked the pictures of the room, and it looked like Mary was expecting her visiter, so contact could have been made at any time. It did not have to be only on the night of the murder.

Mary and the murderer could have been meeting for some time. She could have even introduced the murderer to George if the murderer brought up the subject of him being in San Francisco. Then again, Mary could have told the murderer that George was here. That seemed like a more reasonable answer to Franklin. Whoever was meeting Mary found out where George was, through her, or at least the area where he was likely to be found.

An important thing to find out now was if any of George's friends saw him with anyone new in the last months or even days. In the circles he traveled in, someone new would certainly be observed.

Make a note, Frank told himself.

Margot walked into the room with a flourish.

"You've either solved the whole thing without my help, or you are completely stumped. Which is it?" she asked as she dumped all her books and her brief case on the floor next to his desk.

"Neither. I've gained a few answers, but I've gathered many more questions than I had to begin with. I sure hope we have some kind of witness that saw the murderer with either Mary or George. I'll check that out later"

Franklin looked a little dejected and said, "Last night I had a meeting with the brother -- yes, I said brother -- of

Miss Geraldine Gallagher. She was listed as the only living survivor of the Gallagher family, as of last June. This was in the obituary of one Mrs. Emily Gallagher, who I might say I was sure, was our murderer. Mrs. Gallagher, it said, was preceeded in death by her husband George Gallagher, in nineteen-sixty-seven. As for Mister George 'Fuzzy' Gallagher, seems the town editor thought it would be a nice thing to do, so he listed George as dead. Being nice to the deceased, Emily, and to the daughter, since George, up and dumped them in nineteen-sixty seven and left them to fend for themselves. Does this make any sense to you?"

"I think it does," she answered.

As he rattled on Margot began taking notes. Everything he said was written down, even though right now she couldn't put any meaning to it.

"Now that those facts are perfectly clear, Margot, have you come up with any new ideas? I hoped you would have something to discuss with me this morning."

"I only came up with new questions, like you," she said. "Why should anyone feel the need to kill these people now? Why wait for all these years? Frankly, I think they should have been done away with years ago.

I'm like you, I felt sure that dear Mrs. Emily had something to do with it, but if she died last year, how can this do anyone any good now? There must be something to connect these happenings now -- and one other question, Frank. How did she die? Was it positively natural?"

"Yeah, that was one of my first questions. By the way, I did go down to St. John's yesterday. That was what most of my tirade was about. I spoke to some of the old residents, and George positively left in nineteen-sixty-seven. He just up and left. Some of them knew Mary Carlin too. They knew about her fooling around with someone. One of them said he thought it was George. I have a feeling they knew he was involved there.

152

One old man was pretty strong in his description of George. -- mean, drunkard, womanizer, wife-beater, probably child-beater, and all around <u>Bastard Extrardinaire</u>. He gave me a pretty good picture of him. It fit with what I felt about George from the diary pages."

Margot was taking notes, "Did they say if anyone had contact with him recently? I mean, how could the murderer find either of them if they've been gone for that long -- and why now? What could cause this to come up now, and with such a violent conclusion. It seems to me that all the parties involved knew what was going on. Why wait so long to do anything about it? If there is some new person involved in this, why are those diary pages so important? They seem to be the central part of this puzzle, I think. Who could they affect now that wasn't affected before?"

"Thanks, Margot. You have just exhausted my list of questions that I was about to ask you," Frank sighed.

He walked over to the boards and assumed the position of a standing "Thinker", his head going back and forth, as he compared pictures, diary pages, and letters. Something here had to mean more that it looked like on the surface -- but, what?

Margot joined him in his study of the boards, and they stood for almost fifteen minutes before any sound was heard from either of them. Finally Margot grunted, reached back to the desk and picked up the copy of the obituary of Emily Gallagher, and brought it over to George's board.

She leaned closer and said, "I wonder."

"What? What? You wonder what? For God's sake, don't do that unless you have something." Frank was starting to perspire and become a little flushed.

"Here, Frank, look at this old article from George's board and the obituary on Emily. The print looks a little alike. I'm sure most of the print in the world looks alike, but this has the same spacing and the typeface isn't the usual. Looks like it came from an old fashioned type of newpaper."

"Gimme that. Where? Show me." Frank was now jumping around, trying to look over her shoulder.

"Down, boy. Don't give yourself a stroke. It's not all that earth-shattering. Here, see what I mean. The first letter of each paragraph has that old fashioned script. Could these possible come from the same newpaper?"

When he turned the clipping over Frank found an ad for a grocery store sale in St. John's that was held last July.

"Oh, brother, the old man that was killed in this article and there is another one in the other article -- these must be the grisly killings that Chief Michaels was talking about. Why would George keep these articles?

Where did he get them? Maybe Mary Carlin gave then to him, or he was able to get the paper from one of the stands around here. I doubt very much if he went down to St. John's very often."

Franklin went back to his desk and started to rummage through the file and envelope that Michaels had given him yesterday.

"Michaels said he put some information on his old killings into the envelope, just in case I might have some time to read them. This might have some connection to this case.....here it is. Two separate articles on two old men killed last July. The dates are just ten days apart," he said excitedly. "Michaels gave me the full page with each article."

"They're exactly the same articles," Margot's speech was getting a little quicker. "Here, read this. It says a man named Hendrix was murdered in his home by what could have been a troop of "Manson-like" hippies, looking for money and kicks."

"That's the same article Fuzzy had. What's on the other one?"

"It's about a local doctor who was murdered by someone looking for drugs and money," she answered.

"Bingo. Michaels' grisly murders are the same ones Fuzzy carried in his wallet. Now I know I have to go back to St. John's. The chief said there was more to them than was in the paper, because they were so grisly. He sure likes that word."

Franklin was beginning to glow. He was an athlete preparing for the arena.

"Now, Margot, you get your notes together. I'd like you to go with me in the morning. I think I have a few ideas to put into the mental file," he said as he tapped his temple. "Then first thing in the morning, I want to get down to St. John's."

"Sure, but, I think you should go alone. I have been assigned to this case, and I have the time," she replied with a questioning look, "but how would Chief Michaels react to a new face.? And a woman's at that?"

"He's a good old boy, you're right. He might talk easier to just me. Let's get this mess cleaned up and get out of here."

"I've got to see Miss Gallagher at six-thirty this evening and right now I have a meeting with the mayor and a planning commission on pension funds for police widows. How the hell they ever got me on that committee, I'll never know."

"It's your sweet, glowing nature," Margot said, as she chucked him under the chin.

Chapter Sixteen

It was lunch hour. The girls from the library wanted to go shopping over at the Sales Depot, after work.

"Gee, I'm sorry, Ilene, but I'm really strapped for time. I promised Terry I'd get home as soon as I could tonight. I have a six thirty appointment."

Gerry wondered why they kept asking her, but they did not realize why she had to be with him as much as possible right now.

"What are you now, a babysitter? Ilene prodded. "Come on, Gerry, just a little shopping and then we can get a bite to eat at The Pub. It will be fun. We've got to do something different, for a change. "

Gerry's shoulders came up, and they could tell she was angry.

"Why do you keep on about my wanting to be with Terry? He won't be here very long.   What's the big deal anyway? You can go shopping without me. Besides, I'm short of money right now." Her voice was getting shrill. "You all have other family. Terry's all I have ever really had, and I'm not going to waste time away from him right now."

Of course, they all apologized for teasing her. They did not realize how close Gerry and her brother were. As a matter of fact, they didn't even know about Terry until last July.

Last June they were surprised when she came to work and told her boss she would be taking off a few days for her mother's funeral. Later in July she went back to clean out her mother's house and to see to selling it and the remainder of its contents. It was a very hard time for her. When she came home, she started talking about Terry.

When Gerry left home and moved to San Fransisco, into the same apartment where she now lived, she had been twenty-two. Shortly after moving in, she obtained her job at the library. Her quiet ways had made a very good impression on the manager of the South City Library. Gerry enjoyed the long hours of peaceful filing and reading.

Today she sat off to the side of the lunch table, lost in her own thoughts.

She asked Ilene and Sue, "Why do I feel so uneasy? I have my friends. Terry is with me again, but I can't relax. I wonder what he has been doing. I don't know if I like it when he's with me or if it makes me frightened. Sometimes he scolds me like I was a little child. I'm just as old as he is, but he can treat me so mean. I guess that's just his way of showing me that he loves me."

"Don't worry so about it," Ilene responded. "Brothers are like that.

One day you're great, and the next they treat you like you're some kind of an insect."

"No, Terry isn't like that. I remember, Mama always said we would always have each other and we should always have our own way of showing love. She was so right. I sure wish Mama was still with me. Maybe I shouldn't have left St. John's so early." Gerry smiled and sighed, "That was such a nice time."

"What did you say, Gerry," Sue was staring at her and Gerry was shaken back into the present.

"Oh, nothing, I was just thinking about when I was still living with Mama in St. John's. That was really a good time. I'm really not sure why I left. I had the same kind of job at the local library. I guess I thought it was my turn to set the world on fire. Just like you two did, right?"

Sue and Ilene felt much better, this was the old Gerry.

Sue wiggled to the end of the bench and said, "Yeah, we haven't exactly turned San Francisco on it's ear, have we? Why, at least once a week I put a book on the wrong shelf, just to let the world know I'm still alive."

Ilene giggled and grabbed the empty lunch bags, "Let me do the cleaning today."

Gerry loved her lunch hours with her two friends. When she first moved to San Francisco, she looked for a job for about three weeks before she found the opening at the library. Every one was so nice to her and she became friends with these two girls, from the back office.

They all had their lunch hour together either downstairs in the employee's lounge or across the street in the small public square. After a while, they began to trade lunch, just for a little variety, so they usually had a great time trying to make something special and save money at the same time. Over the years they had grown as close as sisters.

One day, about eighteen months ago, one of the maintenance men approached them late one morning and asked, "How 'bout I join you at the park for lunch? You all seem to have a good time, and it sure gets boring down there with all those pipes and motors. I bring my lunch, and I could use the company of three lovely ladies."

They giggled to themselves and Ilene spoke out, "Sure, come on along. We need a fresh face to look at."

Sue and Gerry were a little shocked by Ilene's forwardness, but they were also excited at the prospect of having lunch with this man who seemed so worldly to these three small-town girls.

As he left, Gerry whispered, "How could you?"

"What's the big deal? Just yesterday we sat out there and complained how bored we were with the same lunch in the same place, day after day. Now we have a new challenge. We can figure out who will win the heart of this knight in shining armor."

"You mean knight in greasy armor," Sue giggled. "If he would only get some of the grease and oily smell off of him. Maybe he will for lunch." "This is really exciting, isn't it, Gerry?" Sue asked.

Gerry looked up with a slightly frightened glint in her eyes, "I guess, but something about him scares me."

159

As they sat waiting for him to come over to the park, they all speculated as to where he would sit, who he would talk to the most, and which of the fair maidens would win his heart.

Their frivolous mood did not last more than ten minutes. After he sat on the bench between Gerry and Sue, he proceeded to curse and use vulgar sayings. He then began to tell off-color stories to the shocked girls. He must have assumed their awed look was a sign of approval, for just as quickly as he started with the filthy language and stories, he placed a hand on the knee of each girl along side of him.

Then he told Ilene, "Now, don't you worry none, honey. You'll get your share of me. I'm man enough for all of you. Why I could take you all on at the same time." With this statement he reached over and smacked each one's thigh. "Don't any one of you feel left out."

The girls grabbed their lunch things and left him sitting there staring. When he realized how he had shocked them, he started laughing like a mad man. They could still hear him roaring as they went in the employees' side entrance. The girls went back to work silently. Nothing was ever said between the three friends about the episode, and it was as though it never happened.

About three days later, on Saturday, the maintenance man was found dead in the boiler room. He was trying to fix a valve on the furnace and was overcome by gas, by all appearances.

The gas valve was shut when they found him, but the police thought he was probably strong enough to get the valve closed. He probably passed out, and the room was still filled with enough gas to kill him as he lay on the floor. He appeared to have fallen and hit his head on a pipe that came up through the floor to the furnace.

The same weekend was another of the times she was sure that Terry had come. She missed him after all these years. It had been a long time since she had thought of him. When she awoke from a nap on that Saturday afternoon, a bath towel was wet, there was a smudge of grease on the kitchen floor, and some old clothes were pulled from the back of the closet. She knew at once why they were there. Terry didn't mind closets, but she could never bring herself to go into the far corners of even the smallest closet. When Terry made one of his visits, there was always some sign. He either moved things around or he'd leave her some mysterious note.

This time Gerry looked in the kitchen by the sink, and there was the note from Terry: Hi, Gerry. <u>Stopped by to fix a few things. I've made a few adjustments here and there. Take better care of yourself. I get tired of fixing all your problems.</u> It was signed with a big swirling <u>T</u>.

This note was almost cordial, but this was not the standard. She was never comfortable with her feelings about Terry. When there were small, there were so close, they could almost reach into the other's mind. Now it felt the same, but still different, and she couldn't remember why it should be different. That bothered her, too.

She hadn't had any of those problems for a long time. When she was younger, around high school age, she had a memory problem. The doctor said it was the stress of being a teen-ager. It had been several years since she'd forgotten what she had been doing or had blank hours in her day. At times, she even had blank days.

If these quiet evenings could just continue, soon things would be back to normal. She really loved him, but things were always affected by the presence of Terry. His personality was one of great demands and sometimes severe reactions. No one was immune to his moods and the domination he demanded in any situation.

Gerry wondered what she would do with the dark room when the time came for Terry to go. Maybe he would get rid of the equipment, himself. After all, he had just purchased it last summer after he arrived.

When he left this time, would it be for good? She never knew. What would it be like to be alone for good, to know he'd never be back. Surely he would not do that to her. She didn't like to think about that.

Bringing herself back to the present, Gerry said, "There are some feelings time cannot benumb".

Ilene grinned, "That's easy. That was Byron."

"Okay, girls, time to go back to work." Sue said and started clearing the park bench as Gerry and Ilene folded the small tablecloth they always brought for their picnics.

Just before reaching the back door, Gerry paused, stiffened slightly. "Here within these hallowed walls, lives and dies the wisdom and joy of the minds of the universe. Yea, to seek the wisdom, is to be singly fortunate, but to have it, is to be doubly blessed."

Ilene looked at Gerry with a puzzled glance, "Who said that?"

Gerry, with a haughty shrug and a cold tone in her voice, answered, "I did, you twit."

Chapter Seventeen

Frank entered the lobby as Ed was rounding the corner from the back hall.

"Evening, Lieutenant Franklin. Right on time I see," Ed gave a quick half-salute, barely touching the brim of his hat.

"Good evening, Ed," Frank said with a smile. He enjoyed the crispness of this very sharp 'protector of the lobby'.

"First, sir," Ed paused, "May I announce you?"

"Of course, Ed. Sorry, I didn't think. Please call upstairs first. I believe I'm expected at six-thirty. Right?"

"Right, sir, that's what you said last night," Ed was punching in the apartment code number on the red house phone. "Yes, Miss Gallagher. It's Ed. Yes, miss. Oh, fine, just fine...Yes miss, she's fine too, thanks. Miss Gallagher, Lieutenant Franklin of the San Francisco Police is here for your six-thirty appointment. May I send him up?....Very good. Yes, right away."

As he returned the receiver to it's carriage, Ed turned to Frank and said, "Lieutenant, Miss Gallagher says she'll be happy to see you."

"Thanks a lot, Ed. I appreciate it."

They walked casually over to the elevator, and Frank waited as Ed reached out and punched the elevator call button.

"Thanks again," Frank said, as the door slid shut.

His last view of Ed was a smile and his tip-of-the-hat salute.

<u>Crispy clean, that's what that guy is. Sharp and crispy clean.</u>

Frank thought he must ask Ed if he was in the service in his younger days.

"Nah -- none of your business, Franklin," Frank said to himself as the door slid open on the second floor.

163

As the elevator door opened and Franklin stepped out, a small voice said, "Lieutenant, over here. I'm Gerry Gallagher. Please come in."

Frank Franklin was immediately in love, at least puppy love. As he followed her into the apartment, Gerry Gallagher took on the appearance of a woman-child. She was small, but not little., delicate, but not fragile.

She closed the apartment door and turned to him with her hand outstretched.

"Lieutenant Franklin," she said quietly, "I'm Gerry Gallagher. Oh, I said that already, didn't I? I'm a little nervous. I've never had the police come to my apartment before."

"Miss Gallagher, I'm very happy to meet you and please don't worry. Most people get nervous with the police. It's natural."

Her hand felt small and delicate, but the handshake was solid. Not like so many small women who's hand usually felt like a piece of soft cloth with no bones.

"Did your brother tell you why I wanted to see you?"

"Terry? Yes, he did. I still don't fully understand. He said you would explain more when you came tonight. Something about my father."

"Yes, there seems to be some confusion, but we believe this man George Gallagher, who was --er, who died last Saturday here in San Francisco, was your father."

"Lieutenant, I--we thought he died long ago. That's what my mother said. It was around Christmas or New Year's Eve in, I think, nineteen-sixty-seven. He left and then she said he died."

Frank started moving from one foot to another.

"Oh, I'm so sorry," Gerry said. "Where are my manners? Please Lieutenant, sit down. Here on the couch. It's much more comfortable than that old chair. May I get you some tea? I was just getting ready to have some myself. It's made and ready to be poured."

"Yes, tea will be fine."

After Gerry poured the tea, Frank took the cup she handed across the coffee table to him.

Sipping the hot tea, as quietly as he could, he said, "Very good. Is it a special blend?"

"Yes. It's one of my few extravagances. I get it down in China Town. It's really inexpensive. It cost more to go there and get it than the tea costs. Lieutenant Franklin, could you get back to this man who died and is supposed to be my father?"

"Of course, Miss Gallagher. Last Sunday morning he was found over by the harbor. He had identification on him that gave his name as George Gallagher. He also had a voter's registration -- a very old one, that is -- from St. John's. We had other reasons for going to St. John's and when we inquired about anyone named Gallagher, they found the obituary of your mother from last summer. It mentioned the fact that her husband died in nineteen-sixty-seven, and gave your name as a surviving family member"

Franklin purposely skipped the wording on the obit that said "only surviving member"

"Oh dear, yes. My mother passed away last June. I still don't see how your George Gallagher could be my father." she was becomming teary with this last sentence.

"When I was down in St. John's yesterday," Frank said, "I checked into it with Chief Michaels. You remember him, don't you? He said he spoke to you last summer when you came down for the funeral."

"Yes, he was so kind. He made all kinds of arrangements for me."

Frank explained, "Well, he took me to see some of the older residents, and I believe they cleared up the question of your father's previously reported death. When the obituary was printed, they felt it was easier to agree with what your mother had been saying for years, that your father died in nineteen-sixty-seven. This was their small way of avoiding any confusion or leaving any open questions concerning your family. Now, does that make more sense," he asked as he returned his tea cup to it's saucer.

"Of course. Now I see it much clearer. I've been a little confused lately, but that surely makes more sense." Gerry paused for a moment and said,"Confusion now hath made his masterpiece."

"Very fitting. I see you're a reader. Mr. Shakespeare, I presume?"

"Yes, I'm delighted you know. Working in the library, I use all my spare time reading. My friends and I have a game we play at lunch. We try new quotations on each other. It's quite enjoyable."

Gerry reached for the teapot and said, "Lieutenant, I can't thank you enough for coming here and telling me about my father. Was there anything else?"

As he motioned that he didn't want any more tea, he said, "Yes, there is Miss Gallagher. I don't really know how to say this, I don't want to frighten or upset you."

He watched her small perfect face take on a puzzled look as she brushed her hair back. He noticed how nice her hands were with long perfect nails polished with a red enamel, though the red color didn't seem to fit her. She seemed more the soft pink type.

"What will upset me? I don't feel sad about my father, since I've thought he was dead for so long. Does this make me a bad person not to feel sad?"

"Oh, no. Not at all. I understand how you feel. You've had years to think he was gone, now you find out he just died -- but I can certainly understand how there would be a lack of sorrow now. What worries me is the fact that your father, George Gallagher, was killed. Murdered, that is. There was another killing that's connected to St. John's and to your family when you were a child. A schoolteacher from St. John's. Mary Carlin. Do you remember her?"

"Oh, my goodness. Yes. She was our teacher and my mother's friend."

Now her eyes began to fill and she seemed to shrink into the corner of the couch.

"We're investigating both of the murders. Miss Carlin was killed sometime Thursday morning, and Mr. Gallagher was killed late Saturday or early Sunday morning. We're hoping someone saw either of them with a stranger, or saw anything unusual."

"Will that help?" she asked.

"The area Mister Gallagher frequented is pretty full of bums, and he was known by most of them." At least Frank didn't say that Gallagher was a bum, too. "Hopefully one of his buddies will have seen something. Mister Gallagher was a little down on his luck, so he was on the streets some of the time. When he didn't have his job at the market."

"I don't know what to say. I feel bad, but I don't know what to say"

"I understand. This must be quite a shock. There is more, Miss Gallagher."

Gerry Gallagher looked like she was about fifteen years old now as she sunk back into the cushions of the couch.

"Is your brother here? Maybe it would be better if he was here for the rest of this."

Franklin was beginning to worry about the young woman. She was growing very pale.

"No, he's out for the evening. What's the rest you talked about?"

"I'm afraid you and Mister Gallagher, your brother, may be in danger. I've alerted Ed the doorman to watch for anyone or anything out of the ordinary. Here's my business card. Please call me if you think of anything that may help."

"All right, but what would that be?" Her voice getting more childlike with every sentence.

"Any contact from old family friends, any strange events around work or here at the apartment house. Have your brother contact me if anything new turns up. Please, Miss Gallagher, if anything unusual occurs, be careful. Try to keep to areas that have lots of people. We'll have this cleared up soon, I'm sure."

"Yes, sir. I'll try very hard to think about this. I'll be careful, too."

"Okay, I'm going to go now, but you be sure to lock the door behind me and only let your brother in. Will you do that?"

"Yes, sir, of course."

Frank let himself out and waited for the click of the inner lock.

Downstairs he briefed Ed on calling him for anything of a suspicious nature. The doorman grasped the seriousness of the situation, without trying to overdramatize it. This pleased Frank.

He'll be good to have around if we have an emergency, he thought to himself.

Chapter Eighteen

The streets were fairly quiet, but then, it was three-thirty in the morning. They should be.

Sitting with their backs against the wall, the two men were barely visible from the curb where the slightly built figure stood. They shared the early part of the morning here under the canopy with a small treasure of cheap whiskey. The bottle was held in a small brown paper bag. They seemed to think this bag would hide the bottle from the world.

It was almost time for them to start their rounds of corner trash cans and alley dumpsters. Peggy and Frisky went their own route at this time in the morning. Usually they met around seven in the morning over on Market Street.

Their names, acquired so long ago, had lost any meaning. Peggy's left leg was stiff. He was probably known as "Pegleg" at one time, and Frisky loved to talk about women. Maybe he was frisky at one time, but now all he did was talk, constantly.

Seeing a young woman walking down the dark street at this time of night made the two men take a second look.

"What 'cha think she's doin' down here at this time of the mornin'?" Peggy asked, as he put the bottle into his back pocket. "Now there's someone lookin' to get into trouble real bad. This ain't exactly the best neighborhood to be takin' a stroll."

She took one small step from the curb and glanced at the men as she started across the street.

"Don't know. Maybe she's lookin' for some action. We sure could give her a good time, don'cha know." Frisky answered with his usual cackling laugh.

"Hell, Frisky, how long has it been since you even seen a woman's bare ass, let alone had any of it?" Peggy snickered as they both got up and started down to the corner.

Before she reached the corner, the woman crossed the street and disappeared, forgotten by both men. Now they parted at the corner and began their nightly routine of rummaging for any usable item or some discarded half of a sandwich to eat.

Frisky shuffled around the corner and into the alley. He heard the slight sound of foot steps before he saw the small female figure. He started to back out of the alley when she called to him.

"Frisky, don't be afraid, it's just me. Don't you remember me? I saw you last week when I was talking to George. You remember that, I'm sure. I brought him a bottle and a few sandwiches."

"Oh, ya mean Fuzzy. Yeah, sure, I remember, I just didn't get a good look at 'cha down there on the street. I couldn't figure out who ya was. Now I see. Sure, I seen ya with Fuzzy. What 'cha want with me?" he asked. "How'd ya know my name?"

"Oh," she said as she neared the filthy old man, "George pointed you out to me when we were talking. He told me you were a good friend, so I felt that I should bring something for you. I wanted to help you out a little, like I did George. That's his real name, you know. George."

"George or Fuzzy. Bull shit, he ain't no friend of mine. Ya don't make no real good friends down here on the streets. Ya might have friends, but they ain't never what ya'd call real good. Cut yer throat for a bottle, most of them would, don'cha know?"

"Have you seen George, lately, Frisky? I've been looking for him but he hasn't been at his usual place by the flower stand."

"One good reason he ain't been there, don't 'cha know? Some 'good friend' sliced him up the other night. Down by the harbor. Damn fool, don't know why in hell he went down there, anyways. He never did like to leave this here area , so how come he goes down there, and get hisself cut up anyways? Cut the shit outta him, they did. Clean out."

Frisky started walking toward the dumpster as they talked, and he added with a twisted face, "I hear tell they even made mince meat outta his head, don't 'cha know?"

"Have you talked to anyone about him lately?" she asked. "Maybe the police?"

"Hell, no police or nobody talks to us down here. They just walk around us with their noses up in the air, like maybe the air is fresher up there. Nobody cares when one of us buys it. They figure we been dead for a long time. We just don't know enough to get buried, don't cha know?"

"Here, Frisky, I brought a bottle of whiskey for you and some sandwiches, just like I gave George. Fuzzy, I mean. Why don't we go on over to your place? We could have a little privacy before your friend shows up. Wouldn't you like that?"

"Sure, little lady. Ya sure are a cute thing. How come ya want to spend so much time down here with bums, when ya could be out dancin' with some rich dude at one o' them fancy places?"

"I just want to get to know you, that's all. I feel there must have been some terrible injustice to put you on the streets like this, and I'd like to lend you a helping hand. Let's go to your place now, where we can have a drink and a little conversation."

They rounded the last corner, walked through the open archway into the back of a building that had been deserted for years.   Back in the corner were three stacks of cardboard and some wood from some crates.   The two bums had been collecting these for months.   Next winter the boards will be added to the sides and give them a little more protection from the weather. One side of the building was torn down, and bricks were strewn all over. A window hung from one side.

"Welcome to my castle." Frisky said. "I seen a sign down on Market Street, in a window, that said, Mi casa es su casa. Tried to steal it one day, but they almost caught me. Had a buddy say that was Mex talk for, "Welcome to my castle". Don't know if he was shittin' me or not, but I like the 'Merican way of sayin' it. Sounds pretty nifty, don'cha know?"

They made their way to the back of the building. Frisky pulled out a few boards and made them a seat in front of the larger enclosed area. He and Peggy usually slept here.

"Now, then, let's have a go at that bottle," he said.

"Certainly, Frisky, let me open it for you. Would you like to have one of the sandwiches now. I have ham, cheese, or turkey. I didn't know which you preferred."

"Shit. Ya got to be kiddin'. I ain't preferred nothin' since I hit the streets." He laughed. "What ever hits yer hand first, little lady. I'll take that and save the rest for later, don'cha know?"

"Of course, dear. You just sit down here and let me serve you, like you were in your castle. You can be the lord of the manor."

"Sure, whatever a lord of the manor is. It sounds good. Ya never did tell me why ya was comin' down here to be with us bums. Ya some kind of a god damned do-gooder?"

"You could say that. I'm trying to clean up a few things. You just happen to get involved when you saw me with George," she said as she handed him one of the sandwiches.

"Involved in what. Was George and ya gettin' it on?" He snickered as he stuffed his mouth with the first bite of the sandwich. The bottle, sitting at his feet, was left opened.

"No, George was.... an acquaintance from many years ago. I had some unfinished business with him. It took quite a while to find him. I finally found him through a mutual friend who knew he was living down here around Market Street. Perhaps you knew her. Her name was Mary Carlin. She told me where to find him. I think he saw her once in a while when she would walk home from work."

"Nah, we don't talk 'bout nobodys past, or nothin'. 'specially to some guy who ain't from the streets. Talkin' 'bout the past can just make ya feel worse, don'cha know," he said between gulps on the bottle and bites of the ham and cheese. "Hey, where ya goin'?"

"I'm just looking around. Stay seated and enjoy your treat. I just want to see these boards," she said as she walked behind Frisky and moved a few boards out from behind him. "This looks like it might do. I can't make up my mind."

"What the hell ya' doin', cleanin' house, missy?" he asked as he rose and reached for her arm. "Here, let me help ya. I'll take yer arm and ya can climb back over here and talk to me."

With the gesture of reaching out, his companion jerked back from him and snarled, "You don't ever try to touch me. Do you understand. Do not touch me. I cannot stand to be touched."

"Sure, little lady, just tryin' to help, don'cha know? Just tryin' to be a gentleman."

She walked around and sat down again in front of him and relaxed.

As he took ravinous bites from the sandwich, he took a few large gulps from the bottle. It was not taking too long for the alcohol to take effect.

"What's your name, sweetie?" he asked.

"You may call me Emily Geraldine, but please do not call me sweetie," She stood again, and started to walk around the area of the cardboard enclosure.

"What 'cha doin' there, Emmy," He slurred as he took another long draw on the half-empty bottle.

With this, she spun around and almost screamed, "Don't you dare call me Emmy! My name is Emily

Geraldine. Don't you say it any other way. Is that clear? Emily Geraldine. I detest nicknames. Emily Geraldine. Did you hear me?"

She towered over the semi-slumped figure, holding both of her fists in front of his face.

"Sure, Sure, Swee....I mean, Emily Geraldine. No nicknames fer yer kind. Emily Geraldine it is. That's a real purty name, too. Tell me, Emily Geraldine, why in the hell ya got on rubber gloves? What 'cha 'fraid of, ya think we got germs down here?"

He was sitting up a little straighter now that he saw the pure anger in her pale blue eyes. Gone was that sweet look she had when they met out at the alley mouth Now he felt he were looking into the face of a very angry animal.

They sat in silence for several minutes after she returned to the seat across from Frisky. He was so drunk, he did not notice when she rose and started to walk around him again. This time she pulled a long slender knife from the bag she carried -- so long and shiny that she stood and admired it for a few seconds before moving closer to Frisky's back.

"Sorry, Frisky, the two-by-four would be my usual preference, but this will have to serve as an able alternative." In the semidarkness of the old building, she reached forward from behind him and said, "Here, my dear, let me fix your collar."

She carefully stepped nearer to him and said, "Don't forget. My name is Emily Geraldine and it was George, not Fuzzy. I detest nicknames."

She reached out quickly out with her left hand and grabbed his hair. She pulled back so suddenly, there was a loud crunching noise from his neck.

She remembered seeing an old neighbor woman snap the neck of a chicken she was butchering when Gerry was small. With a flash of the knife, Emily Geraldine reached around in front of Frisky and brought the blade evenly across the front of his throat making an ear-to-ear cut about one inch deep.

She stepped back, allowing him to fall, and waited a few seconds for his body to stop quivering. Then she reached forward, changing the knife into the other hand and made a tiny little puncture on the left side of his neck.

"Now, isn't that just grand?"

The slight spasms continued for a few more seconds. Then there was silence.

"I can't wait to hear the comments when Terry hears about this one."

She made her way over the rubble to the outside alley and left the building.

As she disappeared down the dark alley, a light voice sang out, "And I did it their way,"

A few more throaty laughs could be heard as she strode confidently down the dark alley.

Chapter Nineteen

"Gerry, why are you sitting in the dark like this? What's wrong?"

"Oh, Terry, I just don't know what's going on any more. Haven't you noticed things are getting more confusing?"

"What things are you talking about? There are a few things I want to discuss with you, but they sure are not all that confusing. I think you just don't pay enough attention to the things you're doing. I know we have a problem, but it's almost over."

"Terry, do you always make everything my fault? Some of this could be your doing, too. You know more of what's going on than I do. You always did know more of what was happening to us. I wish I could be more in control, like you."

"I'm not so sure, Gerry. There have been some things going on that I can't explain myself. I wanted to ask you about some junk that was left on the kitchen table last night. Did you go out?"

"Of course I didn't go out, " she replied. "Why on earth would I go out in the middle of the night. I went to bed at ten-thirty, after the news. You know that. You made a sarcastic comment about the frilly nightgown."

Terry's voice was low and almost growling, "Then why do you have your flannel gown on now?"

"Do I? How on earth did this happen? What did I do, change my gown in the middle of the night? This can't be happening again. I've had trouble with that same thing happening for the last few months. I guess I'm really getting addle-brained. That's what Mother used to call it. Just plain old fashioned addle-brained."

"Don't talk about her that way," Terry snaped. "I will not discuss her. She's gone, and George is gone, and all the rest. Now everything is cleaned up. Maybe we can start fresh,"

"Why do you get so cross when we talk about our parents. They weren't too bad. I'll bet all parents are just like them."

Terry started to mutter.

"Terry, what are you mumbling about. Please tell me. I don't like it when you're mad at me."

"Has Emily Geraldine been here?" he asked slowly.

"Emily? You mean Mother? Don't be silly. Why would you ask such a question. You know she's dead. I don't like it when you talk like that."

"Emily. Emily Geraldine, that's who. You know who I'm talking about. We haven't seen her since high school. I'm pretty sure I know why she picked now to show up. This could really mess up the plans we have, and you know she can't be controlled. Tell me the truth. Has she been here?"

Gerry had not stuttered since she was fourteen, but she started it now. "I d-d-don't th-tthink s-s-so. Wouldn't y-you know if she was h-h-here? She w-was so mean. Y-you told me so."

Terry's voice was getting lower and lower, as it usually did when he became angry, "That's what worries me. I've usually known when she was here, and this time I didn't. I'm positive she's been here. I think she has been up to some of her old tricks. You remember how she would do something, and we got the blame. We have too much at stake now to have her mess around with our plans."

"Terry, I d-don't want to t-talk about it. I r-really don't know what you m-mean," Gerry said with a somewhat detached tone.

"You've got to be kidding. Don't hand me that garbage. You know damn well what I'm talking about. We've got to talk about it and get it over. It's rotted in our minds too long now. Every since we found the diary, it's gotten to be more of a sickness in us. Let's get this mess finished. If we're careful, we may be able to stay together. Now, we have to talk."

178

Gerry rose from the sofa and reached for the light on the end table. "I d-don't know what I want. I didn't want all this to happen. Most of this was your idea. I don't even like to think about. I just pretend it never happened. Just like I did when we were little and Daddy would....never mind. Why can't we just go back to the way we were in high school? Things were so simple then. I did what I wanted, and you did what you wanted. No one ever knew the difference. That was so nice. Terry, why can't we do that again, please. No one has to know what's happened in the last year. I still can't be sure what went on, I keep forgetting things. Don't tell me anything else. Let's just start again. We can even move and get a new place. The people here haven't noticed anything strange. I'm sure we could live someplace else, and it would work out fine."

"No, no, it just won't work. You have to start using your head and figure out what's going on. You just don't realize what is really happening.

Can't you see what's happening? Stop indulging in fantasies, and look at the situation. Remember what all has happened to you in your life. You have to figure out the real truth, even if it means that I'll have to go away. Maybe if you can work on it and clear out your mind, you and I can really be together."

Gerry started to cry as she walked into her bedroom whispering,

"Why can't we just have it like it used to be. That was so nice. Just me and my sweet brother. Not someone who crabs at me all the time. Please be nice to me again, Terry. I need someone to be nice to me again. I remember when Mama was nice. She was sometimes, when she had time, after she wrote in her book. Honest, she was nice. She never hurt me, did she? I know she did that funny thing to Terry sometimes, but she never hurt me....when she had time....after she wrote in her book. As long as the book was finished, she had some time for me.

179

She brushed my hair and tucked me into my bed. My mama was nice to me."

As Gerry closed the door to her bedroom, all that could be heard was the small voice talking about her mama. Over and over the words "nice to me" could be heard.

At eight thirty, Thursday morning, Terry called the library and told the head librarian that Gerry was sick and would not be in today. "In fact, she'll probably miss a few days of work. Sorry."

As he hung up the phone, he shoulders seemed to be stooped this morning. From the back he looked like a sad old man who felt his time on earth was almost over. He shuffled back down the hall without so much as a glance around him. The cockiness of the young man had disappeared completely.

Chapter Twenty

Franklin walked through the front door of the St. John's police station, and was met by a hearty handshake from Chief Michaels.

"Frank, I thought you were bringing your assistant down with you. Isn't that who you were talking about when you called yesterday?" the chief asked as Franklin walked across the office.

"Yes, Chief, but I changed my mind. Actually, she changed my mind. Since you had expressed the opinion that these murders were of a somewhat vulgar nature, she thought you might be a little more at ease just telling me about them. A lot of people would rather not talk about touchy subjects in front of a stranger, let alone a woman. You know what I mean, don't you?"

Margot forgive me, Frank thought.

The chief shook his hand strongly and answered, "Frank, I think your assistant showed a lot of common sense. I most definitely would have been ill at ease talkin' about one of the murders in front of her. It surely was a messy thing. I'm afraid she might have found it just a bit too upsettin'."

"Well, Chief, we won't have to worry about that now, will we?"

Franklin made a note to tell Margot how close she had the chief pegged -- Southern thinking and all, including the delicacy of the little woman, no matter how she was trained.

It made him laugh a little to himself. He remembered how she talked about castrating some guy who took a swing at her chin and connected. She would have done it, too, if they hadn't gotten that knife away from her. Chief Michaels was standing with the coffee poured. He was holding a tray of the greatest-looking cakes and Danish rolls. Franklin fixed himself a plate with three pieces of pastry and returned to get his coffee. As he took his coffee, he was sorry he had taken the blueberry, and contemplated taking an extra cheese Danish.

With his food and drink seen to, he settled himself down. He waited for Chief Michaels and Deputy Hays to get to the business of their "grisly" murders of last summer. Frank could only think of them in these terms, since this was the only way both the chief and Hays referred to them.

"Frank, I surely hope we can be of help to you. I've laid out both folders on these cases. Now I'd like to go through everything just as it happened. You don't mind if I do it that way, do you?"

"Of course not," Frank answered. "If it's all right with you, I'll just take notes as you go along, and then at the end, if I may, I'll ask my questions."

"That will be fine," Chief Michaels replied. "Now, the first victim was Doctor Mason, found on the twentieth of July last year. That was a Sunday...er, let me look here....yes, that's it. Around six in the evening. His nurse, Miss Sally Jenson, was passin' the office and saw a light in the back window. This wasn't supposed to be on, so she stopped to check it out."

"There in the back office, the one he used, not the examination room, was Doc. He was tied to a chair . Looked like he'd been sittin' there for at least twenty-four hours. We figured it was dopers come through town and stopped at the first doctor's office they came across. Doc musta seen them and went in to stop them. They must have caught him and killed him. We couldn't find anythin' out of place, and Miss Jenson said there were no drugs missin'."

"Chief, why does her name sound familiar?" Frank asked.

"You met her daddy over with the Park Bench Bunch. Don't you remember? He was the one that gave us such a grand and flowery description of George Gallagher."

"Oh, yes. I just wanted to keep my characters straight. Thanks. Please go on. Sorry I stopped you."

"No problem. The only thing we could figure was they got nervous when they killed the doc. Ran out without lookin' for anythin'. He even had his money clip still in his pocket. Nothin' ever showed up on him. No clues, nothin'. Like the murderer just slipped in and out of town, and disappeared. That takes care of number one."

"Chief, I hate to keep interrupting, but how did Doctor Mason die?" Frank asked, trying not to be impatient.

"Oh, yeah, I did forget that. Don't know how I could forget that part. It was the darndest thing you ever saw. The poor man was tied to a chair. He had a scuff on the right side of his head, but that didn't kill him. Must have just knocked him out for a while, but he probably didn't regain consciousness anyway. Frank, you won't believe this but his throat was,"

Frank coughed and cleared his throat, trying to remain calm and let Chief Michaels continue. He wanted to hear more before he told them of the similarities in these cases.

"As I was sayin', his throat was cut, Frank, all the way across. From his right ear to his left, just as clean as it could be. Almost through too -- but the other side, from the left ear to the center, looked like someone hacked at it with the knife, but didn't give it enough "umph" to make it a good cut. Can you beat that? The throat was cut one-and-a-half times."

"Oh brother," moaned Franklin.

"I can see you don't believe me, but I've got pictures and....."

"No, Chief Michaels, I certainly do believe you. I have two victims in San Francisco with exactly the same ...ah, terminal illness. One-and-a-half times across the throat. This is getting pretty close."

183

"What about your second victim. Was his throat cut?"

"Naw, but his was done by someone that was really sick," Hays said. "We figured it was done by the same guys that got to Doc."

Hays started to squirm when he saw the look on Michaels' face.

Michaels continued, "But the throat job wasn't all that was done to Doc, Frank. His hands was all cut up. They was just hangin' in ribbons of flesh. Not cut off, just hacked up. Over and over."

"Chief, if I may interrupt, again." Frank was afraid the chief might turn that stare his way, "Was there any sign of forced entry at Doctor Mason's place? Any footprints or signs of someone else being there?"

"Oh, yeah. We did find some cracker crumbs on one corner of the desk. It looked like the doc spent some time talkin' to whoever it was. The doc smoked, and there were some butts in the ashtray. All his brand. That was it. Nothin' else. The office gets cleaned on Saturday, late afternoon, so all that had to be from Saturday night."

"Doc's assistant," he continued, "says she was there Saturday evenin' at six. She forgot her good shoes and had to go back for them. She said the place had been cleaned and everythin' was in order when she left. The only arguement against Doc catchin' them after they broke in is, why did he smoke those cigarettes? If they had him tied up, he couldn't smoke, and if he wasn't tied up, he must have considered them friendly. Sally said he made no mention of meetin' anyone there on the weekend. If he knew them, it must have been a last-minute meeting. Maybe they called him at home, but we didn't see any sign of them bein' in his house. That's it on Doctor Mason."

Michaels said as he reached for his coffee. "Any other questions, Frank?"

"No, I'll save them all for the last part. Thanks, Chief."

The chief quickly emptied his cooled coffee, gulped down a cheese Danish and began again. "Now, for victim number two.   This was about ten days later,   on the thirtieth of July on Wednesday the week after we found Doc. It was about three in the afternoon, one of the local kids was having trouble with his dog.   Seems   the dog wouldn't get off old man Hendrix's porch. The dog took to howlin' and raised such a ruckus that the kid went home to get his ma."

"That was Billy Compton," Hays offered.

"Yes, Billy Compton," Michaels said.   "His ma thought the dog had gone mad, so she called the dog catcher. Took about thirty minutes, 'cause he's also the barber in town and he had someone in the chair. Well, anyways, when he got there, the dog didn't look mad, but just to be on the safe side, he used that pole and loopy thing they have to catch animals and keep them away from the people doin' the catchin'. When he got the dog all looped up, he went up on the porch to see what set the animal off. That's when he caught the smell."

"That smell coming out of that house would set anything to howling," Bill interjected.

"Yes, Deputy," the Chief Michaels said in a low growl. "Anyways, he had a pretty good idea that it was a body, so he called me right away. We went over there, and me and Hays went in the back door. Well, I'll tell you, I ain't never seen any spectacle such as that before.   The kitchen is right off the back hall, and when we come in that back door, we saw right into the center of the kitchen.   That's where the table sits. Lordy, Lordy, right there in the middle of the kitchen, nailed -- I say nailed -- to the table is Old Man Hendrix. He's got big nails in both hands, holdin' him to the tabletop, and ropes around his ankles holdin' both his legs to the legs of the table. On the floor off the side of the table from between his legs is a great big dark-brown spot. No, it was more like a dried-up puddle. Blood. Lots of it. You wouldn't think an old man like that would have that much blood in him, being so skinny and all."

Hays added as he took out his hankerchief and started wiping his forehead and neck. "It sure was terrible. He was just.....

"Bill, let me get there in my own time. There's things to say in the right order."

Frank smiled to himself. Old Ralphie was not going to be cheated out of his time in the limelight.

"Well, Old Man Hendrix was most assuredly dead, seein' to the blood and the smell. I believe I failed to mention the fact that he was all swollen up, somethin' fierce, too."

"Now for the biggest shock. Well, sir, I'll tell you, this here is somethin' really sickly. Sittin' up there on the old man's chest, lyin' about six inches from his chin, was his own, ah.... er, penis. I can't tell you how horrible his face looked. The horror and fear just yelled out. He died, lyin' there, starin' at his own peck...umm, 'scuse me, penis, while he bled to death. Can you imagine what must have gone through that poor old man's mind as he was lyin' there? He had one of his own dirty socks stuffed in his mouth, I guess to keep him from screamin'."

Hays squirmed and whispered, "I'da died just from the sock."

"Thank you, Deputy, we might just be able to arrange that," Chief Michaels offered. "We had a coroner from the county seat come down. Everythin' was just as simple as it looked, 'cept for the blood on Hendrix's chest. The coroner said the old man must have had a hard...., I mean, he must have had an erection for there to be so much blood on his chest. 'Course, these details were kept confidential also, for the usual reasons.

"After a brief investigation of the premises, I surmised that he -- the old man, that is -- was the victim of a breakin' and enterin'. The house was a mess, but it looked like that some of it was from someone going through the drawers and closets while they looked for somethin'. Maybe they thought the old man had some money stashed away. He never had anythin' in his life, so it had to be strangers. 'Course the house was always a mess, so it might have been that way all the time. We're thinkin' the intruders did most of the messin' up."

"Yeh," Bill interrupted again, "and there was some foot prints in the back yard. They were pretty small, so we figured it was just Billy's prints when he tried to get his dog to come home."

"Bill, please," the chief said, making a motion towards to back room, "Why don't you get some more coffee?"

The veins on Chief Michaels' temples were beginning to stand out more, and he wiped his face again with his hankerchief.

"Sorry, Chief." Bill Hays got up and went into the back room, looking properly chastized.

Chief Michaels continued, "We put out an APB to the neighborin' communities to see if any one else had any problems like this, but we came up dry. No one held a grudge against the old man. He's lived here all his life. Used to own a hardward store over in Shoreville. Had a little money put away and it was just about enough to live on. I did see him pickin' up some pop and beer cans out along the roadside one day, here a time back.

"Now the coroner said the old man was lyin' there for about ten days, so we figure him and Doc Mason got it on the same night. They must have left the Doc's place, and then they tried to get somethin' from the old man. We think he caught them, too. They must have been pretty sick people. There was a cracker box out on the floor. Looked like someone sat and ate dry crackers while they watched the old man bleed to death. At Doc's there was the crumbs on the desk, remember. Since then we haven't turned up a thing on either of the murders. Does this help you with any of your questions, Frank?"

"Chief, it answers a few, and it adds a few to the list," Frank said as he wrote in his notebook. "You say they were both killed the same night. The paper says they were a week apart. Is this another of the paper's convenient lies?"

"We didn't really say when the second victim was killed. We just left that out to keep the town from gettin' too riled about havin' two murders on the same night. We -- the authorities, that is -- were aware that the murders took place the same night. This was just somethin' we wanted to keep to ourselves, not give away any secrets, if we had a bunch more killin's on our hands. Save some facts so's we could have better proof. You know what I mean, don'cha, Frank?"

"Yes, Chief, I'm afraid I do."

With the chief's report finished, Frank reviewed his notes quickly and went to the back of the office to refill his coffee cup and get a couple more of the sweet rolls that were waiting on the sideboard.

Frank returned to his chair, and as he picked up his notes, he asked, "Chief, when you went over the rooms where the victims were found, did you come across anything that looked out of place? Something that could have been left by the intruders?"

Chief Michaels swallowed the last bite of his blueberry Danish quickly and answered, "Naw, Frank. We went over everythin'. Made sure that the intruders, as you call them, didn't drop somethin' that we could have used as a clue."

"Chief," Hays said, as he returned from his desk, "what about those flowers at Doc Mason's place?"

Frank looked at the chief with added interest, "Flowers?"

"Yeah," Michaels grunted, "seems like either Doc or his visiters brought in some flowers. It was just a small bouquet of diasies. Yellow. We found them on the front desk. Miss Jenson said they were about the only thing she didn't recognize there. Everythin' else belonged there .

Frank's interest increased as he asked, "What happened to the flowers?"

Michaels glanced at Hays and he answered after a nod from his chief to finally say something.

"We checked them, and there wasn't anything different about them. I do remember Miss Jenson getting out a vase and putting some water in it for the flowers that night. I guess she saved them until they died."

"Could I possibly talk to Miss Jenson? I'd like to find out if anything else was different in the office."

"Frank," Chief Michaels voice seemed a little tight at the moment, "I just told you, nothing else was out of place or different."

"Oh, right Chief. I'm reaching for straws right now," Frank added.

Frank made a few more notes and asked , "What about in the old man's house? Any books, for instance. Some papers with some old writing?"

"Frank, that place was such a mess, there could have been an alligater there and no one would have noticed."

At this Frank knew something would come out of Deputy Hays.

'less it bit them." Hays said this so quietly that Chief Michaels missed it, although Frank did not, and he gave Bill a slight wink.

"Chief, I hate to be such a bother, but my department is something like yours. We've kept a few secrets for our own reasons. Would it be possible for me to go through Hendrix's things and Doctor Mason's also?

Have their things been stored, or is it too late to hope to find something? I do have some particular thing in mind. I know it's an imposition, but I'm really in a jam."

"Sure, Frank. No problem. The old man's house hasn't been touched. Nobody wants to clean it, so it just sits there. We boarded it up to keep the kids out. Doc's practice was taken over by a youngster, but I'm sure he still has all the files. Most of the junk.... I mean, things were in the office when he took over. Miss Jenson works for him, too. You might be able to find out somethin' from her about the things they saved and the stuff they pitched."

Frank's face was showing his excitement now as he stood from his chair and said, "Would it be all right to stop by the Hendrix house right now. I'll call Miss Jenson today, too."

"Frank, I hate to put you off on this, but could you possibly do it tomorrow? This afternoon starts our Crafts Festival and there's a parade with speeches later and then our Fun Fair. You know how it is? All the booths with the crafts for sale. It's pretty important to the town, and the things you want to look through have waited a year. Another day won't hurt."

Frank had mixed emotions on this. He didn't want to start looking through the belongings of the victims at this hour. He also did not want to come back out here tomorrow . He did not dare tell Michaels that he did not know what the hell a Crafts Festival was, nor did he give a damn.

"Sure, Chief. I understand," he lied. "I'll call Miss Jenson and make an appointment for tomorrow, and I'll go through Mr. Hendrix's house then too. Well, my thanks again. As usual, you came through for me. I've certainly added more information to what I have. I hope I can do somethng with it when I get back," He rose to leave. "Bill, thanks again, for all your help, too. I'll be in touch tomorrow."

Chief Michaels said, "I tell you what, Frank, tomorrow morning, first thing, I'll have Hays go over both places, and we'll call you early as we can. Bill can work tonight after the parade too. If we can find what you need we can get it to you by messenger tomorrow soon as possible. What should we be lookin' for?"

"Thanks a lot, Chief. I really appreciate this. I'm looking for anything that looks like pages from a diary, probably on notebook paper. This is really good of you, Chief. It can save me some time and possible save some lives if our killer has some more victims in mind. Don't forget, anything that could be a diary or notes made about their lives. It will be signed by "Emily". They're mostly on loose leaf paper, but some are from those school notebooks with the spiral back."

As Frank left the office, Hays and Chief Michaels were sitting very quietly as their respective desks. Franklin had a feeling that Chief Ralph Michaels was about to tear his deputy a brand new ass. Bill didn't look too happy about Frank's departure.

Frank was anxious to get back to the station and talk to Margot. This case was getting crazier with each day.

As Frank entered his car, he heard Chief Michaels and Deputy Bill Hays fussing at each other inside the office.

"Chief, It's just like the story about the chicken with the tire tracks on it's back."

"Shut up, Bill, I don't want to hear it."

"But Chief, it's a quicky."

"Bill, if you don't be quiet right now, you'll never tell another dumb chicken joke for the rest of your life. In fact there will be no "Rest of your life. Understood?"

"But!"

"Understood, <u>Deputy Will 'um Hays</u>?"

"Understood."

"Understood, what?"

"Understood, sir."

Chuckling as he slid into the driver's seat of his car, Frank mimicked the chief's drawl. "That Hays is somethin' else."

Chapter Twenty-one

All the way back from St. John's, Frank had a nagging realization. This spree didn't start just this week. It started last year when Emily died. Or more exactly, it started three weeks later.

That was one week after Gerry Gallagher, and her brother came back to clean out the house. When they cleaned, Chief Michaels said some things were burned and some things were given away to organizations such as the Salvation Army. What else was found?

<u>Damn,</u> Franklin thought. <u>What else? Their mother's diary, of course.</u>

That had to be the explanation. As much as he hated the idea, it looked more and more like the brother and sister were involved in doing the killings and were not prospective victims. Frank had a hard time believing that Gerry could be involved in this. The brother certainly could. He was hard, cold, and most assuredly aggressive.

As soon as he returned to the station house, he started the ball rolling to see if any of the street people who knew George, had seen anything. There had to be someone.

The people of the streets have a warning system, that tells them that a newcomer is around. They can spot a cop or an interloper from fifty yards -- probably something in the clean smell of their clothes. A stranger on the streets around here must have been seen by someone. They were just too thick on the streets to let even the most casual of meetings go unnoticed.

The biggest problem was to get any of them to talk. These street people were a leery lot and did not usually go around offering any kind of information to just anyone, maybe if a bottle of the right type of liquid could be offered in return. That usually loosened a tongue here and there.

Franklin reached over to his desk, picked up his phone, and punched the number of the front desk. "Kelly, could you send one of your officers up, I'd like to have him go down to Market and Eighth to ask some questions for me."

"Lieutenant, right now I have about three of my officers in that approximate location. They're taking the statements of some bums over there. One of the regulars bought it last night. His name was Frisky. His buddy, named Peggy, found him this morning about eight o'clock. He was out back by his sleeping place, a carton from some old furniture. Seems like he was missed when he didn't show up on his corner at seven. It wasn't exactly what you'd call a natural death. His throat was slit from one ear to the other. Must have died instantly."

"Sounds like it was pretty terminal," Franklin answered. "By the way, I didn't know these guys actually kept schedules. Who found him, his broker?"

"No, sir," Kelly snickered. "Just his buddy. He says Frisky always shows up early when the office workers start coming to work. I guess they panhandle a little in the morning.   Then   they go down to MacDonald's for a sandwich if they get enough,"

Kelly was reading from his note book.

"If he didn't get enough change, he'd hit the trash cans out back of the fast-food spots."

"His throat, was it cut once, or twice?" Frank asked.

"Just one time through, Lieutenant. Ear to ear, but there were little marks, almost like punched marks, not really cuts, just little hacks. You know -- little tick, tick, ticks," he said as he poked his neck with an imaginary knife.

"Kelly, this is probably the guy I was looking for. Looks like someone is thinking a little faster than I am. Damn."

"Jeez, Lieutenant, that's the kind of stuff you got up there. I didn't connect them. I'm sorry. We think his neck was broken, and then the throat cut from behind from the right side to the left. Being an old Perry Mason reader, I'd make it to be left-hander. Right Lieutenant?"

"You watch too many reruns. "

"Have the officer in charge come up here as soon as he returns to the station. I'd like copies of everything. Have them make a written description of the scene and lots of pictures. You know what I like. Call them now, before anything is moved. This could be very important."

"Yes, Lieutenant. And Frank, I'm sorry I didn't connect this thing with the job you're working on. I just didn't think."

"That's okay, Sergeant," Franklin said as he put the phone back onto the cradle.

He walked over to the boards of Mary and George, started pulling out some pins, rearranging them. He made room for one more victim. He was sure he would need it.

He stood there wondering what this guy saw -- perhaps a meeting between Mary and George, or the murderer and George. It had to be something like that.

While he waited, he thought this might be a good time to check on Gerry Gallagher. He opened her file folder and checked the phone number of the library. He had written both her apartment number and the library number on the inside cover after he received the folder from Chief Michaels.

He dialed and waited for the phone to be answered on the other end. When the library operator answered, he asked if he could please speak to Miss Gallagher. He was answered by a very businesslike explanation that Miss Gallagher was not allowed to receive personal calls at the library. She explained it was library policy.

Then in a soft, almost whisper, "Besides, sir, she's not in today. Her brother called this morning and said she was sick. He said she might be out for a few days, too."

"Thanks. Thanks a lot," Frank answered, surprised to find himself whispering too.

He placed the receiver back onto its cradle and began to worry. <u>What kind of sickness does she have?</u>

His first impulse was to call the apartment, but he thought better of it. "Maybe I should go over there."

"Maybe you should go over where," a voice asked from the doorway.

"Oh, hi, Margot. Gerry. She didn't go to work today. I just called the library, and they said her brother called in sick for her today. That scares me."

"I don't think the brother would actually hurt his own sister, would he?" she asked.

"I don't know -- and now I've got another victim. It seems to me that the brother and sister are just about all of the people left who were involved in this thing from the start."

"Tell me about the other victims. The ones from St. John's. Did Chief Michaels give you a good run through on them. Are there some more questions involving them?"

"Oh, brother." Frank moaned as he got up to go over to the boards again. "Where do I start?"

"Get a chair and read my notes, while I stare at the information we have up here. Then I'll give you a run-through."

Margot pulled a chair closer to the boards but didn't sit on it. She reached for the notes that Frank was holding out and began to pace. Frank motioned for her to sit down several times and finally gave up. He was used to her pacing, he just didn't like it.

"Last year's murders," Margot said, "had one throat cutting like we have this year and one very different kind of cutting,"

Frank looked up and sighed, "If you can call having your pecker wacked off different, yeah. That's different all right."

Margot almost ignored the fact that Frank had even spoken.

"They were probably killed for different crimes, so to speak. Were there any diary pages with these two men?" Margot asked as she paced the floor with Frank's notes in her left hand and a stale pretzel in the right.

"No, at least not yet. I asked Michaels if there was anything different found with the bodies. He didn't find anything that stood out. Of course, he wasn't looking for anything like diary pages either. They're checking it out now. If they find anything, they'll send it by messenger."

"Frank, have you thought what it must have been like for the Gallagher twins, when they found their mother's diary.? To read all the things in there and possibly to be reminded of past horrors? I have a feeling that they may not have even remembered what they went through as children. That happens often in abuse cases."

"Yes, I can imagine the horror at reading the diary. I didn't realize that they might not have remembered those things from when they were kids. Is that really possible?"

"Yes, sure it is. I have a theory about the twins, but I'm a little shakey on it right now. I need a little more information before I can come out and explain it to you. Just be patient, and don't worry about Gerry. If my theory is correct, she's in no danger."

"Oh, thanks, you're a great help," Frank said as he started pacing right alongside her.

"Frank, why are you pacing the floor? You look like a caged animal."

"You gotta be kidding. Come on, let's go out for a drink and get something to eat. We can discuss this all evening."

"Let me get my notes. I definitly am going to call Gerry at home. I don't care what you say, I need to know she's there and she's all right."

As Margot began to straighten the desk and put her notes in order, Frank dialed the number of the Gallagher apartment.

He heard the firm, gruff answer of "Hello, Gallagher here."

Frank said, "Hello, Mister. Gallagher, this is Frank Franklin. Lieutenant Frank Franklin. I talked to you Tuesday night about the two unfortunate victims from last weekend. Mary Carlin and the gentleman we discovered to be your father."

"Yes, Lieutenant Franklin, I remember you quite clearly. What can I do for you?"

"I'd like to talk to your sister. I tried the library today, but I was told she was ill. Nothing serious, I hope. You remember I said I was worried about the safety of both you and your sister."

"No, it's nothing like that. She has the flu."

Franklin thought the brother sounded a little distracted. Maybe there was more to this than he was saying.

"Mister Gallagher, may I speak to Miss Gallagher?"

"No, you can't. She's in the well," Terry answered almost as if he hadn't heard the question properly.

"I beg your pardon? She's in the well. What does that mean?"

"Er.....I said she isn't well. You misunderstood me. She isn't well, and I won't disturb her. She's sleeping. The best things for illness is to sleep. If she sleeps for a few days she'll be as good as new."

"Call back next week, Lieutenant. Thank you for your concern, but she will be fine after she sleeps for a few days."

"Yes, that's what you just said. Thanks, I'll keep in touch."

Margot was hovering over him, as he replaced the phone to it's cradle, "So. What? What? Tell me. Don't stand there like that."

"He just said the strangest thing. First he said, "She's in the well". Then, when I asked what that meant, he corrected it and said "She isn't well."

Margot grabbed her briefcase and said, "That frosts it. Let's go. I want that drink. We have a lot of work to do and I've got to get to the research center the first thing in the morning. If I'm right, we have one monumental problem on our hands. Come on, big-time spender. Let's fold our tents for the night."

"Sounds good to me. Your camp or mine? I'll furnish the wine."

March 6, 1960

Dear Friend,

This was one of the Sundays when Miss Carlin came for dinner. I guess it wasn't so bad. She helped with the cleanup just like she usually does, but one time I saw George looking at her with that funny look. He looked mad when she said she would help dry the dishes. I wonder if he hits her like he does me, when he gets mad.

We sat and talked after dinner, and she seems to get along pretty well with the babies. She won't call them anything but Terrance and Geraldine. It sounds pretty strange when she says their proper names, but they seem to like it. She says that they have nice names and they should not be shortened. She says they don't sound proper if you cut them off. Can you believe that? Would I call my babies something that isn't proper? Some day she should be taught a lesson. Any good mother wouldn't do anything that wasn't proper to her own babies.

She also said that I could call her by her first name, now that we was such good friends. She isn't too bad, but I sure don't consider her such a good friend. Nobody does what she does to the husband of her friend.

I heard her and George laughing in the front room before dinner. I guess they think I'm too dumb to know what is going on, but I can hear and I can see those little signals. Well, someday someone will give them what for. I'd sure like to be around when it happens. Wouldn't that be fun. Maybe catch them doing those nasty things and take pictures for the newspapers. Can you just see that headline? That would sure embarrass them.

After dinner Terry and Gerry went out front to play. That crabby old Mr. Hendrix started yelling like he does, when they get just a little noisy. You'd think he could be a little more patient with children. Everyone knows they are just being kids and having a little fun.

Last week I caught Terry throwing rocks on the old man's roof. If he wasn't so mean to the kids, I'm sure they wouldn't pick on him like that.

There's been some talk around here about that old man, but I don't quite understand it The lady at the store said he liked little kids. I'm not sure what she means. He sure don't act like he likes them. Sometimes I don't understand what people mean when they say some of those silly two-meaning things. If he likes little kids, why would he be so crabby with my babies?

Miss Carlin -- I mean Mary -- says my babies are real smart in school. I always figured they might have trouble with school work, like I did when I was in school. I think she might just be saying that so I will feel better about all the trouble they get into.

Gerry is still acting mean once in a while to the other kids. At recess yesterday she got into trouble again for hitting some boy. She took Terry's coat, and the boy thought it was Terry beating up on him. This time she just about went crazy. The principal said she used a fence board on his head. He didn't bleed very much, but his mother sure did yell at me. I told her that Gerry was sorry, and she would never do it again. That woman was going to hit my poor Gerry, but I sure pushed her right off of our porch.

I told Miss -- Mary , that she should watch out for my babies at school, if she would be so kind. I'm afraid of what that crazy lady might try to do to them if I'm not there.

Gerry is making me worry. She keeps doing things, but she won't take the blame. She always says Terry made her do it, or she even says she didn't do anything at all. I don't like it, but I think she sneaks out at night like he does.

I still want George to take down that old trellis but he just laughs and says boys will be boys. Then maybe the next time he wants to beat him for just looking out of the window and yells at him to not even think of going out for one of his night-time strolls, he'll remember that.

I remember talking to an old friend of George's one time. He said George was a real mean kid in school. He sure don't act much different now.

Why does my family make me worry so? Can't they see the problems they give me?

Goodnight, my special friend,

Emily

September 14, 1960

My dear friend,

This is a sad time to write to you, Diary. My poor Gerry. She just cried and cried. Real tears too. That dirty old man next door got her into his house and did the most horrible things to her. She wouldn't say exactly, but from what I saw, it must have been terrible.

Yesterday after school, Gerry was playing in the back yard all by herself. I don't know where Terry was, but he should have been with her. That man next door, Old Man Hendrix, got Gerry to come into his house after school. She said he promised her a tea party. You know how much she loves tea parties. She was gone for a long time when Terry came in and told me he thought she was inside the house next door. I didn't know if I liked for her to go in there or not, so I went over there and knocked on the back door and asked him if Gerry was in there, and he said she wasn't. That's when I heard her scream.

Can you believe that old disgusting man had her tied to the kitchen table and had her panties down? He had his pants unzipped and was showing her his -- you know, he was showing her his thing. She was crying real tears. I've never seen her with real tears in her eyes. She kept calling for Terry, but he wasn't around.

I stormed in and took her off that dirty table and hit that old man as hard as I could. She quit crying as soon as I got her out of the house, and when Terry heard what happened, he started to cry. He had some real tears too. They started to talk in that silly talk they use sometimes.

When I got home I called the police and told them what he did to my baby. They said that he was just a harmless old man and couldn't have done much to her. Can you believe they feel that way. George didn't come home last night, and tonight I was afraid to tell him. He would say it was my fault that I let that old man touch Gerry.

I made Gerry and Terry some hot chocolate and put them to bed early, but my poor babies were so sick and upset. I hope Gerry isn't hurt real bad. I mean, you know, Diary. I think he used his fingers to hurt her, and like I said, he had his zipper undone too. I don't know if -- you know, that can be done to a little girl Gerry's age. I still think Terry should have been there to protect Gerry from Mister Hendrix. Maybe, Terry will pull one of his tricks on him that would show him not to do things like that to little girls, especially when they have a brother to protect them.

Tomorrow I might just take her to a doctor and have him look at her. I wonder if the doctor would have to touch her to see if Hendrix did anything to her.

The babies are in their room right now, playing their silly 'turn-around' game. They took turns reading to each other for a while after Terry got home from school. I think it was both of them. Gerry is so good at imitating Terry's voice now, I can't tell if it's her or him.

Good night my secret friend,

Emily

April 25, 1961

Dear Diary,

Things are pretty quiet around here. George has just been a dream lately. He even brought me some flowers. They was only dandelions, but he stopped and picked them along side the road on the way home from work, and I think that is really romantic, don't you?

The babies are doing better in school, but Terry is still a problem with sneaking out at night. I still wish George would take that old trellis down, and then maybe Terry wouldn't have a way to get out of his room. He can't get down from the porch roof without those slats. The roses are long gone anyways. I'd love to have some climbing roses on that thing again. Remember, when we first moved here, how pretty things were? The roses and the lilacs out back made everything smell so nice. George says flowers need too much care, and I need all my time for the house and the babies.

The school hasn't complained at all this week. I think the kids are really growing up. They've even been playing with some of the other kids in the neighborhood. One day they even brought some little boy home with them to play. He didn't stay too long. I don't know why. Terry said he had an upset stomach. Probably something Terry put on the little sandwiches I saw him making. It probably didn't agree with the boy.

The man next door complained again yesterday. He's just an old crab. He says the kids make too much noise when they play out back. He even blamed them when his flowers died. Now, how could some noise from kids playing make flowers die? I told him it was because the racoons had pulled them out, and he said we don't have no racoons, that the kids had pulled them out. Why would my babies pull up his old flowers. They love flowers. He's really mean, that old man, Mister Hendrix.

Tomorrow I have to go shopping for school shoes for Terry. George has been making him take his shoes off when he comes in the house. He says that will save some wear and tear on the soles. Terry is so neat, he likes to have everything so straight on his side of the closet. Sometimes when George gets mad, he goes and messes up the closet just so he can upset Terry.

Poor Gerry gets it, too. George hasn't been mean to them at all for a week or so. That makes it nice around here. Then we can be a normal family like everyone else.

I've been able to save a little from my grocery money each week.

When I go for the shoes, I'm going to see if I can get some of that new kind of knit material that the fancy stores are showing. They make some of the fanciest suits and dresses for the rich people out of this cloth. I'd be proud to have something out of it, and I know George would be proud to be seen with me if I had something like that on.

Do you think he might take me out to a movie? Maybe we might even go to dinner. Oh, diary, I would dearly love that.

Good night my friend,

Emily

August 25, 1964

Dear Diary,

Today was one of the nicest days of my life. I've been so worried about what goes on around here, but I had an appointment with Doctor Mason, and now I feel so good. I can't imagine how bad I felt before I went to him.

My periods were bad the last few months, so I went to get something to make me regular. He talked to me so much, and made me feel so good.He said I had to forget my problems and relax. He even gave me a back rub. It seemed like we were in that back room for hours. He said he didn't have any patients coming and his nurse was gone for the afternoon. He gave me the whole afternoon. He didn't charge me any extra either. He rubbed my back and my legs. I was so relaxed. He gave me a shot and it really made me relax.

We talked, and he rubbed my back the whole time. Over and over he said I didn't really have any problems, and I could tell him everything. He is so wonderful. His hands are wonderful, too. Oh, my dear Diary, I just had the most wonderful day. I guess I'm saying wonderful an awful lot, but that is the only word that can describe this day.

Doc gave me an appointment for next Tuesday at the same time. He said I needed the time alone with him, so I could really get myself relaxed. I tried to tell him about the twins and George, but he said I should just relax.

He's going to give me another shot next week, so I won't be so tense. That was his word, "tense." I must remember to use it and add it to my list of new words. That will be the only way I can ever hope to improve myself. I'll add a new word as often as I can. I'm sure Doc Mason will help learn me some new words every time I go to his office. He said I could come to his home if I ever needed a friend or needed to relax some more. Doesn't he sound just like an angel?

My Dearest Diary, I guess I must say good night, but I hate to stop talking about Doctor Mason. He makes me feel so good.

Good night, my sweet. That's what he called me today. Doctor Mason, I mean. When I left his office, he said, "Good Bye, my sweet." Isn't that just the most wonderful thing you ever heard?

To my dearest friend, good night.

Emily

September 1, 1964

My Dearest Diary,

Today was my regular time to go to Doctor Mason's office. He makes me feel so good. Last time I started to tell him about what George does to me, but he wouldn't let me talk. He said sometimes a person's mind works in strange ways. That was his way of saying that I must be making these things up, but I don't care if he don't believe me, as long as I can go and talk to him and have him rub me all over like he does.

I think he enjoys it as much as I do. I peek into the glass on his cabinet in the office and watch his face. The glass is almost like a mirror.   Sometimes he'll be rubbing my back and my bottom, I mean my hips, and he almost has a content look on his face. That's one of my new words, content. Doc says a person has got to be content with his life, or it just isn't worth living.

He said that was why he didn't mind giving me these extra treatments, even though they're free. They're to make me content.

When I look at his face, I think he's making himself a little content, too. He just smiles and rubs and rubs and smiles.

Just between you and me, dear diary, today Doc rubbed just a little close to some bad parts of me, but I didn't say anything to him. It felt pretty good. It gave me a warm feeling all over. I never felt like that when George touched me there. Course, when George touched me, he was real mean about it and made me hurt. When Doc got close he just moved real slow, but he didn't really touch my -- you know, my private place. I felt so warm, I caught myself wishing that he had really touched me there.

We talked about the babies a little. I told him some of the things that happened when they was little, but he said my mind was just wandering, and I probably read a book about such things. Doc said daddies don't do those kind of things to their own babies. Maybe he's right. Maybe I didn't see some of those things either. I could have just been tired and imagined them.

Like the time I thought George made me watch him do that thing to Gerry. I was probably asleep and dreaming. Why, dear Diary, should I be cursed with such bad dreams. There must be something evil in me, to let me make up such things in my mind.

I'm sure if Doc says that's the way it is, it must be true. They shouldn't do those things to each other either, because that just isn't the way for a brother and sister to act. Maybe I imagined that too.

That's all I have for tonight. Goodnight, my sweet diary, goodnight.

Your friend,

Emily

September 15, 1964

My Dearest Diary,

The twins are in their room pouting, but I just couldn't help it. I don't have time to read to them when I have so much to tell you.

Today was my regular appointment time with Doctor Mason. He says I should call him Alexander now when we are alone for our special visits. He put me in his book that has a listing called <u>Regular Appointments</u>. Isn't that just the most fancy thing you ever heard.

Oh, today was just wonderful.

First, we sat and talked. He even had two small glasses of wine for us to sip while we talked. George would just die if he knew about the wine. I really had trouble. You know how sleepy I get when I have even one sip of wine. He said it was the best thing for me. It helped me relax and got me out of my anxieties. That's my new word, this week. Course Alexander had to write it down for me, but he said I should practice it and use it when ever I can. This will help me improve myself. He said the funniest thing. He wrote this down for me, too.

If you don't use it, you lose it.

Have you ever heard anything so great? I just love it. I sure can't say it in front of George, but I can think it when ever it fits. I'm getting so many new words and sayings from Doc -- I mean Alexander.

Today my rubdown was something special. I never thought I would see the day when I would liked to be touched -- there. Alexander makes it feel so wonderful. It's not dirty and it even makes me feel strange and nervous.

Alexander says I have to let my nervous feeling do what it wants to do. Let my body have some fun, too. I'm not sure what he means about my body having fun. I don't know what happened, but I sure did like it. I had the warmest feeling. I even caught myself pushing up against Alexander's hands. It just felt so good. Was I being an evil person for liking that feeling so much?

I wonder if that's the way George feels when he does that sex stuff to me. I know he is doing those bad things to the twins too, but I don't try to tell Doc anymore, cause I know he don't believe me. He must think I really need help because of the stories I tried to tell him.

Now I'm afraid if I stop trying to tell him about the mean things that go on in our house, he might think I don't need no more treatment. I would surely miss my special treatments. I never had such a feeling as I do when he rubs me all over, like he does now.

Alexander sure enjoys it, too. I guess a medical man can get so much satisfaction from taking good care of the sick. They most certainly must have a calling from heaven to make them doctors. At least Alexander must be that way. He just has the most heavenly look on his face when he gives me my rub-down.

Good night for today, my dear friend. I am so happy I have you to tell about the great things that are finally happening to me. I think I better find a better hiding place for you. There surely would be trouble around here if George got to read any of this.

Love,

Emily

212

September 28, 1964

Dear Friend,

I know it's early in the day for me to be talking to you, but I feel a little guilty, and I don't know what to do about it.

I made the twins play in their room after school today. I got a note from the school today, and Gerry is in bad trouble. She says she didn't do it, but the teacher saw her and some of the other kids agree with the teacher.

The twins were playing on the slide at recess, and some boy from down the block was picking on them. Now it should have been Terry's place to see that bully, cause he knows how to do things the right way. He should go tell the teacher on the play ground, when someone is picking on them, or he and Gerry should have left and got away from that mean bully.

I guess this was one of those times when Gerry was the mean sister that Terry talks about. When that bully kept pushing on Gerry, she finally lost her temper, and she shoved him off the top of the slide. That boy fell about six feet down to the ground, and someone had left their bike there at the foot of the ladder. That poor boy, I think his name was Chester Carson, he broke both legs and his collarbone.

Gerry says she didn't do it. She cried and said that over and over. Well, she didn't really cry. She never cries. She just sort of whined and pouted, but she still says she didn't do it. Terry told me the bad sister did it. I do wish he'd stop calling her that every time she does something different.

He acts like she's another person, when she does that. I say she just has a mean streak like her daddy. It comes out once in a while. She used to be like that all the time. Then she got real sweet and quiet. I like her much better when she's the real sweet little girl. That mean one can go away and stay as far as I'm concerned.

I'm so tired. Tomorrow I go to my appointment with Alexander. I just can't wait. He'll makes me forget about the mean sister and all the proplems these twins give me. He almost makes me forget about George and his mean ways. I wish I had met Alexander years and years ago. I'm sure he would have liked me then, just like he does now.

Week before last at my appointment, he said that he had a new way of rubbing and we would try it this week. I'm so excited. Last time he rubbed my shoulders and down my back with his hands, but before he quit he ran his lips all over my shoulders and went down almost to my hips. I got so nervous. I guess it was nerves. I felt so warm, all over. I couldn't breath. He said he'd do that for me again.

I noticed he was breathing a little fast like I was. He's getting pretty old. It was probably the strain of stooping over like that, to rub his lips all over my back. He must be close to fifty or fifty five. I guess that's pretty old for a man who has to give rubdowns so much. His legs must hurt, too. Last time his knees started jerking and he had to stop rubbing. He just held on to me around the waist until his body stopped shaking and jerking.

He sure is a good doctor. Sometimes I think I love him more than I do my own family.

This is all for today. I must be sure to find a good place to hide you, now that I've told you all these new things about Doc.   Alexander, I mean. He means so much to me.

Goodnight Dear Diary,

Emily, your faithful friend.

214

October 6, 1964

Dear Diary,

    I can't talk for too long today. Things have gotten real bad. I feel like this is the end of the world.

    You know how happy I've been since I started having my regular appointments with Doctor Mason? Well, today -- it's so hard to talk about -- I don't know if I can even write about what happened. Today he did something to me that I think may have been bad. You know, something like -- like George does sometimes. Something that nice people don't do.

    He was sweet and kind, at first, just like usual. Then he did something that George does sometimes, and it made me afraid. I guess it made me afraid because my body did somthing it never did before. Doc Mason called it a climax. That was the word he used. He said it was a natural thing for a body to have happen. I don't really believe him. I never did it before and I never heard tell of it. My mama never mentioned anything about that happening.

    It made me feel real good when it was happening, but after it was over, it was bad. I know I did a bad thing. When he did that thing to me, it felt good, but then he kissed me in that bad place, and that wasn't a good thing to do. I don't think you're supposed to like to have that done to you. That made me cry, and I left the office as fast as I could.

    I don't think I can ever go back to him again. He said I would like it the next time, but I can't go back to that office again. I just know everyone there would know what kind of things I have been letting him do to me. He made me feel as dirty as George does. That's not a natural thing to do to a nice lady. I kept saying I was a nice lady.

I feel so ashamed. I've been crying, and now my eyes are all red. When George comes home, he's going to know I done something bad. I just know it.

The only thing I can think of, is to go cut up some onions. I guess I'll have to make that onion casserole that George likes so much. Maybe that will make him not notice the red eyes and the guilty look on my face. I feel so dirty. Just like when George does those nasty things to me.

I think that men must be the worst things on earth. Why did God put them here anyway?

I have to go. The twins will be home soon. I sure hope they didn't have any trouble at school. I just don't need any other problems to think about today.

Good bye, my dear friend,

Emily

December 17, 1964

Dear Friend,

Everything is pretty much the same. The twins have been pretty good for a change. They haven't had any notes from the teacher for about four days. I hope that means they are growing out of their troublesome ways.

Their daddy has been kind of quiet, too. I always get afraid when things get too quiet around here.

I talked to Mrs. Jenson at the grocery store yesterday. She said that some of the mothers around the neighborhood were afraid that there was someone around here that likes to hurt little kids. One of the neighbor ladies said her little girl was crying when she came home from school. All they could get out of her was something about an old man who showed something funny to her. The poor little thing didn't know what it was, but I sure can guess.

I'll just bet it's that disgusting old man Hendrix, next door. The women in the neighborhood have always watched their kids when they had to come near his house. These are new people on the block. One of the fathers said he would sure take care of him if he caught him doing any funny stuff with the kids again.

Yesterday something else happened. I guess you remember what I wrote and told you a couple of months ago about Doctor Mason. Well, he sent me yellow daisies. He had the florist deliver them. All the note said was "Concerned about your nervousness". Please call me if you need more treatments."

Can you imagine the nerve of that man. After what he did to me, and now he's sending me flowers. If George finds out, I will probably get killed for sure. I threw them out in a trash can down the block. If George looked in the can and found something like that, he'd know for sure that I had done something bad. He might even hurt the babies too.

I sure wish that doctor would go away. I hate that man. I don't feel so good, but there is no way I'd go to him, again. I'd die first.

I can't dwell on all the bad things that have happened to me in my life, or I'd be a sorry sight.

I bought some pretty red and green material. I'm going to try to make a fancy table cloth for Christmas.

I hope George stays nice until the holidays are over. I remember one year we had a real nice Christmas. George even brought home a bag of chestnuts, and I roasted them in the oven. Those darn nuts just exploded all over the oven. Nobody told me you had to cut a hole in them, so the steam could come out. The babies sure laughed at all the popping and noise in the oven. George even laughed at them. That was the nicest Christmas. Maybe we'll have another one like that, sometime.

I hope we can all have a Merry Christmas. That's all for today.

Good night, Dearest Diary.

Emily

Chapter Twenty-Two

Franklin replaced the receiver of the telephone and sat back, sighing. Chief Michaels had just told him about diary pages found with both of the St. John's victims.

Dr. Mason's were wrapped around the small bouquet. Miss Jenson found them on her desk in the outer office when she entered the office that night to check on the light. She saw the flowers but thought the doctor was just in to pick up something special and brought the flowers for the next day. She removed the pages and the cone shaped plastic bag to put the bouquet into a small vase with some water.

She then went into the examining room and discovered the body of the doctor. The papers lay on her desk until Monday when she came back to tidy the office and prepare to close it until told what to do with the records and doctor's belongings.

When Chief Michaels called her Thursday afternoon, asking about any books or notes, she remembered the pages immediately. She remembered putting them in the call-up file. She didn't know what they were, but she was afraid to toss them out.

With such good fortune at Doc's, the Chief decided to go to Mister Hendrix's house himself.

After questioning several people who helped that day at the Hendrix murder scene, Deputy Hays remembered some papers falling off the table when they moved the old man. Deputy Hays was sure he stuck them in something on top of the "ice box", as he called it.

When Michaels looked on top of the refrigerator where Hays had placed the papers, they were still there, in an old cookie jar.

Chief Michaels called Franklin as soon as he returned to his own office. Franklin listened as the chief read a few sentences from both groups of diary pages and asked

Chief Michaels to get them to him by messenger as fast as possible. Frank promised to explain the situation to Chief Michaels as soon as things were cleared up and finished.

He gathered his notes together and noticed it was time to leave.

Margot and Frank had arranged to meet in the park when they were finished with their alloted chores for the morning. If their timing and luck were good, they hoped to try for a conversation with Gerry's friends from the library.

Margot was fifteen minutes late, but as she skipped up to Frank's car, she was smiling.

Frank matched her smile with his scowl. "What is so great? Did you find what you were looking for? My morning was pretty successful, Chief Michaels called. He contacted the nurse from Dr. Mason's office and checked out the old man's house. They both had diary pages. The nurse found Doc's the night she discovered the body. She didn't know what to do with them, so she stuck them in a file until something came up. The ones from Hendrix were shoved in a cookie jar. They're being sent in right now by messenger. I can't wait to read them. The Chief says there aren't many pages, but they are definitely what we are looking for. He read a few lines from each. What did you get at the center?"

Margot was adjusting her skirt as she sat in the passenger's seat of Franklin's car. "Frank, most of what I was looking for was possibilities. Comparative situations in like cases of mental instabilities."

"In English, please."

"Right. First, my theory. I believe that Gerry is in a severly confused state and isn't exactly sure of her own identity. She may know who she is on most occaisions, but with her childhood background, the condition of her mind can certainly be fragile.

"One of the strongest causes for this fragile state of mind, of course, is the sexual abuse. From a family member, especially, it can cause what could be described

220

as actual fractures in the mind. This would certainly fit this situation. Another is the distancing of the nonabusing member of the family -- in this case, the mother.

"From what we've read in the diary pages, the father abused both children, sexually and mentally. The mother spent hours with her diaries. She often told the children they must rely on each other, while she found her own way to remove herself from the family situation by writing in her diary. In some cases, this has actually resulted in multiple personality disorder, often called MPD, but that is a very rare condition.

"When you mentioned that Terry said she was in the well, it fit another criteria for this fractured, or fragmented, mental state. A person with this problem usually has a place mentally, where he or she feels safe. Some express it in terms of who is in control -- that is, who has the limelight, so to speak. Which part of him is doing the thinking. In one book on the subject, the patient referred to the waking times for any one of the personalities as "being on the spot". Do you remember the story Three Faces of Eve? She referred to it as being 'out'."

"Gerry's is a negative reference. Terry called it being 'in the well'.

He must have known about her condition for a long time. I believe this must be the reason he shows up when she in any kind of stress. He knows what could happen. He comes to her to take care of her until she gains control of herself."

"I believe there's a good chance that Gerry is our murderer. Do you remember when Emily talked about the mean sister. I think this was Gerry's other self -- her other personality, if that makes it clearer. It's quite probable that Gerry isn't aware of this personality. I'd be willing to bet that Terry knows about her problem. He's probably been covering for her for years. From the way Emily described it in the few diary pages we saw, this must be what happens when Gerry faces stress. Well, Frank, any comment?"

221

Margot leaned back and waited for Frank to digest the lengthy report she had just given.

"I'm flabbergasted," he said. "I don't know what to say. I still find it hard to believe about Gerry. You haven't met her. She's such a quiet, fragile little thing."

"Yes, but from what Emily wrote, she also was mean and vicious at an early age. This certainly follows with the kind of person we're looking for, don't you think?"

"Yeah, and it means something else too," Frank said. "It means Terry could be in trouble. He didn't sound too worried about her being "in the well", but he has to know that the other one will be able to gain control. Isn't that how it works?"

"It doesn't work in any set fashion. No one can tell exactly what will occur as the personalities come and go. They may both be asleep and nothing occurs. Just a sleeping person. It is still a very serious mystery to the doctors who work with this illness."

Frank started the car, "I think it may be important to get to the girls Gerry works with. Maybe they can confirm some of this theory of yours. See if they've have noticed any changes. Maybe we can catch them at lunch."

They spotted the girls sitting on the grass in the park and pulled over to the curb.

"I'll go first. I think I can convince them that we are trying to help her." Margot said. "You stand there and look official. Show them your badge and look intelligent."

Margot greeted the girls first, then motioning to Frank introduced him.

"Ladies, this is Lieutenant Frank Franklin of the San Francisco Police Department. We know you are both friends of Gerry Gallagher, and we wondered if you would help us. The reason we came today was to talk to you about her. We know she's been ill. We're very concerned about her."

Ilene looked at Frank and said, "Could we see your identification again, sir? We like to be careful when we talk to strangers. I hope you understand."

"Of course, ladies," he said as he extended his wallet to the girls for inspection. "Most commendable. In these days it pays to be careful."

"This looks fine, Lieutenant. Please, what can we do for you. We have been concerned about Gerry ourselves, but why is the police department involved. She just has a case of the flu."

Margot stepped forward again and answered, "Yes, miss, we know about the flu, but we have reason to believe she may have another illness that isn't quite as apparant as the flu. Has Gerry shown any unusual reactions lately? Acted differently from, say before her mother died? That's been a year, now. I know I'm asking a lot, but it is very important to Gerry's well-being."

Ilene glanced at Sue and said, "She does get a little testy some times, especially where her brother is concerned. Just the other day she was almost angry when we teased her about baby sitting. She has some idea that she and her brother will never have any other friends. It really hurts our feelings to have her think that way. We consider ourselves her friends. We feel almost like family, but she has this thing about never having any one but Terry. That's the way she puts it."

Sue raised her hand at though she was in school.

"Miss Kent, she gets....well, different some times in the library. One minute she is sweet and kind and the next she comes out with a caustic remark that can really hurt. Just the other day she said Ilene was a twit. That usually wouldn't be a mean thing to say, but her tone of voice was almost sneering."

Ilene leaned forward and added, "Yes, I noticed that too. We play a little game at lunch some days. One of us will recite some line of poetry or quotation, and the other two must tell who said it. She said somthing that sounded

223

very philosophical, and I asked, "Who said that?" She almost snarled, "I did, you twit". It just wasn't like her."

Sue was beginning to look uncomfortable, "I don't like to be talking about a friend, like this. Maybe she just doesn't feel well."

Margot continued to take notes and Frank stood there, looking impressive and intelligent.

"Ilene, Sue," Margot started, "please. You're helping Gerry by telling us these things. If we're correct, she may need much more of your help. Is there anything else you can remember? It's very important."

Sue responded, "Did you know we had no idea she even had a brother until her mother died? When she came back from cleaning her mother's house, she mentioned him one day at lunch, just as though we had known about him all the time."

"Yes, Sue's right. And then, every time we said we wanted to meet him, she gave us the excuse that he didn't like to meet new people. He sounded like he might be a little mean to her. At times she sounded afraid of him, then she would say something about only having each other to rely on. Do you know why she felt like that?"

"Gerry had a very unusual childhood," Margot explained. "That, coupled with the fact that her mother continually stressed she and Terry would only have each other to rely on all their lives, gave her some very different ideas. By next week, we hope to know more and be able to help Gerry with her problems."

"Miss Kent, that's another thing," Ilene said. "In the last few months, she was always referring to her 'problems'. When we would ask her what they were or if we could help, she usually said she wasn't sure. She seemed to forget a lot of things, too"

Frank finally came forward and said, "Ladies, if I may ask a question or two. In the time you have known Gerry, do you recall anything unusual happening to anyone around you? Have there been any strange occurrences that might have concerned Gerry's life or her job here at the library?"

"No, sir," Sue answered. "Nothing ever happens around here. The library would be a pretty boring place to work if we didn't like our books so much."

Ilene added, "Yes, the most excitement around here was over a year ago. It was pretty tragic. One of the maintenance men fell and bumped his head on a floor pipe. They found him dead on a Saturday. It was a little scary, to see how easy an accident can take a life."

Frank glanced at Margot, but did not skip a beat, "Could you be more specific about the date?"

Ilene looked at Sue and they answered in unison.

"March" Ilene said and at the same time Sue answered "February".

Frank looked from one to the other and said, "Which is it?"

Ilene reached into her purse, pulled out her checkbook and said, "February. Sue's right. That's the week I bought that book on barns from the fancy book store downtown. I had it with us that day that maintenance man embarrased us so much."

"Is that the same maintenance man you just mentioned, who fell and was killed?" Frank asked.

"Yes, as a matter of fact."

"Could you tell us more about the day he embarrased you?"

Frank was adding some to his notes too. Margot sat down on the bench next to Sue.

"We -- all three of us, I mean -- were coming over here for lunch almost every day. One day Mr. Kelsey -- I think that was his name -- asked us if he could join us for lunch. We were pretty excited, I must say. We'd never had any of the men employees ask to have lunch with us before.

"When we got to the park, he came over and started to talk dirty and say the most outrageous things. He even touched both Sue and Gerry on the knees. He was really disgusting. I remember feeling a little guilty when they found him the next weekend. He was working down in the furnace room and fell and hit his head. They said there was a gas leak and that's what killed him."

Frank looked up from his notepad, "Did Gerry say anything about him after he died?"

"No, sir," Ilene answered. "We never even mentioned lunch that day.

He was so vulgar. We never mentioned that day or him again."

Margot stood. "Ladies, thanks so much. I may want to talk to you again. Would that be all right? I'll call first."

Sue looked a little shy. "Please, Miss Kent, don't call the library. They're pretty strict about the phone. Just come to the park at lunch time. You could even come over to the library. We can usually be found someplace in the building. We help a lot of people find books, so just ask for us by name. We want to help Gerry. We're very worried about her."

As Frank and Margot got back into the car, Frank said, "I think I'll check into the maintenance man's death. It could be something."

Margot answered with a soft, "Ummm. I think so too."

Frank started to pull the car from the curb and Sue skipped over to Margot's window.

"Oh, Miss Kent," she said, "we just thought of something that surprised us last summer. Gerry changed her hair color a little. It really took us by surprise. It wasn't much, but she changed the color and the style just a little. Does that mean anything?"

Margot smiled. "When did she do this?"

Sue thought for a minute and answered, "About two or three weeks after her mother died."

"Thanks, Sue. I'll remember that."

Chapter Twenty-Three

Terry was sure Gerry would sleep for most of the weekend, and now was the time to sew up the loose ends around the apartment.

The closet was cleaned of any old clothing that had been used during the past year and needed to be disposed of. She certainly didn't need to find the old butcher's apron that he had stolen from the back door of the butcher shop in St. John's last July.

One thing made it easy for him to put things away for use at a later date. Gerry hated the backs of closets and therefore never ventured into the back of the extra deep closet in her bedroom.

Last year he had placed this apron and some old high-top boots back in the far left side of the closet. There was also a burlap bag with a two-inch dowel and one very sharp butcher knife. These both came in handy on several occaisions during this past year. Terry was remembering more and more of what had been happening.

The neccessity for some special tools had sent him on a few excursions. A few were gathered from backs of stores at night, and others were taken during the day. Some proprietors did not watch too carefully when a clean-cut young man came in and was so friendly and needed extra help with finding things. So much of the time the owners had to go to the back room to find the required item, only to return to the front of the store to find the interested young man gone.

The closet was cleaned, and the box was by the door, waiting to go to the basement, for it's appointment with the compactor. One more box remained in the kitchen closet, but this would be the last thing to be destroyed. It contained the remaining thoughts of Mrs. Emily Gallagher, written during the first thirteen years of her marriage until

George Gallagher left, and she lost the need to tell her innermost thoughts to her beloved "Dear Diary".

This box contained the remnants of sixteen notebooks, the very soul of Emily Gallagher. In these notebooks, containing thirteen years of her life, lay the answer to the riddle of the twins and the murders. Soon they would be tossed into the compacter in the basement. Then they would be crushed into the solid mass of waste from the entire building to be picked up next Tuesday.

When Terry found the books after Emily's funeral, he systematicaly read each book in order of date. When he found an offensive entry, he removed it and made a separate pile. Then he began to tear at the remaining pages. After tearing at a few pages, he gave up this idea and covered the books with the scraps. He finished the reading after they returned home.

The thing he did not know about now was a small green notebook that was hidden under some scarves in Gerry's top dresser drawer. Gerry herself was not consciously aware of the book's existence.

As Terry left the elevator at the basement level, he held the door open with one box while he carried the other box over to the table in front of the compacter. Walking back to the elevator, he picked up the remaining box and carried it to the table. He tossed a box of clothing through the compacter door. Standing next to the electric switch that set the plunger to work, he thought how much better it would be if this was a coal furnace. Even a trash incinerator would be better.

He picked up the burlap bag filled with more clothes and the wooden dowel and started the compacter again. Moving away from the noise, he decided to take a look in the dark room. There might be some things in there to be destroyed too. He was determined to get all the loose ends cleaned up today.

As the darkroom door clicked shut, the elevator door quietly opened. Ed Spatro, the doorman, entered the basement room with a large box on each arm. Shuffling across the room to the table in front of the compacter, he shoved the boxes across the table and let out a sigh of relief at the easing of the heavy load in the boxes.

"What the hell do you want?" Terry snapped as he came out of the dark room.

Ed jumped as though he had been shot, "Oh, Mister Gallagher, I'm sorry. I didn't know you were down here. I hope I didn't disturb you. I can come back later. I just have some boxes of paper backs novels that my sister-in-law gave me. You know how I like to read these great..... "

"I don't give a damn what you like to read. Can't the residents of this place get a little privacy when they want it without the hired help getting in the way? Come back later when I've finished. I'm doing some very private work, and I certainly don't want some hired hand nosing around."

With this he slammed his fist on the table to make his point.

Ed nodded and started backing away. "Yes, sir, right away, sir."

As long as this young man was around, Ed would always feel like he was a bug, about to be smashed under someone's heel.

Terry went back to the door of the darkroom and started locking it.

"Mister Gallagher, I'll just put my things over here under the table and out of your way. I'll be right out of your way. I can do this any time. I'm leaving now, Mister Gallagher."

Ed grabbed two boxes and quickly shoved them in the corner under a table filled with old jars.

"Okay stop your jabbering and go," Terry growled as he picked up the remaining box from the table. "You don't have to tell me your every move. Just leave me alone."

Ed breathed a sigh of relief when the doors of the elevator closed. His last sight of Terry Gallagher was seeing him drop the box into the compacter chute. That young man made him so nervous. He could not think straight or even get a handle on his own nerves. No one ever talked to him like that. All he could think about was getting out of the room and away from this maniac. Ed's heart was beating so fast, he felt he had been chased by a mad dog.

"God, do I hate that little son-of-a-bitch," Ed said aloud in an almost hysterical voice, as he entered the lobby.

Almost running to his desk in the corner, he sat down and tried to catch his breath. He had to compose himself in case any of the other tenants entered the lobby. He felt it was not professional to appear unkempt or not in complete control of ones self while on duty.

Finding it hard to control his nerves after several minutes, Ed reached for his keys and unlocked a small wooden box at the back of the bottom desk drawer. He removed the caps from two airlines liquor bottles and emptied them both into his coffee cup printed with red letters on one side , <u>One good turn deserves another</u> and a picture of revolving doors on the other side. Topping off the scotch with approximately one-quarter cup black coffee, he took one long drink from his cup, and a glow appeared on his cheeks.

Now, his old calm returned. All was right with Ed's world again.

Chapter Twenty-Four

Frank and Margot were just arriving at his office when the messenger arrived from St. John's. They sat at the desk, reading the diary packets from Chief Michaels.

"Oh, brother," Frank said. "Poor Emily sure can find the creeps. This first one that was with Doctor Mason's, it's dated Tuesday August twenty-fifth, nineteen-sixty-four. The twins would have been around ten. There are five entries here for Mason. Seems the kindly doctor liked to rub and touch. He actually had Emily thinking these were treatments for her nerves. His nerves must have enjoyed it too. Sounds like he sure came closer to turning on Emily than George ever did."

"Frank, that's disgusting."

"No, I think it's the truth. Listen to this. 'Just between you and me, dear Diary, today Doc rubbed just a little close to some bad parts of me. I didn't say anything to him. It felt pretty good. It gave me a warm feeling all over.' She goes on to compare the good doctor with George, here. She certainly was naive about the doctor's motives. She really thinks these are treatments. I just don't believe this."

"Frank, shut up. I'm trying to read too. I'll get to Mason's pages. There isn't much to Hendrix. He was just an old letch who liked to expose himself to children. Just finish your own reading, please."

"Yes'm," Frank said obediently.

Frank finished his small stack of pages that were left with Doctor Mason.

The doctor seemed fond of touching Emily and had her returning every two weeks for her "nervousness". These treatments consisted of rubbing her on all parts of her anatomy and finally kissing her in some unusual paces. This last episode caused her to stop going to him. She was frightened by his actions and her own reactions.

Frank and Margot traded packets. The entries from Hendrix consisted of only four dates -- March and September 1960. The twins were around six then. The last two were from December 1964 and April 1967.

"In the first entry," Margot said, "Emily complained about the old man being such a crab, and in the second, he tricked the six-year old Gerry into his house, tied her to the kitchen table with her panties down, and exposed himself to her. Sounds like he may have done some touching."

Frank muttered, "Seems to be his weakness too," and added as Margot replaced the Mason pages to the pile on the desk, "Well? What do you think?"

"Terrible. These kids suffer all their early years and then forget, only to have it all brought back with their mother's diary. I can see what started the killings. The first two were easy. They still lived in town. George and Mary must have taken quite a lot of foot work. I wonder if they tried to find the vet that performed the abortion. He may still be on their list."

Frank walked over to the boards and. staring at them, asked, "What if Mary Carlin communicated with Emily sometime in the recent past? She'd been living in that same place for a long time."

"You're right, Frank," Margot agreed. "If Mary wrote, there could have been letters with the diaries. The twins may have found them and looked her up. The building manager said a kid had visited Mary several weeks ago. Terry probably made the contact. The manager also said Mary was seen talking to some bum. I'll bet she got them together. George and the twins, I mean."

Frank punched the air. "That's it. That's got to be the way they all got together."

Margot walked to Frisky's small report on the board, "What about him. Where does he fit?"

"The poor slob was just in the wrong place at the wrong time. Probably saw one or both of the twins with George."

"That's it then. We've got them all connected, but we can't do a damned thing about it. Now where do we go?"

Frank took a deep breath and slowly exhaled. Walking back to his desk, he sat down and leaned back. "I guess we wait. I still want to look into the death of the library maintenance man. Maybe something will come from that."

"Frank, the best thing that could happen to us would be to find the rest of Emily's diary."

"Yeah, you're right -- And there's a Santa Claus, too."

Chapter Twenty-Five

With Gerry Gallagher back to work at the library for a week, everything seemed to be just as it had been before the murders started.

Gerry called Frank on Wednesday and told him Terry had left. She did not bother to say where he had gone. She explained that now that she was recovered from her flu, she didn't really need Terry any more.

Ed Spatro also called Frank last Wednesday night and reported that Miss Gallagher went back to work on Monday and the brother had left. All seemed back to normal.

Margot managed to meet the girls at the park Tuesday and Thursday, and Ilene introduced her to Gerry, saying Margot was a friend of Sue's aunt. This made it easier for a relaxed lunch, and Margot was accepted quite easily by what appeared to be a fully rested Gerry. She was even included in their quotation game and mentioned to Frank that Gerry seemed to be just as she had been described when he first met her.

On Friday, when Margot met Ilene at the library, Ilene said, "Gerry is just fine now, and I don't think we have to worry about her. She doesn't seem nervous or snippy to anyone here. The few days' rest must have taken care of the jitters she had when she became sick. Really, Margot, I think she was just run down. Her brother made her nervous, and I think she'll be fine, now that he's gone."

"Okay, Ilene. I'll keep in touch with you. If you notice any changes -- you know what to look for, the nervousness or the abrupt mood swings -- if any unusual actions from Gerry appear, please call me as soon as you can."

"Sure, Margot. No problem. I want to help Gerry as much as you do. If anything different comes, up I'll call you first thing. I've got to go now. My supervisor is watching, and I'm not supposed to use library time for personal reasons. Come by the park for lunch again any time, please. We all enjoy having you join us."

"I will. I enjoyed the lunches, too. I'll sharpen up on some new quotes for the next time. Maybe one day next week. I'll be in touch."

Margot made a few more notes and closed her book. Leaning back, she realized she was moving in place just as she had seen Frank do a thousand times.

"Now I'm moving like him," she said half-aloud. "That's a bad sign." Going to the public phone in the entry lobby of the library, Margot called Frank at the office and reported on her last conversation with Ilene.

"Well, Frank, everything seems to be back to normal. The girls say Gerry is just like she used to be. No nervousness and no sharp, sarcastic remarks. She's just back to sweet little Gerry again. Have you come up with anything new?"

"No, it's all come to a standstill. No more murders and no more action or information on the old ones."

"I'm sure the twins were in on all these killings, but until something new comes up I'm stumped. I still think Terry may be in danger. Did anyone really see him leave? If they did all this together, she might still want to get rid of him. Frank, we've got to get to Gerry before something new sets her off and we have some more dead people on our hands. Just call it a hunch, but I thing Terry will show up again, and that will mean trouble."

"What pulled your chain? You were the one that thought it was only Gerry. Did you learn something else from her this week?"

"No Frank, it's just a feeling of unrest I got from those two days at the park when I had lunch with the girls. Gerry is too relaxed and refreshed. She acts like some of this didn't happen. Do you know she didn't even mention her brother on Tuesday or Thursday. It was like he hadn't been living with her for the past year. She didn't mention any of the questions about her father and mother either.

236

She seems to have blocked out all of the happenings of the past year completely."

"That doesn't sound too natural, does it?" Frank said, staring at the boards across the room. I think we need to have a brainstorm on this case. How about starting Saturday afternoon, at my place? We can take a break for dinner and continue on Sunday morning. I'll even eat your burned bisquits, if need be."

"Francis, you are such a gentleman. How could I refuse an invitation so grand. If you look in your freezer, you'll find those bisquits from two weeks ago. I can always wet them and toss them into the oven for a few minutes to warm them."

"Great. Forget it. I'll make omelets on Sunday morning. You can make the hash browns. They're supposed to be charred. The English muffins will do fine with both of those."

"Great, I'll see you at one o'clock tomorrow afternoon. Be sure to have some bubble bath in stock, in case the phone rings Sunday morning. What's for dinner tomorrow night?"

"I don't know. I guess you'll have to take pot luck."

"Pot luck at your house? Sure, Francis, sure."

Chapter Twenty-Six

Frank brought home the contents of the two bulletin boards in his office. The papers and books were spread over the floor in the living room of his apartment in the same order as they had been hung on the boards.

Margot, with her shoes off and the sleeves of her pale grey sweater pushed up past her elbows, was ready for work.

"Here," Frank said as he held out the wine glass to Margot, "some liquid knowledge. Maybe we can find something we overlooked before."

"Thanks, put it on the end table for me, please."

"Frank, I'm taking all the diary pages and putting them in date order. Including the ones from the two men in St. John's. Is that okay?"

"Sure. It may make the St. John's years fit together a little better." "Yes, I read them last Friday afternoon, but I didn't read them in date order with the others. I thought it might give a different picture with the others. Some of the sheets left with George are the sickest things I've ever read -- where she talks about George forcing her to have sex, and here where he starts making the twins watch. That's enough to give anyone a complex. These came from the box at Mary's apartment.

"Here's another one when she talks about George's girlfriend, Mary Carlin. The next page we have was from Mary's packet, also. Here, Mary is mentioned by name. George brought her to Sunday dinner. He said she was an old family friend. Now the next entry was with Mary, also. This one mentioned Dr. Charlie and Mary taking Emily to him for an abortion. I have another sheet from Mary's batch,. It seems to be after Emily's abortion.

"Now following the date order, we can fit in some from the old man's house -- the old man who had his penis cut off. There are four entries for him. He molested Gerry when she was about six years old. The mother sounds very upset, but other than going to the police the day it happened, it doesn't sound like she did much about it. It probably hurt Gerry more to have her mother do nothing about it than the fright of the old man fondling her and exposing himself to her. The mother sounds like she wanted to forget it. She didn't even tell George about it. It would have probably caused too much trouble for Emily."

"Where does Doctor Mason fit in?" Frank asked.

"I was just coming to him. His five entries are dated nineteen-sixty-four, and they are all within about two months. Looks like she went to him about every other week, once he got her started with her 'special treatments' as she called them. I wonder how many other female patients he had hooked like that. Well, the way his hands were sliced up tells us the murderer was seeing to his offending parts, just like the old man's penis. There were five diary entries on Doctor Mason. At least that's all that were left with his body."

"That must have been all there were, then," Frank surmised. "If the murderer went to all this trouble to place each victim's pages with the body, I'd bet all the pages were used that pertained to each victim. Don't you think so?"

"I agree. That was the vengence, I guess. Sort of paying them back for that ugly part of their lives."

"It has to be both of them," Frank said, as he raised himself from the floor stiffly. "The twins I mean." Rubbing his lower back, he moaned, "Damn, that floor gets farther down there every day. Here, let me fill our glasses."

"Frank, unless we catch them in the act, or get some real evidence, we have nothing against the twins. Terry's gone, and Gerry doesn't talk about him. She acts like he doesn't exist. We have to get her in a controlled situation and see if we can break that calm she maintains all the time. I don't think she's as stable as she appears. There has to be something that will shake her up a little. No one can stay so controlled."

"Yeah, the best thing that could happen would be to have some more of these diary pages show up. Chief Michaels had his deputy go over the Gallagher house twice and there was nothing that even remotely resembled these pages. My bet is they got them when they went to clean out after the mother's funeral. They must have burned them when they got rid of the clothes and things there. Michaels said Gerry burned some things there, and Gerry said so herself -- or was it Terry that said she burned some things? Which ever one said it, there were a lot of things burned that day. Michaels said she was outside burning for at least forty-five minutes to an hour. He passed there twice that afternoon and noted the time. That has to be when she got rid of them."

"I don't know, Frank." Margot leaned over the diary pages again. "When would she have had time to read all this and pick out just the pages that contained the information on the victims? There wouldn't have been enough time that weekend. Remember she, or they, only stayed for Saturday afternoon. There's no way she could have read all the diary pages. We only have part of them here. There had to be books and books, just to cover the years involved. Why here alone we have at least twenty entries, and these are isolated entries taken out of at least eleven or twelve years of keeping a diary."

"You're right. They must have brought the diaries home to have time to read all of them. Then, to pick out just these entries of all the abuse and trouble caused by these people. The diaries may still be in the apartment -- if we could get in there and check it out."

"Frank," Margot said as she shook her head, "don't even think of it. There's no way we can get a search warrant without probable cause and any other way is downright breaking and entering."

"Maybe we could talk to Ed. You know, the doorman. He might be able to get us in. How about for a good cause?"

"Forget it. I'm not going to jail. We just have to think of a different way." Margot settled back against the couch and sipped her wine. "Maybe....no, damn it! Francis, you've got me thinking like you now."

"Let me call Ed. Perhaps he's seen inside of their storeroom down in the cellar. He said they changed it into a darkroom, but they may use it for storage, too."

"That sounds too far-fetched. Anyway, why would they keep the diaries once they finished with their victims? Unless....do you think there will be some more victims?"

"We can't tell without the rest of the diaries. There haven't been any other people mentioned in any of the pages that we have. If someone new were to pop up, they may have their own entries in the diary. I still wonder about the veterinarian that performed the abortion. I think we are back to the waiting game. I can't see any way to stir things up with Gerry. I wish Terry would come back. Ed Spatro says he is quite an excitable guy. He'd be the one to spook into some action."

Margot raised herself from the floor and settled back onto the seat of the couch, "I think the way to get Terry back is to get to Gerry. That's what the girls keep telling me. Gerry told them that Terry always showed up when she had a problem and needed his help. She must know how to get in touch with him. She has a problem, she calls her brother, and he always comes running. I think that's the only way to get him back. Let's try to get to Gerry and upset her. I know it sounds cruel, but I think we are dealing with a pair of very sadistic killers. No matter how innocent and sweet Gerry seems, I still think she is in on these killings."

She took a sip of wine.

"Okay, I'll call Ed tomorrow and...damn, no. It's Sunday and I think that's his day off. I guess I'll call him on Monday. I'll sound him out about getting into the apartment. I can't make it sound official, but if I talk about the brother enough, I think he'll go for it. Now, my lovely," Frank said with a sweep of his hand, "let's put these things away for the evening and get down to some serious business,"

"Serious business or monkey business," Margot said as she stood up from the pale gold couch. "I thought you were going to feed me."

"Of course I'm going to feed you. Everything is ready and waiting. The wine is ready to be poured. The only things I have left to cook, are the egg noodles to go with my beef burgundy. Does that sound like monkey business?"

"It sure sounds like it may lead up to some. Quick, let's eat." With that Margot patted Franklin's rump as though he was some cute little kid on the corner.

"Chauvinist," he cried.

Chapter Twenty-Seven

Sunday morning Ed received a call from the managing office, asking him to come in for the Sunday man. Ed's wife wasn't too pleased, but he reported to the building as soon as he could. By nine o'clock he was rummaging through the side drawer of his lobby desk, looking for something to read. Finding nothing, he settled for the Sunday paper.

"I'll go downstairs later and get a new book," he muttered.

He started with the magazine section, with plans for the crossword puzzle after he finished reading.

It was almost noon when Ed finished the puzzle and began to look for other things to do to pass the time. He was beginning to pace when he decided to go to the boxes from his sister-in-law. He put them downstairs last week, when Mister Gallagher was so ill tempered..

Checking everything to see that the lobby was in order, he entered the elevator and went down to the basement. He left his two boxes of books in the corner just a few days ago. As he left the elevator, he saw the corner of the boxes, just where he had so hastily left them on the day Terry Gallagher yelled at him.

Ed shuttered and glanced upward with a quiet, "Thank you, Lord, for sending him away."

Things were certainly nicer now that he was gone. All was peaceful, and Miss Gallagher was relaxed and sweet again.

Pulling the boxes from under the old table, Ed tossed them up on the counter in front of the compacter.

As he dug through the first box he said, "Darn you, Liz."

His sister-in-law had given him the wrong box. These were all magazines and do-it-yourself craft books. The church rummage sale probably received his mysteries.

He reached for the other box, hoping this one was filled with mysteries. Liz was known for her warped sense of humor, she may have done this on purpose.

He had one flap pulled free on the second box when the buzzer went off. That meant someone was at his desk in the lobby, looking for him. Raising the other flap on the box, Ed noticed the whole top seemed to be covered with tiny scraps of lined notebook paper. It would have to wait now. He wondererd if Liz had filled the box with torn paper to keep the books from moving around. He looked around and decided that it wouldn't hurt to leave the boxes out on the table. Not many of the residents came down here at this time on Sunday.

Moving quickly, he rushed to the back stairs. If someone wanted him, he should not waste time by waiting for the elevator to come back down to the basement. Ed missed the movement of the elevator door opening as he rounded the corner and opened the stairwell door.

Gerry was humming softly to herself as she walked across the basement room to the door of the darkroom.

As she glanced around the room, she noticed the boxes on the table and reached for some of the magazines. Ed had removed these from the first box. They were the kind of magazines she enjoyed so much, and she wondered whose they were. If someone was throwing them away, maybe they would let her look through the box first.

As she shuffled through several of the magazines, she pulled the other box forward. Perhaps this box held the same thing. She peeked around as though she were really being a sneak thief, then lifted the corner flap and tried to see into the dark box. As she pulled the corner flap up she heard the door at the stairwell open and she moved back from the table.

"Good afternoon, Miss Gallagher. May I be of any assistance to you?" Ed asked, as he walked across to the table.

"Ed, are these your magazines?"

"Yes, Miss, they sure are, but they're the wrong kind. Seems my sister-in-law gave me the wrong box of books. It was supposed to be a box of paperback mysteries, and instead I got her craft magazines by mistake. Do you like them? You sure can have them. I'm not into sewing and needlepoint, myself," he laughed, as he repacked the books.

"Oh, Ed, I'd love to have them," Gerry answered.

"Well, then, I'll just carry them right up to your apartment for you. Did you want anything else? You look puzzled."

"No, I don't think so. I'm not sure just why I came down here. Just to look around I guess. It couldn't have been too important. Ed, this other box looks familiar. What's in it?" Gerry's voice was beginning to sound a little shakey.

"Why, Miss, I'm sure that's just some of the mysteries that were supposed to be in both boxes. I'll check it out later, but if it's these artsy-craftsy things, I'll bring it straight up to your place. Will that be all right with you?"

Ed was so happy to see Gerry back to her old self.

As Gerry started to walk from the table, she again lifted one corner of the top and saw a small torn corner of yellow lined paper caught in the fold of the carton. Pulling it from the box, she quickly put it in her skirt pocket.

"I'd sure appreciate it," she said happily. "I just love these magazines."

After Ed put the box of magazines on Gerry's kitchen table and left, Gerry put the kettle on to make some instant coffee. Her supply of tea was gone and she hadn't been up to the trip to China Town to replenish it.

Now, coffee cup in hand she sat at the kitchen table and began to look through the stack of craft books. It was as though she had found a treasure chest. All afternoon, as she leafed through book after book, something kept trying to come to the front of her thoughts. Every once in a while she would pause between books and stare thoughtfully at the mirror on the wall.

What was it that was trying so hard to come forward in her mind? A name, an action? Something she had seen or heard today was nagging at her. She just could not remember what was bothering her.

Ed hadn't returned to the basement since he left Gerry's apartment. He felt he had been away from the lobby too long. He planned to get to the other box of books when he took his dinner break at four-thirty. He could eat his sandwich and pick out a book to read for Wednesday, when he came back for regular day shift.

At four o'clock Sunday afternoon Ed's wife called. She asked him to run over to the drugstore for her cough medicine. He started out the door and he remembered he still had that second box of books lying on top of the table downstairs. Dashing down the back stairs to the basement, he grabbed the box and slid it back under the table filled with canning jars.

Then he went up the back stairs and out the side entrance on his way to the druggist.

Wednesday he'd get his book picked out. Right now his wife needed her medicine. This was much more important than some old paperback.

Upstairs, Gerry sorted her new magazines into several stacks and was enjoying each book. Dinner was in the oven. Her evening was planned -- eat and read. What better activities for a Sunday evening?

Chapter Twenty-Eight

Monday morning was a disaster as far as working on the Gallagher case.

"Mug Thy Brother-In-Law", as Frank had it labeled in the file, had come up with a new incident. Now the brother had been mugged. Frank was sure the husband had just returned the favor and gave his wife's brother a taste of the same medicine. He was having the whole family brought downtown for a session of questions.

By ten-thirty Frank got around to dialing the lobby phone at Gerry Gallagher's apartment building.

After six rings, a panting voice answered quickly. "Ed, this is Lieutenant Franklin. I talked to you several times a couple of weeks ago. About Miss Gallagher? Do you remember me?"

"I'm sorry, sir. This isn't Ed. I'm the fill-in for Ed. My name is John Whitson. May I help you?"

"No, I really need to talk to Ed. Can you give me his home number? I'll let you call me back at my office if you'd like to check me out."

Frank hated to waste time like this. He also did not want to have to go looking for a telephone book. His had disappeared long ago. He could never bring himself around to swiping someone else's.

"I think I'd better do that, sir. Just to be sure," Whitson sais. "I hope you understand."

"Certainly. No problem," Frank answered, his voice not giving away the tight look on his face.

After giving the doorman the number of the station, Frank hung up the phone and waited. The switchboard relayed the incoming call back to him. The door man very sheepishly gave Frank the home phone number and address of Ed Spatro.

Ed's phone was answered on the third ring. After a lenghtly explanation of the diaries and what he and Margot were looking for, Ed was quiet on the other end of the line.

"Ed, did you hear me?" Frank said as he raised his voice a little.

"Yes, Lieutenant. I heard you. I was just wondering."

"Wondering? Wondering what? Have you seen something like these books?" Frank was trying not to sound anxious.

"No, Lieutenant, but I remember about a week ago, just before Mister Gallagher left, he was getting rid of some things down in the basement storage room."

"Oh, damn. Did he burn something? What did he have?"

"Well, I think he had already thrown some of the things away before I came down. These things don't get burned, Lieutenant -- at least not here. We only have a compactor. The city collects the trash and they incinerate it. When I came into the basement, he was just putting a box into the compactor. He yelled at me to leave him alone, so I took my boxes and put them aside to work on at another time. He was in a rotten mood, as usual, all screaming and red in the face. I thought he was going to attack me for a minute. I got the hell....'scuse me. Anyway, I sure got out of there. Just as the elevator door closed, I could see him put the last box into the compactor drawer."

"Goddamn. I guess that blows the diaries. Thanks, Ed. Oh, has Miss Gallagher seemed any different. Is she still relaxed and quiet?"

"She sure is. Just last night I gave her some magazines. She was just her old self again."

"Thanks again, Ed. Sorry to bother you at home. I really appreciate your help. I'd like for you to still keep an eye on Miss Gallagher for me, and if you happen to go into her apartment, I'd sure like it if you could look around for some old notebooks. Mostly yellow lined stuff. Call me for anything, Ed. I owe you for all this help."

"Thanks, Lieutenant. I'll probably be going up there Wednesday. My sister-in-law gave me the wrong books and I already gave Miss Gerry one box. As soon as I get the scrap paper off the others, I'll see if I have an excuse to go up there. I'll call you, Lieutenant. 'Bye for now."

Hanging up the phone, Frank was a little confused by Ed's remark about craft books and his sister-in-law's mistakes. He shrugged. It must make sense to Ed.

Frank still had no direction to go.

"Now what?" Frank yelled at his desk, piled with five folders from five victims.

At eleven-thirty Frank finished reading the report on the maintenance man's death at the library, last year:

Victim died from gas inhalation. Death was preceeded by blow to the right temple, thought to be received when victim fell, hitting his head on floor pipe. Lividity was normal for position of body. Gas was turned off, but victim's hand was on valve. It was surmised that victim found a leak in the gas pipe, but slipped and hit his head. While dazed, he was able to close gas valve, but with his face so close to floor, the victim inhaled enough gas to result in death.

Conclusion: Accidental death."

"I wonder," Frank said as he tossed the report off to the side of his desk. "I just wonder. A blow to the right temple?"

Ed replaced the phone, and started thinking about the two boxes of books he had in the basement. He reached for the phone and called his wife's sister Liz.

The phone call took about ten minutes. After all the "How are you?" and "How's Mike?" questions, Ed learned that Liz had indeed fixed two boxes of books for him. Both of Ed's were filled with mystery paper backs. There were three boxes for the church book sale. All of the boxes for the church sale were filled with craft books. None of these five boxes were topped off with yellow scraps of paper.

With this news, Ed started rummaging through his billfold, looking for Lieutenant Franklin's number. After finding the card he hastily dialed.

"Lieutenant Franklin. This is Ed again. I've got it. I'm sure I do."

Franklin, caught in a moment of deep concentration answered with a sharp, "Ed who? And what have you got?"

"Ed Spatro. You just called a few minutes ago. I think I know something about the yellow papers you were looking for. I'm pretty sure I have them down in the basement. But, Lieutenant----they're all torn to pieces. A whole box full of pieces, I think."

"Ed, are you sure? How did you get them? Never mind. Meet me. Can you get away right now. Meet me at the apartment building. Please, it's very important."

"Sure Lieutenant. Right now. I can be there in five minutes."

"Okay, Ed, go there, but stay away from Miss Gallagher or her brother, if he shows up. Stay away from both of them. Hide or sneak around. Don't let either of them see you. If they find out you have that box, it could be very dangerous for you. You can explain to me how you got it when I see you there. Again, Ed, stay out of sight and away from the Gallaghers. Got it?"

"Sure thing. I'll wait in the alley for you to get there. I'm just sure this is the box you're looking for. I'll bet we swapped them on the table."

"Explain when I get there. I have to get in touch with Miss Kent, so hold on till I get there."

Frank slammed the phone down and yelled for someong to dial Margot. As he reached the outer office a phone was handed to him.

Ten minutes before Ed's return call to Frank, Gerry Gallagher walked back to the desk in the reference section of the library. She was still having a hard time concentrating. Sue and Ilene asked her several times during the day if she was feeling well enough to be at work.

Now the confustion and stress from the questions were beginning to show. Gerry sat down and tried to work on some catalogue cards. As she felt a sneeze coming on, she reached into her skirt pocket for a tissue. She felt the small scrap of yellow paper that had been quickly dropped into her pocket on Sunday when she was in the basement store room.

Looking at the paper with the same puzzled look, her expression rapidly took on a snarling scowl.

With no care of where she was, her voice rose in a shrill scream, "No-o-o-o-!"

As she screamed, she flung her arm across the desk. The cards, files, and everything that had been on the desk went flying as Gerry swept the desk clean. She turned quickly. With the stance of a soldier, she walked toward the back door of the library.

"Gerry," Sue called, "where are you going?"

"If you really believe it is any of your concern, I am returning to my apartment. Kindly mind your own business after this."

With that Gerry was out the door, and Sue was left with the same feeling she had experienced before when Gerry had snapped at her. Sue realized that this must be what Margot Kent had been talking about when she said Gerry might start acting up again. She quickly dialed Margot's number.

"Miss Kent, Gerry's at it again. She started screaming and throwing things. Then she just snapped my head off, and went out the door. I hope it was all right to call you at work. She looked real strange. She was just wild back there, when I came into the room."

"Sue, did you see what upset her?" Margot was reaching for her purse and notebook.

253

"No, I just heard her scream the word "no" over and over. She sounded like it would go on forever. Is there anything I should do?"

"No, I'll look into it now. Thanks for calling me. I'm sure we can help Gerry," Now Margot was walking around her desk in anticipation of leaving the office as soon as she hung up the phone. "Thanks again, Sue. I'll call you as soon as I find out anything."

Margot walked as far as the door when her phone rang again. Returning to the desk she placed the phone to her ear and said, "Margot Kent here."

"Margot, I think we've got the diaries. At least Ed Spatro thinks he has them. Get a squad car with a driver and meet me at the apartment -- fast. Use your sirens, if you have to, but make it fast."

"Frank, I just received a call from Sue at the library. Gerry's been set off again. It sounds like she's really gone off the deep end this time.

Sue said she was violent and throwing things and yelling 'NO! NO! over and over. Gerry left the library. Just a few minutes ago. She said she was going home. If Ed is there, he should be warned. She may be dangerous."

"I've already done that. Just get over there. I'm leaving now."

Frank was out the door before the officer had the phone back on it's cradle.

Chapter Twenty-Nine

Ed was just coming out the rear door of the apartment building as he saw Gerry rounding the corner at the end of the block. Her head was held high, and her stride was long and firm. He couldn't quite believe this was Miss Gerry. As she neared the alley beside the apartment building, Ed was sure it was her. He dashed back to the rear doorway that was used for deliveries and stepped inside to the small vestibule. His surprise was evident when the door swung open behind him and Gerry Gallagher stepped inside, not ten feet away from him.

"Oh, hello, Miss Gallagher. Fancy seeing you back here. I'm just here to pick up a few things."

"Really, Mr. Spatro. I couldn't care less. Now get out of my way. I have something to tend to, and I certainly will not dawdle in idle conversation with you."

Ed couldn't believe his ears, but his eyes told him this was most assuredly Gerry Gallagher. She sounded more like Terry Gallagher. She had never talked to him like this before. She was so firm -- and almost rude.

She brushed past him, and entered the back hall of the lobby floor. Going to the elevator, she did not notice as Ed followed her down the hall from a fairly safe distance. Ed came into the front lobby, and he looked at the floor indicator on the elevator. He noticed that she was now in the basement.

Remembering Frank's warning, he slowly decended the back stairs to the basement. Very pleased with the fact that when he first arrived fifteen minutes ago, he slipped downstairs and retrieved the box that he believed to hold the prized pieces of paper Lieutenant Franklin was so anxious to see. He brought the box back upstairs to the front desk.

Checking the lobby for tenants and the relief man, he slipped the box into the small closet in the corner of the lobby. Not many people even knew about the space. Ed felt this was a safe place for this mysterious box.

As Ed slowly opened the door to the back hall in the basement, he heard the first of the wild raving and shouting. Puzzled, Ed could not figure out who was in there with Gerry. He could separate at least three different voices. They were jumbled with unfinished sentences, and there were crashing sounds of things being thrown around in the furnace room.

Ed remembered again the warning from Frank. Backing out of the hall, he went up the stairs and out the back door.

Both cars came at the same time. Margot was getting out of the squad car, thanking the driver.   Frank had just come to a jolting stop at the curb behind the squad. Leaning into the window, Frank instructed the officer to phone in a request for another car and a medical unit, including paramedics trained for psychiatric care.

Ed motioned to Frank and Margot to come to the back door and began to relate his meeting with Gerry.

"You mean," Frank asked in a horrified voice, "she got to the box that had the papers in it?"

"No, sir, I hid it when I first got here. She sure was going crazy though. I could hear her screaming, and I think she had her brother down there. Maybe someone else, too. They sure are making a lot of noise. I think she was throwing things around. I guess she's looking for that box. When I first got here, I snuck down there and grabbed it and stuck it in the lobby closet. I think she went upstairs then. When I was coming out, I could hear her yelling and talking to the other ones. She was on the steps when I came out the door to meet you. She sure was mad. I just can't believe that was Miss Gerry. She looked so....mean, I guess is a good word for it. She looked just plain mean."

Frank and Margot took the back stairs to the second floor.

Listening at the apartment door, Margot called out somewhat quietly, "Gerry, it's Margot Kent. May I come in and talk to you. I know you're upset, but I'm here to help. Will you let me in, please?"

Ed walked up behind Frank and Margot and said, "Here's the master key. I thought you might want it if she won't let you in."

They slowly opened the door and found an empty apartment.

"Now where do we look?" Frank asked.

Ed motioned to the stairs, again. "I'll bet she went up on the roof. She told me once that she goes up there to look at the stars and relax. She sure needs relaxing now."

"Thanks, Ed. Come on, Margot. Up we go again."

They neared the door to the roof and Frank motioned for Margot to wait.

"Margot I hear voices, they're out there on the roof. Here, let me get the door."

"Frank are you sure? I just can't see either of them coming up here. Why would they? They didn't know we were coming. I wonder what set Gerry off. Sue didn't know, either."

"Listen. I can hear them out there. At least I hear some voices. They aren't yelling anymore, like Ed said they were doing down in the basement. I wonder when Terry came back, and why."

"Do you think they would try to hurt each other?" Margot asked.

Frank moved his ear closer to the crack around the door and said, "I don't know. It seems strange. I'm sure he thought all the evidence was destroyed. He cleaned all those loose ends a week ago."

Margot looked at him with a puzzled glance. "Well, what do we do next? I think we should get out there and talk to them. Try to reason with them. I hope they'll realize they both need help."

"First things first. Let's just get out on the roof and look at the situation. I'd like to hear them talk for a minute to check their state of mind, before we go barging in on them."

They crept slowly through the door onto the roof.

Then came the small voice, almost pleading, "Terry, why did you make me come up here?"

"Oh, come on. Don't start," Terry said as the neon light on the apartment across the street buzzed. "I had to come up here to think. I'm afraid that Lieutenant Franklin is getting too close. He knows something is different about us. He doesn't know exactly what it is,"

"Terry, I'm getting confused again. I'm not sure I remember what is going on. Can you explain it again? Please, don't get mad at me. I'm just having trouble keeping things sorted out. Are we playing "turn around" again?"

"Sure, in a way I guess we are. Now I don't want you to worry," Terry said, almost tenderly. "I've taken care of any of the papers that may have gotten us in trouble. I got rid of them last week."

"That nosy-parker Ed was poking around down there, but I took care of all the books and papers that you brought back from St. John's. Now the past is dead, and all the mean people that hurt us when we were kids are gone. Even a couple that we didn't know. I think someone else took care of those for us. We took care of the ones who hurt us, but she may have helped there, too."

"Terry, what do you mean someone else took care of the others? We only talked about the ones who did things to us or Mother. Did someone else get....you know, hurt? Who would do something like that for us? I can't remember who she is. Do I know her?"

Terry was trying to remain patient and calm, but the stress in his voice was beginning to show. "Gerry, don't you remember? When you were little, if something happened that you couldn't take care of yourself, there was another person who always showed up to fix it. Mother didn't believe you the first time she came. After that, you always forgot about it, so nothing was said. Remember the time when that fat slob from the next block kept pushing you off the slide. This other Gerry came just as he started to push you. She knocked him off the top of the slide. He broke both legs and all you did was stand and laugh at him."

"Don't. You're scaring me. I don't remember any of that. Why would she help me? And who is she? I get afraid when you talk about things that I can't remember."

"Oh, Gerry, sometimes I think you understand, and then you get like this. You just can't figure out anything for yourself. Don't be afraid. I'll take care of things from here on. I thought for awhile I was going to leave, but I guess I'm going to have to see to things for a little while longer. Don't worry. I'll take care of you, just like I used to."

Chapter Thirty

Frank and Margot waited for what seemed an eternity before there were any more words from across the roof.

Frank made a motion to move toward the voices, but Margot whispered, " Frank, wait, don't go to them yet. I want to listen to them talk some more. We may learn more this way than with questions."

Margot slipped down behind the ventilation stack and sat down on the pebble covered roof.

"Gerry, are you listening to me? Don't go back to sleep. This is not the time to leave me. You've had your rest, Please don't do this now. I need to have you here with me."

Terry's voice was beginning to show the strain of the past few weeks.

"Gerry, can you hear me? Come on, now. Don't go into the well. I need you awake. Who knows what will happen if you sink now. Please, wake up."

"What? Oh, yes, Terry, I hear you," Gerry answered in a drowsy voice. "I'm just so tired. All this has been almost too much for me. I surely would like to just go to sleep for a while."

Frank leaned over to Margot and whispered, "See what I mean, Margot. She's still sick. Could he have been giving her something to make her sleepy. It's not natural to be so sleepy all the time. The girls said she was back to normal at work. Ed mentioned that she seemed to be in a rage when she came in from the library this afternoon. This changing from one extreme to another is strange."

"No, Frank. I think I know what it is. It's something we haven't come up against in either of our careers. Let's listen and let them get relaxed. We don't want to cause any panic up here on the roof."

"Yeah, you're right. We don't need an hysterical confrontation up here."

Gerry asked in her dreamy way, "What did you say, Terry?"

"I didn't say a word. Why?"

"I thought I heard you whisper to me. You used a lot of big words. You said that I was being a confounded ass about this whole absurd situation and I didn't really deserve to live. That's a terrible thing to say to me. How could you?" With this Gerry started to sob quietly.

"Gerry, it's not me that's talking to you. I haven't said a word and I'm afraid I can't explain it simply enough to you."

Frank and Margot edged closer to the corner of the stack and were barely able to see Gerry sitting with her back in the corner of the wall that enclosed the roof of the building.

"Where's Terry? He must be over there, just to her left. I can't see behind that pile of boards."

Frank was stretching farther out and putting himself more into view from the side corner where Gerry sat.

"Get back. She'll see you," Margot hissed as she tugged on Frank's sleeve.

"But, I can only see one of them. Where's Terry?"

"He's probably just behind the boards, like you said. Now shush."

"I'm going over there," Frank said to Margot. "I'll be careful and very gentle. You wait here. She might get upset at seeing you here. She doesn't know about our connection yet."

As Frank rose from behind the ventilation stack, he slowly moved out into the line of vision from Gerry's position.

"Miss Gallagher, please don't be alarmed. It's Lieutenant Franklin. Remember, we talked last week. I'm here to help you. Please let me come over there next to you. Mister Gallagher, where are you? I've come to help. Please answer me. I don't want to get your sister alarmed. Are you still here, Mister Gallagher?"

Frank glanced behind the pile of boards and saw only empty space.

"Mister Gallagher, would you come out and help me with your sister? I really need your help right now."

Frank was beginning to wonder just how Terry could have disappeared so quickly. The door was behind Margot and he surely hadn't gone out there. He would have to worry about Terry later. Right now Gerry was rising from the corner.

As Gerry stepped forward, Frank heard her say, "Lieutenant, this farce has progressed as far as I intend to permit it. Will you please cease your caterwauling and leave me alone. There have been some drastic changes, and I am now in charge. There will be no need for the inept services of the judicial forces of this city, who, for some unconscionable reason, continue to harrass me. I am fully recovered and in complete control of the situation."

Frank involuntarily stepped backwards at the long statement from Gerry, completely surprised by the strength in her voice and by the firm stance she had taken. Her hands on her hips and her feet slightly apart, her body language was telling him that he was no longer needed or wanted. It was also telling him that this was a completely different Gerry Gallagher.

Margot, still behind the ventilation stack, was as shocked as Frank, at the total change in the usually shy and timid Geraldine Gallagher.

"Gerry," Margot said, as she stepped from behind the stack, "remember me from the park? I'm also a friend of Lieutenant Franklin's. I thought I might be able to lend a hand to you and your family if you were still upset. May I come forward? That wouldn't upset you, would It?"

"Madame, I see no reason on earth why I should seek any comfort or anything else from you. I am in complete control now. There is no need for any outside interference. I shall deal with the situation revolving around my....family, as you call it. I certainly don't need strangers sticking in their unwanted assistance. It has not been requested. Please cease to hover over me and allow me to return to the apartment. The vulgarity of your impudence astounds me. If I require aid, in my fashion I most assuredly will seek it from someone in which I have more confidence."

Gerry Gallagher walked across the roof and to the door to the staircase. Frank and Margot stood starring at her as though she had slapped them both across the face. Was this the gentle, timid "little miss" they had seen just weeks before? Here was the calculated, firm woman declaring how much she was in charge. Where were the hysterics and the fright that Ed had heard in the basement? This was not the same person they had just been listening to on the roof just a few minutes ago. Frank and Margot were astounded.

They followed her to the door until she turned, and politely, but firmly said, "I have no further need of your attendance. Please, be so kind as to leave this building. If I find later that I have need of your services, I will be in touch. In other words, don't call me, I'll call you."

Margot stepped up quickly and said, "Miss Gallagher, I think you should know, Lieutenant Franklin and I have the box of old books and diaries that belonged to your mother."

With that statement Gerry Gallagher slammed the door firmly in their faces and left them standing on the roof.

"Well, I'll be damned!" Frank exclaimed. "Did you ever see anything like that? And why in the hell did you tell her about the diaries?"

He took out his nasal spray and gave each nostril a dose of inhalent.

Margot reached for the door knob and said, "I'm not totally sure why I said that. I think we have one very sick lady on our hands. Now is the time to force our hand. Let's get down to that apartment and see if we can ruffle a few more feathers while she's thinking about those diaries. Did you notice how many times she used the word 'control?' That's the key word. Now it's our turn to be in control."

"I sure hope you know what you, or I should say , hope you know what we are doing. And another thing. How in the hell did Terry get off this roof?"

With that Frank held the door as Margot slipped through, and they went down the back stairs to the second floor.

"Frank, are you sure the box that Ed found is the right one? Is it definitely the one that has all the remaining diary pages in it?"

"I might be in big trouble there. He said he had a box full of yellow scraps. The torn bits had small writing on them. I could be totally wrong on this, Margot. We have to look at this box, before we confront her anymore tonight."

"No, Frank, she's upset, in spite of the way she acted upstairs. We must make our move while she's on edge. I think it's the only way to break her. You just follow my lead. She seemed to be more ill at ease when I appeared. I have a feeling that she thinks she can manipulate you. I was the surprise on the roof."

"What do you mean manipulate me? What makes me so easy?" Frank asked in a true, injured male-ego fashion.

"You'll see. I have one of my famous theories that you usually laugh at, so let me prove it first. Let's go."

Margot knocked at the door of the Gallagher apartment,and she and Frank stood there and waited. After a few minutes they could hear a muffled conversation from inside, but couldn't make out any words.

"Margot, wait, I'm going to get some help. I don't want Terry to disappear on us again."

Frank ran over to the elevator and pushed the alarm bell giving it one short blast and one long blast.

"What was that all about?" Margot whispered.

"I told Ed if he heard that, to signal the med unit to come up. Just planning ahead. Okay, now what have they been saying?"

"I can't make out any of the words. It sounds like two or three people all talking at the same time. The voices come and go."

The door to the elevator opened and Ed Spatro crept out, " I told the guys. They're bringing up their stuff. Can I help some more? "

"No, Ed," Frank said, "just stay to the side of the door when we go in. As soon as we're in, wait for my men and the paramedics. Have them ready."

"Yes, sir. Right away." Ed felt flushed and excited but kept calm and did exactly as he was told.

Margot put her face near the door and called out, "Gerry, it's Margot Kent. Please open the door. It's very important. It's about what your mother wrote in some of her books."

After a few quiet minutes, the door opened slowly. Behind it was Gerry Gallagher, trembling like a small child. Margot and Frank cautiously entered the apartment, while Gerry stayed behind the door, almost holding it as a shield.

"Gerry, it's all right. We've come to help. Please come with me. Sit beside me here on the couch."

Frank walked over to the large over stuffed chair he sat in on his first visit to this apartment. Gerry slowly closed the door and reached out one small hand to Margot. Margot led her to the couch. They sat wordlessly for a few minutes.

"Frank, would you go to the washroom and get a wet facecloth for me. I think Gerry would like to rinse her face and forehead. Don't you think that would feel good, Gerry?"

"What's wrong with her?" Frank said as he leaned over to Margot's right side. "She's back the same as before, only more so."

"Get the wash cloth, " Margot said flatly.

When Frank came back into the room, Margot had Gerry leaning on her shoulder and was rocking her back and forth, comforting her as a mother would do when a little girl had fallen and hurt herself. Frank handed her the washcloth, and Margot began to gently pat Gerry's face with the cool cloth. As she started to push Gerry's hair away from her eyes, Margot made a short gasp and motioned for Frank to sit in the chair across from them.

Margot continued to hum to Gerry and wipe her face. At the same time, she motioned for quiet from Frank. As Frank sat down, Margot slowly reached up and pushed again at Gerry's hair line, slowly removing a wig of beautiful long redish brown hair.Frank stared but could not have made a sound. Sitting before him on the couch sat Terry Gallagher, leaning on Margot's shoulder. He was quietly moaning and pouting.

"Shh, it's all right," Margot said gently. "I'm here to help you. Just try to stay calm. We'll stay with you, and everything will be just fine."

"Margot, what happened?" Frank asked. "How can this be?"

"Later, Frank. Let's see to Terry first."

Margot slowly eased Terry's head up from her shoulder as the paramedics entered the room.

"Here, Terry, these nice gentlemen will take you to the hospital.

I'll be there very soon. Please don't worry. They'll take very good care of you."

Terry looked around as they eased him down on the stretcher, "Gerry....I have to take care of Gerry. She needs me so much. That mean sister might hurt her. Please, keep Emily Geraldine in the well until I can help Gerry. Now I know her name. It's Emily Geraldine."

"Don't worry. We're here to help. I think now we can get some true answers. Things will be fine again for you and Gerry. That's what you want, isn't it, Terry?" Margot stood over him with her hand on his shoulder as the paramedics started out of the room. "I'll be with you as soon as I can, Terry. Don't worry."

As the paramedics left, Margot gave them a slip of paper and said, "Here's the patient's name. Please see that Doctor Crandall talks to me before any medication is administered. This is very important. If this case is what I believe it to be, no medication should be given without a conference between me and the doctors involved at the hospital. The patient's name is Terry Gallagher. I'll be in touch with the doctor before you arrive. Thanks for the fast service, and please take good care of Terry."

As the last paramedic reached for the door knob to shut the door, Margot added, "Oh, watch this patient very carefully. He can be extremely dangerous in spite of his mild appearance right now."

Ten minutes later, Margot replaced the phone after talking to Doctor Crandall in the psychiatric department.

Turning to Frank she said, "That should give them a pretty good idea of what the main problem is with Terry. He will take some close observation. It's really hard to give a true explanation of what has been going on, until we see just how firm his own personality is established."

"What does that mean? Are you saying he has more than one personality like....what's her name? Sybil?" Frank was still a little shaken by the discovery that Gerry was actually Terry. "Couldn't he just like to act like he's Gerry to get away with the murders?"

"No. Remember, Gerry has lived here for years and hasn't had any problems until they, or she, found the mother's diary. Terry probably has been living his life as Gerry since he left home. When the Gerry personality found the diaries, he -- Terry that is -- felt it time to come out and take charge. It is unusual that he chose to be himself when Gerry was still "out", too. Who can explain how a sick mind works? Now we have to get to those diary pages and read as much a we can, so I can talk to the doctors about Terry."

Two hours later Frank walked into his apartment, where Margot sat on the floor with neatly stacked books piled around her.

"What were the scraps?" Frank asked. "Where are they?"

"Terry must have started to tear the books apart but changed his mind. He probably decided they could go into the compacter whole. These notebooks were under a small layer of paper scraps. He couldn't have torn up very much."

"Okay, but what's that one on the couch? It looks different," Frank asked, as he moved toward the odd sized notebook.

"Never mind that one for now. That's what I found in the back of Terry's night stand drawer. I've been through all of these and have a stack of pages pulled out. I've marked each book with a tab where I pulled out a page, so I can replace them later. I have enough here in this pile to tell us what we need to know. I might also add that I was completely wrong."

"Wrong? About the twins?" Frank sounded a little puzzled.

Margot shook her head and answered, "Just wrong on the whole situation. First, read this pile of entries. I've kept the pages in order by date. You'll have a continuing story with the pages we have already read. Miss Emily Gallagher's diary is quite a shocker. Then you can read this small notebook. It's the icing on the cake. It brings it all together.

Frank reached for the stack of papers as he dropped to the floor and leaned back against the couch.

Taking the remaining diary pages he slipped into the conclusion of Emily's unreal world, told in her most secret words and thoughts.

January 14, 1957

Dear Diary,

Things are pretty nice lately. I'm sorry I didn't write for a while, but when I feel so sad, I just can't think sometimes what I should write about.

George is fine again. Nothing was said about the beating and what he did to me last month. He didn't even act like he remembered.

The babies act pretty quiet around him. They don't know what he does to their mama. They don't ask one question about it either. They just act like it didn't happen.

They sure are pretty, my babies. I just love to dress them alike. Some of the neighbor ladies think I shouldn't dress them like each other, but the babies like to do it, so why can't we do what we please? Well, sometimes, Terry complains, but then I tell them how happy it makes me, and then it's all right with them both.

Just the other day, those stinkers fooled me. They switched their playclothes and I called Gerry by Terry's name. They did that all afternoon and I couldn't tell which was which. I guess I could cut their hair different, but I'd hate to that. I like the new game. They think it's fun to fool me.

I think I'll see if they can fool the lady at the store. You know, Mrs. Jensen, at the check out counter. The one who's so nice to them. Sometimes she gives them a sucker. Maybe we can fool everyone. Wouldn't that be fun?

I haven't done much lately. At first, I couldn't go out because of the bruises, then I just didn't feel like it. I like to watch my babies play. They're more fun then some old group of women or playing cards. I don't know how to play cards very good anyway.

Just taking care of my house and my babies is what I like best. These women who drink coffee and gossip all day are really just lazy. I'll bet they have dirty houses. One thing George used to tell me when we first got married was I sure kept a clean house. Mama taught me that real good. She said that a woman didn't need no twelve years of school to learn how to take care of a house. A clean house was important to her.

I feel better now dear Diary. It feels good to talk to you again, and I won't wait so long next time.

Good night my friend,

Emily

February 19, 1957

Dearest Diary,

I know it's silly to be sitting up so late and writing to you dear Diary, but I can't sleep, so I might as well use the time to talk to you.

I just about have had it with Gerry. Here, she's almost three years old, and she is driving us all crazy. The doctor doesn't know what to do with her, the temper tantrums and the throwing things around. He finally got so mad at her today, I thought he was going to spank her bottom right there in the office. I tried to tell him that she was just a little high-strung. He didn't seem to believe me.

Today was a regular checkup at the doctor's office -- you know, for their shots and to see if they are growing like they should. George gets mad when I take them to the doctor, so I save money from my groceries. That way he don't know when I take them. The doctor says they must have regular checkups and get all the baby shots, so they won't get the measles and mumps and whatever those sickness things are that kids get.

I heard of a boy down the block that got lockjaw. He ripped his leg on a big old rusty nail. Now he's in the hospital over in Wesley. I forget what the other name is for lockjaw -- tegnus or tepnil or something like that. Whatever the name is, he sure is sick. That's why Doc says it's so important that the babies have all their shots.

George don't believe in shots. He says he didn't have no shots when he was a kid, and it didn't hurt him. I think he might be too mean to get sick from any old rusty nail.

Can you believe, when Doc was trying to check Gerry's ears and nose, that little stinker bit down on his finger so hard, she took a chunk out of it. He bled something terrible, all over his nice white jacket and all over the floor. He got some on the nurse, too.

I didn't feel very bad about the blood on Miss Sylvia. She thinks she's something special, the way she talks to the patients. Someone would think she was the doctor, the way she always says, "And how are we today?" That's really a silly way to talk.

She don't dress right for an office where there are sick people and children. Why, one day, when she was sitting at her desk, one of those truck-driver men came in and leaned right over her. Can you believe she just sat there and leaned forward and let that big ugly man look down her dress. Why, I won't even let my babies go up to her desk and take one of their silly toys they keep in the corner box for the kids to play with. I'll bet they are full of some sick kid's germs anyway.

I am so tired. Maybe now I can go to sleep. Do you know that you are the only person I can really talk to. No one else will listen and you have so much interest and heart. You make me feel so good. As much as I love my babies, I think I love you more. You don't ever give me any trouble and you're so understanding.

Goodnight my sweet Diary,

Emily

May 20, 1958

Dear Diary,

Doc called today about the test. He says I'm pregnant again, for sure. He won't do anything about it. I guess I'll have to tell George. I sure hope he don't get mad. Doc says it will be in about seven months. I'd wait, but I'm afraid to do that, because that might make George madder. He gets so funny. I never know what he's going to do. He hasn't hit me or even yelled about anything in so long, I'm just so afraid of what this will do.

We went for a walk the other night after supper. It was sure nice, just a family out for a walk. Even the little ones loved it. They just laughed and skipped. It was so funny. They fooled their daddy when he got home from work. The played their "turn around" game on him again. He even laughed at them when they yelled "turn around" That's what they do when they've fooled someone. They stand next to each other and spin around and yell "turn around" over and over. That sure is their favorite game.

Something real strange is going on with the babies. They're using funny words. I thought at first it was just a new way of saying different words, but I think they've made up their own words. They use them in with real words, but I can't tell what they're saying. George, he gets real mad when they do it in front of him. I noticed last night they just don't talk much when anyone is around, but they sure do go at it when they are up stairs in their room together.

Well, Diary, I'll let you know what happens when I tell George about me being pregnant again. Pray for me.

Your friend,

Emily

February 18, 1959

Dear Friend,

My dearest Diary, I'm really happy with my two babies, but sometimes, I sure do wish they would have both been boys. I don't know what is wrong with Gerry, but now all she does is cry and scream. Nothing pleases her. I have to feed her first. I have to hold her more than Terry, too. Seems like she don't want me to even touch Terry. He is a pretty good baby. Maybe he is just more patient, but she sure does demand most of my time.

Yesterday, she threw her bottle at me when I went to feed Terry. George just can't understand why I'm so tired when he gets home. I spend so much time holding her and carrying her around. He says I should take the bottle away from her, but she likes it so much. I just don't have the heart. After all, four-and-a-half sure isn't too old for a bottle.

Last night, George didn't come home until late and it sure was a good thing. It took me three hours to get the beet stains off the wall. Gerry don't like beets. When I got up to turn off the stove, she threw her plate against the kitchen wall. I really think she was trying to hit Terry, but he ducked, and the plate just spattered the wall. I guess he is really too young to know how to duck. It sure looked like he knew she was aiming at him.

I think today he was trying to get even with her. I caught him taking her toys away from her after their morning nap. He threw her doll out and then wouldn't let her have any of his trucks.

I'm sure it would have to be easier with just boys. He is so much easier to handle. He just gets a little too playful sometimes.

When Gerry loses her temper she makes me think of George. If she doesn't get her way, she starts throwing and yelling. She even hit me today at breakfast. She smacked me in the mouth when I told her she couldn't put both hands in her oatmeal. I think she has a mean streak just like her daddy. She just wants all the attention, and sometimes I just have to pay attention to Terry. He needs that just as much as she does.

It's late, so I better go to bed. I'll write more tomorrow night, dear friend. I promise.

Good night dear Diary,

Emily

July 21, 1959

Dear Diary,

Today we went to the doctor's and he couldn't believe his eyes. He told me he positively didn't believe what he saw when he examined Gerry and Terry. Of course, Terry still pitched a fit, but Gerry was so good, and she opened her mouth for him when he asked her.

He was just a bit nervous. Remember about six weeks ago, she bit a big piece out of his hand. He has a mark about the size of a half dollar from that examination. He couldn't believe it was the same little girl. He said no one could change that much. He kept asking me what I did to make her so good. I told him that I was just patient and I knew she would turn into a good little girl.

Sometimes I think she sneaks and does some of the bad things that Terry does, but I sure don't see her do them. Then after it's done, she always says she doesn't remember. One day she said she had been down in the well. I sure don't know what that means. We don't have a well, and anyway, how could a five year old get down into a well and then get out? I sure don't know where she got that idea of being in a well. Every time she sneaks and does something, then she says she doesn't remember. She always adds, "I go down in the well, Mama."

Maybe when she gets older, she will tell me what being in the well means. Terry didn't know either. He just says that the mean sister is back when one of these times happens. I guess she still likes to get into a little mischief. After all, she is only a baby. All babies like to get into a little trouble sometimes. That's part of being a kid. Don't you think so, my dear diary?

Tomorrow we're going on a picnic. I hope George don't forget. The last time we were supposed to go on a

277

picnic, he forgot and didn't come home. Well, this time we'll just go without him, if he don't come home tonight.

I have fancy white sandwich bread -- you know, the square kind that makes those fancy little sandwiches when you cut it from corner to corner. The babies just love it when I make them. I saw a picture of a rich lady's yard in a magazine and she had these little sandwiches that were all decorated with radishes and parsley. I couldn't get no parsley, but I did have some tops from celery and I'm going to make my own grand picnic. We can act like we're rich sometimes if I can get a nice magazine to copy my meal and fancy decorations.

The babies are excited. They just like going down to the park by the river. They still like to stir up the ducks. They're just babies having fun.

I'll tell you about my picnic next time.

Good night sweet Diary,

Emily

August 3, 1959

My dearest friend,

Today sure has been a bad day. I don't know what I am going to do with Geraldine. She is so mean sometimes and so sweet other times. Just this afternoon, I caught her playing with matches. She is only a baby, but she loves to light matches.

Today she was burning bugs out in the back yard. I saw her digging around under bricks and some of the junk out at the back shed. She looked like she was collecting something. She was putting something in an old can from the trash pile. When I got out back to see what she was doing, she had started a fire. She was burning the bugs. She was pretty cute. She was giggling so hard, she had tears coming from her eyes.

When I came up to see what she was doing, she said, "See , Mama, look how they squirm. They wiggle-wiggle."

I told her that wasn't nice, but she said her daddy did it all the time. I guess he isn't such a good example for the babies. Who would think that a five year-old would enjoy burning little bugs? I guess she just has a mean streak sometimes. Gets that from her daddy, I know.

Now Terry, he is pretty mean sometimes, too, but I haven't caught him huring little things like bugs, yet. I did see him tear the legs from a little lizard one day, but he said it crawled up on his foot. It scared him, so it deserved to die. I guess maybe he was right.

Most of the time I don't like to think of things like that. It bothers me that they do mean things, but I have so much else to worry about. They can't get into much trouble as long as it's just bugs and lizards.

Tomorrow I think I will have enough money to get that pretty cloth that I saw in the window at Clausen's Dry

Goods. It was so pretty. I think I will be able to make myself a skirt.

Tonight I think I'll make George's favorite pot roast. It might help his mood. He's been kinda mean lately. He only hit me once last night, but he made the babies watch us in bed again. They sure are strange when he brings them into the bedroom. They get a funny glazed look on their faces, especially Gerry. She almost acts like she's not inside her own self.

Tomorrow I might sneak over to the park with the babies. They do enjoy watching the ducks on the river there. Of course they like to throw rocks at them. That's only to make them quack. They like to hear the ducks make that loud racket. Guess they think it's funny. They hardly ever hit the ducks. They just like to scare them.

I guess that's all for tonight. My life sure does get humdrum sometimes. Maybe I'll get a new friend some time. There are some other women over at the park with their kids, but just because my babies like to play a little with the ducks, they talk about me.

I think I'm a good mother. I don't spend all my time spanking and yelling at my babies to be good and constantly tell them to mind me. My babies are good babies. They are just a little high-strung and need to let off some steam sometimes. The park is the place for that, so their daddy can't see or hear them when they play loud games. I think some of those mothers are just jealous because I let my babies think for themselves.

Well, dear diary, that's all for tonight.

Your friend,

Emily

September 27, 1960

My dear diary,

Something odd has happened. Gerry started killing chickens. She goes over to the neighbor's yard and hits those old hens in the head with Terry's baseball bat. I caught her yesterday. All she could say for herself was she liked chicken bopping. Can you imagine? She even has a name for it. I punished her twice for it. When I make her go to her room, she says she doesn't know what I'm talking about. I keep buying the hens from the farmer, when she does that. I hope George doesn't ask why we eat chicken so much.

Sometimes I say to her "Geraldine Emily, you're just about the meanest child I ever did see."

How can she be so mean one day and so shy and quiet the next day? Why sometimes I think I have two little girls.

Terry started calling her the mean sister again when she acts like that and the good sister when she is quiet and sweet. I just can't keep up with the way she acts. I never know what she's going to be like. She's like night and day. I think she was mean to start, but when all this looking and watching started, Gerry seemed to get nicer and more timid. Maybe it did her some good.

Now Terry, he was mean to start too, and he's mean now. I guess he always will be mean. I hope I'm not being punished for being a bad wife to George because I don't like that sex stuff. That's the only thing I can figure out when it comes to the reason my babies act like they do.

Our best time is when they play their game "turn around". It's so much fun. They switch places or clothes, and after they've fooled me they sing, "turn around -- turn around ", over and over.

I think they're doing it in school, too. I don't see no harm in that. They're just being playful.

Turn around, turn around. I almost wish I could be someone else, like they can.

Sweet dreams for tonight,

Emily

October 18, 1967

My dearest, only friend,

I'm so shakey, my Dear Diary. I hope I can put all this down in writing. It's so hard to even think about. It's been eight days since the accident and I must finally tell you all about it.

My poor Terry is gone. I don't mean he ran away like some bad boy would do. He's left us for Heaven. That's what Mama used to call it when someone died. Now I know why. It's so hard to say that word.

Monday night there was a terrible fight and this horrible thing happened to my poor baby. Gerry still don't seem to know what happened.

I'm sure she didn't do anything. Like I told the sheriff, they was playing and Terry slipped. I just know that's what happened.

Gerry and Terry was playing in their room all afternoon,and things was getting kinda loud. I told them to hold it down so their daddy wouldn't hear them yelling so much when he came home from work.

Well, he was late as usual, and when he came in he had a surprise for Terry. I told him he shouldn't bring home treats for just one of them, but he said Terry deserved it, because he had been a nice boy and Gerry had been a brat ,and she wouldn't be getting any treats until she learned how to treat her daddy nicer. Gerry was real mad and went up to her bedroom. She was real mad at Terry before George came home, and this sure didn't make it any better when he got the treat and she didn't get anything.

It was just a pack of licorice candy, but that is one of Gerry's favorites. She tried to get Terry to share it with her, but all he did was laugh at her, and then he ate some of it real slow, and told her how good it was.

Later on, when Terry came down he said he wanted to stay down stairs and sleep, because the mean sister was back. I can never tell what he means when he calls her that. He sounds like he's talking about a completely different person. That's pretty silly, isn't it?

He finally decided to go up stairs and go to bed, but then I heard him and Gerry yelling again. Their Daddy hollered at them one time and told them to stop the racket or he'd show them how to be quiet. Then it got pretty quiet.

I guess Terry slipped out for a while. You know how he sneaks out of their window and down the trellis. I think Terry tried to sneak back in the window because I heard the window slam and my poor baby scream with a gargle kind of sound. He always did like to make crazy noises. It got quiet then, and George and me just sat and enjoyed the peace and quiet. It must have been about thirty minutes later when Gerry comes down and very calm like says that Terry is stuck in the window.

George and me went running up to see what kind of trick he was pulling now, but the poor baby was hanging there by his neck, with his body on the outside of the window. The window must have slipped and hit him in the neck and choked him. He had a bump on the side of his forehead but that could have happened when it dropped on him, I guess.

It's really odd that that old window would fall like that, cause it usually is very hard to push down. Gerry was about the only one who could get it to shut on the first try. She had just the right knack for slamming it shut, good and tight. I guess it just slid down this time all by itself.

Gerry acted like she didn't know exactly what happened. She said she was napping on the bed and when she woke up, Terry was just hanging there by his head. She didn't pay him no mind, because he was always playing tricks on her. She thought he was just fooling around like usual. Poor baby, she isn't real sure that Terry is gone. I couldn't get her to understand what was going on at the funeral. It was pretty sad. We didn't have many friends to come to the parlor. Mary Carlin came, and that nice Mrs. Jenson, from the grocery store.

Gerry's still playing "turn-around", even without him. I kind of enjoy it. It makes me think I still have both of my babies when she plays that game. She's so good at it, I close my eyes and I know it's Terry playing there with her. Yesterday I asked her to play "turn around" just so I could enjoy having both my babies with me."

I'm so tired. Something is wrong with George. He don't act like he used to. He sits and looks like he's thinking real hard about something. He almost looks scared. I wonder what's going on in his head.

I must go to bed, now. My dear Diary, what would I do without you to share my life? I get so tired of all this sadness.

Goodnight sweet diary,

Emily

December 11, 1967

Dear Diary,

George is gone. There is nothing fancy to say or no reasons, just that George left.

Last night he came home from work, packed what clothes he had, and walked out the front door. I thought at first he was going to go and live with Mary Carlin, but I don't think he did.

Today, when I stopped at the grocery for milk, Mrs Jenson was just as nice as always. If George had gone over to Mary Carlin's house, Mrs. Jenson would have known about it. Somehow, she knows everything that goes on around here.

I don't know where he went or where he is now, but I think he must be gone for good. I don't know how I feel about that. I don't know how I'll live. Someone has to pay for the groceries and the fuel bills for the house. I just don't know what I'm going to do about them.

Last week there was a notice on the board at the store. They need a cleaning lady at the library. Maybe I can get a job there. Mama always said I was a good cleaner. I think that if I have to earn some money, that will be the only way I can do it.

On top of that, my poor baby seems like a lost lamb. The sadness and the quiet in that upstairs bedroom just tears my heart out.

Things are so bad. I don't know exactly how to describe them. I just don't have nothing left. Since the funeral, nothing is the same -- and now George ups and leaves.

Christmas will be terrible without both of my babies. I miss having them both so much. It's not too bad when I can hear both the voices. I never could tell who was talking like the other one before the accident. When they played "turn around", no one could tell who was who. They were both so good about imitating each other's voice. Now when I hear my baby up there in the bedroom playing "turn around" all alone, I could just cry.

One part of me is sad, and another is so thankful for that silly game. At least with the game I have both of my babies again. I can hear both voices up there, laughing and talking to each other. Only now and then do I remember that there is only one of my babies up there. "Turn around" sure helps both of us.

I called the school. I asked them to please be patient, just a little while longer until my poor Gerry gets used to being alone.

The nurse at school said something like this takes a while. I figure that as long as Gerry has the "turn around" game, it will help ease the sadness of losing a twin. Twins are special, they need special care.

My dearest friend, I think this will be my last time to write to you. I have nothing left of my life to share with you, and things have just ended for me. I don't know how to think about anything or talk about any new things any more. It is just all gone.

Thank you for being my friend all these years. I don't know what I would have done without you when I was having some of my bad times. I always had you to talk to. Sometimes I really felt like you talked back to me. I'll always love you and remember you as the best friend I ever had.

Good bye my dearest friend in the whole world. I'll miss you. But then I'll miss everyone. It seems like just about everyone is gone and I'm the only one left.

Good-bye my dearest, dearest Diary. Thank you for being my friend all these years. I love you.

Emily

Chapter Thirty-One

Frank leaned back and took a deep breath. Placing the diary pages off to the side of the couch, he looked at the ceiling for a while.

Margot remained silent and let the information that Frank had just read sink into his thoughts. Never in all his years as a police department employee had he experienced the feeling he was now having.

"Margot," he said, "I don't know how to start. Now I see why you were so upset when I came in the room."

"Yeah, it does boggle the mind, doesn't it. I didn't think to verify that we were dealing with a male or female. I just assumed it was Terry, when the wig came off. I guess I should have patted him down.....I mean her."

"When I called the doctor to check out 'his' condition, I didn't really say 'Him', I used the name Terry. There are girls named Terry. They didn't have any question's about the sex of the victim. They were only worried about the mental state. She's been placed in psychiatric observation. One of the department specialist will be called in tomorrow."

"What caused all this? Was it her childhood?" Frank picked up the diaries and began to read through some of them, again.

"In my limited knowledge of these cases, I'd say she was always unstable. Add the type of abuse she suffered when she was growing up, and the facets of her personality seperated. When one circumstance came up, and she couldn't handle it, she withdrew. Most of the time when people withdraw from reality, they become dispondent. The actual fracturing of a mind is a very rare thing. In the multiple personality cases we've heard of, their history was parallel with Gerry's young years."

"But, could she actually kill her own twin when they were children? Can that happen, that she would kill someone so close to her?"

"If the personality that killed the brother felt that he needed killing, there would be no hesitation. This other self might not consider Terry her brother."

Margot reached for the odd note book, that was on the end of the couch. "Now, I think it's time for you to read this notebook. This tells the final story."

"The first few entries don't have dates. I've written in an approximate year at the top. I compared some of the events with Emily's diary and was able to get a close idea of when these were written. I inserted Gerry's approximate age, also. Pay particular attention to the vocabulary and intelligence in the writer of these pages. Try to picture what Gerry would have been at these ages. I think you'll see a startling difference. This is the answer to our last mystery. I think it's summed up quite well in the last entry of this diary."

EMILY GERALDINE'S DIARY

1963

About Nine Years Old

To my book,

    The mama writes in her book. That is what I will do. This is my own book.
    Gerry is mean to me. She won't let me talk. The only time she lets me out of the well is sometimes when the daddy wants to hurt her in the closet. I don't like him. He is not my daddy.

    from me

1964

About Ten Years Old

To my book

    I am mad. They won't let me play turn around. I think I will get Gerry in trouble. That will show her.
    They do not know who I am at school. They think I am Gerry. I do not like that.

    me

Ten Years Old

june 1964

Dear Book,

I have a game. I call it chicken bopper. It's really fun.
I take the big bat and hit those old chickens in the head.
Sometimes they smash. The mama found out. I got Gerry
in trouble. I had to quit for a while, but now I do it and no
one knows.
This is great fun. I like to see things bleed.

Your friend,

Me

Twelve Years Old

June 29, 1966

Dear Book,
I've been gone for a long time. I guess Gerry made me
stay in the well. I don't like the brother. He does funny
things to her. She comes into the well,too, but she doesn't
know I'm there. Maybe I'll help her when he's mean to her.
I am sure now. George is not my daddy.
I have a name now.   My name is Emily Geraldine.
Isn't that a grand name. Emily Geraldine.

I love you,

Emily Geraldine

Thirteen Years Old

October 27, 1967

Dear Diary,

That is the real way I should write to you. You are my diary.

I sure fixed it nice for Gerry. Now the brother won't hurt her any more. He started fooling around again the other night. Then, he went out for a while. When he tried to climb back in the room I slammed the window on his head. He sure did gurgle. Next I will take care of the daddy. I told him so, too, when he took Gerry into the closet. He sure looked at me funny.

Good night, friend,

Emily Geraldine

Thirteen Tears Old

November 13, 1967

Dear Diary,

Gerry has changed. Now she is Gerry and the brother, but different. I don't care much for either of them. They don't know I'm here. They only know each other. It feels strange having them in here with me. It's easier to get things done now, especially since I don't have the brother to snitch on me.

Love,

Emily Geraldine

293

Fourteen Years Old

July 25, 1968

Dear Diary,

Now I can do just about what I want to. Gerry and Terry don't bother me, but there seems to be another Gerry. I call her Young Gerry. She's so much like a baby, she doesn't really matter. I just ignore her. I let her come up sometimes when Gerry is sleeping and I'm bored. She is such a child.

Love you, my friend,

Emily Geraldine

Fourteen Years Old

November 28, 1968

Dear Diary,

Gerry and Terry are both being aggravating brats. Somehow these days, I just can't get out of the well. I don't have much to say, but when Gerry takes her nap, I can get this far out of the well to write to you.
I hate high school. Those two snotty girls that tease Gerry are going to get their share of grief some day. I just hate them.

Good night for now,

Emily Geraldine

Almost Fifteen Years Old

March 18, 1969

Dear Diary,

Gerry and Terry talk to each other, but they still don't talk to me. I don't think Gerry even knows I'm here, but Terry might. He's just too mean and stubborn to talk to me. Young Gerry doesn't talk to anyone . She just wants to play silly games.

I can make Gerry do things for me, like read the books I want, but I'm still losing control, most of the time.

I find this very sad. I don't know why.

Your silent friend,

Emily Geraldine

Fifteen Years Old

November 25, 1969

Dear Diary

Gerry had to stay after school today. When she dozed during study period, I wrote some dirty words on her essay. That, dear diary was positively hilarious. I heard Terry try to explain for her, but it didn't do any good.

He's still not sure about me, and he doesn't know anything about Young Gerry. He just thinks it's Gerry being juvenile.

Your friend,

Emily Geraldine

<u>Sixteen Years Old</u>

November 18, 1970

Dear Diary,

It's been a long time since I've gotten out to write to you. I feel so sad all of the time. I think I'm dying.

Gerry seems to be the strong one. Terry doesn't come up from the well very often, and Young Gerry hasn't been up for a long time. I'm the only one who knows about all the others. I get so lonesome.

Good night my only friend,

Emily Geraldine
<u>Sixteen Years Old</u>

February 19, 1971

Dear Diary,
Remember those smart-alec girls from freshman year? Well I settled a debt with them. I smacked them both in the head while they were sitting next to a tree. It made me feel so good to see their heads all bashed in. Just like my chicken bopper game, when I was a youngster.

The neighborhood is all in an uproar. The mother made Gerry stay in the house after school.

The police think there was a mad man coming through town, and he liked to pick on little girls. Cripes, they weren't all that little. They were just snots that got what they deserved. 'Mad Man.' What a laugh.

Good night for now,

Emily Geraldine

Eighteen Years Old

June 22, 1972

Dear Diary,

Graduation was positively a bore. All those sniveling parents. I don't know how Terry and Gerry can stand to be up all of the time. I find it an absolute drag.

Terry doesn't get to participate in Gerry's daily activities, but I hear him whispering to her constantly. I do wish he would shut up some time. He's a constant nag to the poor thing. I don't think the girl can do anything without his constant carping.

Gerry told the mother she was going to work at the insurance office, but I made her apply at the library. I feel a need to learn more. Gerry certainly isn't college material. I can make her read what I want, most of the time. That will help with my education.

Until next time my friend,

Emily Geraldine

Twenty Years Old

September 12, 1974

Dear Diary,

Gerry is getting stronger. Some days I feel as though I'm slowly becoming invisible. When Gerry reads, I can hear it, but I can't see with her any more. Terry is all but gone now. No more nagging. I think Gerry will be the one to live. It's so sad. I'm afraid I'm fading into nothing, but I'm determined to stay. I shall always be here. I promise.

I hope I can keep you. Now I know how the mother felt about her diary.

Good night, my friend. I feel so tired.

Emily Geraldine

Thirty-two Years Old

July 15, 1986

Dear Diary,

So, I've found you again. My promise has been kept. I knew there would be a day when I would return to you. When Gerry found the boxes of the mother's books, I felt as though a breath of new spirit was being pumped into my lungs for the sole purpose of bringing me a new existence. Emily Geraldine really lives. Now, everyone will know.

Good night, my new found friend.

Emily Geraldine

July 1986

Dear Diary,

I must tell you all now that I can remember, and I have you, again, my chronicler.

Last February a piece of scum was removed from this earth -- the maintenance man at the library. How can society live with dross like that, allowing him to mingle with the august people of this world?

He thought I was Gerry when I came into the basement. He didn't see my bat until it was but inches from his head. As he lay stunned, I placed his face next to the gas valve and opened it. I stood by the open window and waited until I was sure he was dead. I rubbed his head against the pipe that comes down into the floor to get some of the blood and skin on the pipe. Then, I placed his head on the floor, next to it. I closed the valve with his hand and left it over the valve.

He will never harass young innocent ladies again. I find the girls terribly boring and trite, but they did not deserve treatment such as that.

I left Gerry a note and signed it with a large garish T. Sometimes I marvel at my own humor.

Tonight you shall have a new hiding place. I feel the back of the closet would be much safer for you, my dear friend.

Until next time.

Your friend,

Emily Geraldine

July 1986

Dearest old friend,

I have read the mother's diaries. How could they do those things?

Those horrible, despicable people! I had forgotten of all the horrors of those young years.

We were only a child.

Terry and Gerry will help. Even the Young Gerry is awake again.

These harsh, disgusting people will pay their debt.

Your lost friend,

Emily Geraldine

July 1986

Dear Friend of Secrets,

We've done it. We have avenged ourself on two of the rotten apples, in the barrel of our life.

This past weekend, Gerry returned to St. John's and we paid a debt to the lecherous old man that lived next door. The lascivious doctor who so wantonly placed his hands on the mother was also dispatched.

What great pleasure we had! I still feel Gerry and Terry don't really understand that I'm here, but they somehow allowed me to participate in this merry occasion. I was the one to hit the old man on the head. He was only stunned, so we stuffed something in his mouth to keep him quiet.

How gloriously gorry it was as Terry nailed him to the table and Gerry removed his penis. Yes, Dearest Diary, I said penis. She brazenly removed it from his trousers and cut it off with one grand stroke of his own butcher knife. Such bravado from her was a great surprise.

Oh, Diary, what a memorable sight it was. I must admit, I was the one who placed it upon his chest where he could stare at it, as he bled to death.

Poor Young Gerry. She sat afterwards and ate crackers. She didn't really understand very much of what was going on.

The doctor was amply attended to. I was called upon again for my talent with a club. Shades of the old chicken bopper game. After my portion of the festivities, Terry tied him to a chair, and both Terry and Gerry cut that scoundrel's throat. Here, Gerry proved quite ineffective with a knife. She only managed to get halfway across. At least she tried.

Young Gerry was more interested in snacking than participating.

As I starred at him, I again read the pages from the mother's diary, and became so enraged, I took up the knife and destroyed those evil hands that so defiled the mother's body.

The pages of the mother's diary, left with each of these monsters, cleansed us of those sins.

Yours in retribution,

Emily Geraldine

June 1987

Dear Friend of mine,

I've found her. That horrid teacher. The mother kept one of her letters, and I was able to trace her. In the letter The Teacher mentioned George.

I shall forever call him George, because he is not my father. He is only Gerry's and Terry's lecherous sire.

Good night, friend

Emily Geraldine

July 1987

Dear Fellow Conspirator,

I've met the wicked woman. She covers herself with an air of innocence and the mantle of poverty. I am not easily misled.

We will deal with her in a most suitable manner.

Farewell, for tonight,

Emily Geraldine

August 1987

Dearest Diary,

The woman has been dealt with in the most appropriate of methods.

We met after she left her place of employment. A sickening little diner on Eighth Street.

This was our third meeting. She asked us up for tea, and was dispatched with the least of trouble.

I, again, with the bat. Terry gave a great slice across her throat. After Terry, Young Gerry attempted to cut her throat also, but her attempt was as ineffectual as the sister's had been with the old man, last year.

For some reason the sister did not rise from the well for this one.

Terry seemed to believe that Young Gerry was the same one who helped last year. He still isn't too sure of who is here. He looked a little puzzled when he realized he held the bat.

I felt I had not repaid enough, so I cut her open, as I so imagined that vetrinarian had done to the mother so many years ago.

We were cleansed again by leaving the diary pages at her door. What a sinful woman she was, and all the world may see now what her sins did reap.

Your retaliating friend,

Emily Geraldine

August 1987

Dearest Guardian of Secrets,

We have found George. The teacher described him to us, and after a few questions on the streets, he has been seen at the marketplace.

This must be done slowly, as he is a wary man of the streets and he will not be as easily fooled as was the simple harlot.

Terry is apprehensive, and Young Gerry doesn't really care. The sister, who knows what she thinks?

Why must I do all of this?

Yours in secret,

Emily Geraldine

August 1987

Dear Diary,

I met George tonight at the corner he calls his "post". He spends most of his evenings there.

The conversation was short and to the point. I took him a bottle and some sandwiches. I then told him who I was. Of course, I used Gerry's name. I said I wanted to meet him by the harbor at one o'clock in the morning on Sunday. I don't know if he will come. He should. It will be settled somehow, no matter how long the wait.

Good night friend,

Emily Geraldine

August 1987

Dearest Friend,

It's done, and I feel I am free. I have a small feeling of apprehension that I cannot justify . Perhaps, it will come to me later.

It was done beautifully. George was sitting alone on the bench. I walked up behind him quietly, and Terry grabbed his hair. With a strong snap backwards, Terry allowed Gerry to strike first. Not Young Gerry, but the sister. As usual, her squeamish nature came through, and she could not finish the cut. Terry switched hands and completed the task. I was so angered because I had not been allowed to hit him first, I gave him repeated blows to his head, even though he was dead.

Vengence has been executed. And so has George.

Your devoted companion,

Emily Geraldine

August 1987

Dear Friend,

Tonight a policeman came. He told Terry that he and Gerry may be in danger.

How idiotic! Just because they identified and connected that woman and George. Terry was his usual obnoxious self. Gerry was asleep, thank goodness. She is such an unfulfilled person. I shall be elated when I have total control and Terry and Gerry have both gone into the well forever. Young Gerry doesn't matter.

The police worry me. This Lieutenant Franklin said there may be a witness. He probably means that disgusting excuse for a human who was sitting on the corner curb when I was talking to George that first night. I believe another visit to Market Street may be needed.

Your friend,

Emily Geraldine

August 1987

Dear Diary,

Dear old Frisky has just held his last dinner party at his "casa". I showered for hours after being near him.

There are no more <u>problems.</u> There is only <u>US</u> and I intend to make that <u>ME</u> very soon.

Terry is getting weak again, and I'm staying up from the well longer each day. Gerry seems to be fading more each day. Young Gerry is the least of problems.

Soon, I will be the only one here.

<u>ME.</u>

Until the day,

Emily Geraldine

August 1987

My Dearest Confidant,

I feel things are closing in, and there are things I must do to tell the world of the truth.

I have finally come to a decision as to the state of mind of this complex person known to all as Geraldine Gallagher. I feel I am the only one to explain to the world the real meaning of her inner being. I have searched the memories and come up with this, the most simple of descriptions.

My dear Diary, this, so basically said, is Geraldine/Terry/Young Gerry/Emily Geraldine Gallagher. Soon there will be but one name. Emily Geraldine Gallagher.

Here, then, from the pen of the talented Longfellow as quoted by E. W. Longfellow, <u>Random Memories:</u>

> There was a little girl
> Who had a little curl
> Right in the middle of her forehead,
> And when she was good
> She was very, very good,
> And when she was bad she was horrid.

Soon, my friend. Oh, so soon. It will be only -- Emily Geraldine. I shall be the only one. I shall be one.

Goodbye my friend,

Emily Geraldine Gallagher

There is a little girl
Who has ----

About the Author

Shirley Byrne is newly retired from a twenty-eight year career as Chief Financial Officer of a manufacturing company that produces plastic bags. Hobbies vary from sewing, painting and reading a wide variety of mysteries and true crime stories, to writing her own mysteries and tongue-in-cheek history.

She has two daughters and a husband who all worked in the same business for most of those years. Two sons-in-law and three grandsons complete this family. She divides her time between homes in Wadsworth, Illinois and Marco Island, Florida, living on a golf course in each place and using neither.

Printed in the United States
124416LV00001B/1-24/A